THREE MINUTES

A STANDALONE DARK ROMANCE

L.D. PACK

PLAYLIST

Lost - Ollie
Voices- Beneath Our Ashes
Fear- NF
Sorrow- Sleeping At Last
What I buried to become me- Bleeding Verse
Rain- Sleep token
I can fix you- Jutes
Can You Feel My Heart- Bring Me The Horizon
Only When It's You-Bleeding Verse
Mine- Sleep Token
Fine Place To Die- Alex Warren

CONTENT TRIGGER WARNINGS

This book is dark-themed and may be unsettling for some readers. It is for adult audiences only.

Please do not continue reading if you are sensitive to the following:

Childhood trauma, domestic violence, endometriosis awareness/complications, emotional abuse, explicit death scenes, explicit blood/fight scenes, explicit sex themes, grief, mature language, mental health awareness, mental illness, night terrors, self-degradation, self-harming, sex themes between minors aged 16-17, substance abuse, suicide attempts/thoughts.

AUTHOR NOTE

Having faced mental health challenges since childhood, I'm a passionate advocate for mental health awareness.

This book unfolds from the perspective of the main male character. This is his story and journey. I created Ezra to embody the silent struggles many men endure. My hope is that by the end of this story, readers will find the courage to voice their feelings and embrace their emotions, rather than suppressing them because society tells them to.

To anyone out there who may be struggling mentally, I encourage you to reach out—whether it's to a loved one, a friend, or even me. I'm always here to listen and to remind you of your worth on this earth. You're not alone in this. Your feelings don't signify weakness; they simply reflect your humanity. Embrace them and allow yourself to feel. You are strong. You are loved.

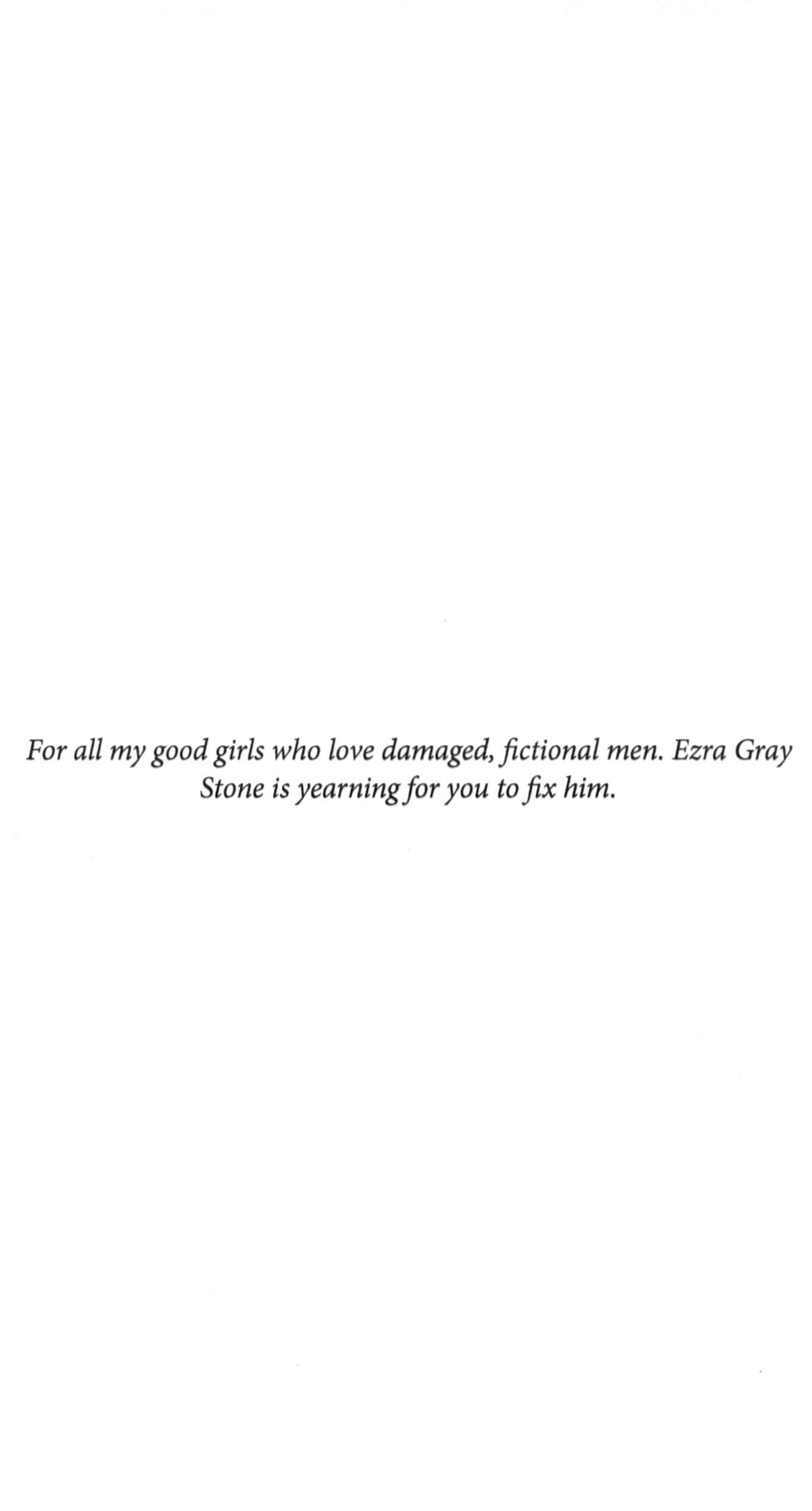

For all my good girls who love damaged, fictional men. Ezra Gray Stone is yearning for you to fix him.

EZRA

Past—September 7th

I bolt upright in bed, the sound of shattering glass ringing through the hallway and plunging me into the depths of night. Rubbing the sleep from my eyes, I swing my legs over the edge and stand up. Distant thuds echo outside my room, quickening the tremors in my hands. I tiptoe to the door with my heart racing, carefully grasping the doorknob and turning it slowly. Peeking out, I keep my body hidden behind the door frame, holding my breath as I strain to catch any sounds. Almost instantly, muffled cries come from my left. The weight of dread sinks into my chest, and I press a hand over my heart to steady it. I step back into my room, my gaze landing on my bed. There's no time to waste—I know what I need to do. Approaching the mattress, I lift the top-left corner, my fingers searching until they find the object hidden beneath. I pull it into view, gripping it tightly.

I slowly turn the bushcraft over, admiring the hand-carved

wood that makes up the base. My thumb brushes over the engraved letter in the center of the wooden handle, bearing the last name I carry. *Stone.* My father's brother Jesse gave me the blade on my twelfth birthday. It was my great-grandfather's, then passed down to my grandfather, who then passed it down to him. I assumed it was because he was the oldest of the two, but he told me to keep quiet about it, offering little explanation. I guess my father would never have approved of me having it, so it was our secret, shared only between uncle and nephew.

At first, I didn't fully grasp its purpose. I thought I'd never use it, or so I believed. I was a calm kid who enjoyed nature and spending time with my two best friends. Violence wasn't my thing, even though it always seemed to lurk around me like shadows in the night. I can't deny that a quiet voice in my head occasionally whispered thoughts I dared not speak. Over time, that same voice grew louder, multiplying and filling my thoughts with anger and sin, urging me to do things no kid should have to face.

Some nights, I couldn't silence their screams. It felt like flipping a switch in my mind. I had to block them out, which led to countless stab wounds in my mattress. I know it sounds ridiculous, but it was the only way to appease them temporarily. Tonight feels…*off.* I don't know what's come over me, but I feel compelled to engage with the voices in my head. I want to give them what they've been pleading for, because deep down, we all know this can't go on forever. As though whatever has been growing inside me is finally ready to be unleashed after being nurtured over time, and is now waiting to be born. I've imagined this moment countless times, never quite sure if I would actually follow through. I didn't want it to come to this, or maybe I did. Right now, there's no time to dwell on that. I need to act fast.

My right hand grips the blade tightly as I move quickly yet

quietly. I need to be clever about this, there's only one chance to get it right. My palms are slick with sweat and my heart races in my chest, drowning out the faint voices behind each thump. As I approach the cracked door, I slowly open it, careful not to make a sound. I scan the dim room and notice the lamp is on beside the nightstand. The strong smell of alcohol immediately burns my nostrils. I step forward, feeling a crunch beneath my foot followed by a slight sting. I bite down on my tongue, trying to ignore the throbbing pain. I lift my foot and see the remnants of broken glass, surrounded by a puddle of liquid. I stare at the mess as my blood drips from the bottom of my foot, mixing with the liquid on the floor: bourbon, my father's favorite.

I turn my head toward the bathroom as the sound of running water catches my attention. I move slowly toward the door, battling through the pain and ignoring the bloody footprints I leave in my wake. With each step, breathing becomes increasingly difficult. Something is seriously wrong behind those walls, and a part of me knows that what I'm about to face will leave a lasting impact on me.

I steady my movements, breathing in through my nose and quietly out of my mouth. Once I reach the bathroom, I slowly peek in, making sure to remain hidden. I crane my neck to the right, where the tiny hall leads to the bathtub. Loud splashing noises come from inside, followed by muffled sounds. The voices in my mind preach louder, urging me to move forward quickly. I pace each step as I get closer. Within seconds, my eyes are fixed on my father, who is crouched in front of the tub, struggling as he reaches into the water. As I approach, my eyes widen in fear. My mother lies naked in the running water, fighting beneath my father's tight grip around her neck. I notice that the water has a pinkish tint, showing that blood has spilled somewhere.

Anger flows through my veins as I creep closer to my father's back. If it weren't for the running faucet and his urgency to harm my mom, he would have already sensed that I was mere inches behind him. I'm also certain his alcohol level has impaired his motor skills, because he doesn't realize that danger is right behind him—I *am* the danger. Once I am close enough, I angle the blade in my hand, preparing myself for what I have to do. I glance at my mom, who is now being held underwater. Her eyes shoot open and meet mine. A moment of shock flashes through her stare before she continues thrashing against his grip.

He's going to kill my mom. I have to do this; I *want* to do this. Adrenaline surges through my veins, shaking my entire body. Before I have a chance to think any longer, I grab the back of my father's shirt and quickly twist it around my fist. My right hand, with the sharp blade poised, moves through the air, striking exactly where I aimed. A loud grunt escapes his throat as I twist the four-inch blade into his right side before pulling it back out. He collapses onto the bathroom tile, clutching his bleeding wound.

I stare down at my trembling hand, at the bloodied blade. This family heirloom now carries fresh human blood, its metal glistening in the dim light. The air is thick with the scent of bourbon and iron. My father looks up at me in disbelief, his face twisted in rage as he hurls insults. "You worthless fucking bastard!" His hateful words are nothing new to me. They used to cut deep when I was younger, but after years of hearing them, I've learned to numb myself to the pain.

With the blade still dripping with his blood, I kneel before him, locking our eyes. "If you ever lay a hand on her again, I'll kill you. Now get up and disappear for good," I growl. Our gazes hold for a moment, a silent challenge hanging in the air. I press the knife closer to his throat, a clear warning for him to think twice before pushing me again.

His breathing becomes labored as his eyes move down to the sharp object threatening to harm him again. I watch as rage fills his stare when he notices the familiar blade used against him. He finally drops his head and surrenders to my command. I stand up, keeping the weapon pointed at him. I was so focused on my target that I didn't realize Mom had already gotten out of the tub and wrapped herself in a towel. I quickly bring my attention to her, scanning her up and down. Tears trickle down her bruised cheeks. My eyes catch on her split-open lip as blood slowly travels down from the crease of her mouth, blending with her tears.

Heat shoots through my insides from the sight of my broken mother, and before I can even process the damage, I look back down at the piece of shit who has caused so much pain. I stare through him as he struggles to get up. He's now sitting in a small puddle of his own blood, the blood loss and lack of friction on the bathroom floor making it harder for him to steady himself. After a few more failed attempts, he looks up at me, almost like he expects a helping hand. But I stand my ground, not blinking once. He catches on quickly, shaking his head. He inhales deeply with a trembling breath and finally gets to his feet. However, just as he is about to fully stand, my foot strikes his face, forcing him back down. My mom lets out a squeal, followed by a long, gasping breath. I keep my focus; I cannot afford to lose it. My father wipes his mouth, now painted with fresh blood. I remain silent as he glares at me with that same intimidating look that once frightened me.

He doesn't waste another moment. After several loud, agonizing groans, he finally stands in front of me, clutching his blood-soaked side. He steps closer, and I instinctively raise the blade just inches from him. I'm prepared to stab him again if necessary, and I can tell he senses that. I've changed; he's turned me into the monster before him.

His eyes flick from the knife and back to me quickly. A slight, devilish grin stretches across his blood-crusted mouth. "You'll regret all of this, boy," he growls.

My father is a tall man; his height and build have always intimidated most people, especially me. And he always used that to his advantage. But now that I'm older, it doesn't bother me as much as it used to. I think he knew someday he'd meet his match. And unfortunately, I am a piece of him. I swallow the kernel of fear he stirred inside me, and step forward. I tilt my head up at him, maintaining eye contact. The sharp tip of the blade touches his stomach as a warning. "The only thing I regret is not doing this sooner…now leave."

His left eye twitches, but he doesn't break eye contact. He then turns and looks at my mom up and down before walking off. I glance at her, telling her to stay where she is. As I follow him out of the bathroom, I keep my distance. I watch as he grabs his wallet and keys, slipping them into his jeans pocket. He turns and looks at me as he struggles to pull his dark, red-stained shirt off. He catches himself and turns his expression to stone as he throws the ruined shirt to the floor. I bring my eyes to the stab wound, staring at the torn, exposed, bloody flesh. I stabbed him good. And the sight of it flares up something inside of me. It almost feels like excitement.

He snatches a black shirt from the dresser top before walking out of the bedroom. I follow closely behind him, the only sound is our feet padding against the hardwood floor. I carefully watch my steps, dodging the blood he leaves in his path. Once we reach the front door, he leans down, biting back the pain from his side, and grabs a pair of his shoes. He then pays me no attention as he heads out the front door. I step onto the porch, refusing to go inside until I see him drive away. Honestly, I probably won't even get any sleep tonight. How could I? This man is dangerous. He's done unforgivable things, and a part of me worries that he won't disappear like I want him to.

My breath catches as he stops at the end of the driveway. He pauses with his back facing me. Slowly, he turns his head to the side. The streetlight shines just enough on his silhouette for me to see the smirk on his face. I grip the knife tightly, ready to lunge if necessary.

He laughs through his nose before opening his mouth to speak. "Enjoy tonight, boy. But know that we'll come face-to-face again. And you won't know when that day comes." He lets his words echo through the night air before getting in his truck, not giving the house or me a backwards glance. I watch his taillights fade into the darkness as I replay his words in my mind—words that weren't a threat, but a promise. A promise that will haunt me forever.

A hand rests on my shoulder, jolting me out of my racing thoughts. I turn and look down at my mom. Relief washes over me at the warmth of her touch. I bring my left hand up, placing it on top of hers and rubbing small circles with my thumb. We stare out at the empty street for a while, saying nothing. This is a moment we've never talked about, but always wished for. The man who brought darkness into our home is finally gone. But will it last? I can't help but doubt it. He's a man driven by revenge, and I fear one day he will seek it.

I take a long, deep breath, letting my shoulders ease a bit. Mom senses the shift in my demeanor and gestures for me to turn around. I comply, still gripping the blade tightly. Wrapping my arms around her small frame, I pull her close, resting my chin on the crown of her head. This woman means everything to me, she's the light in my darkest moments. I'd do anything to protect her, just as she has always done her best to protect me. I only wish I had stepped up sooner. She gently pats my back, and we savor the silence of the moment together. I know we'll need to talk about what happened tonight. There will be questions from people, and we will have to be prepared to answer them. I find myself wondering what Uncle Jesse will think about all of this. A flood of concerns rushes through me as my adrenaline begins to fade. Mom gently pushes against my shoulders to look up at me. She tenderly brushes damp hair from my sweaty forehead, her eyes glistening with tears as she gazes up at me. I can feel the worry hidden behind her look, but she quickly gathers herself, offering me a small, sincere smile.

"Happy thirteenth birthday, Ezra."

"Wake up, birthday boy." Mom's gentle voice softly nudges me awake. I slowly pry one eye open, catching her sitting on the edge of my bed. The sun gently filters through my window curtain, casting a warm glow on her golden hair. It's styled in a high bun atop her head this morning, with small wavy strands framing her face. Her blue-green eyes sparkle with kindness. *She's truly beautiful.*

"What time is it?" I ask.

She gives a soft smile, leaning over to swipe hair from my dampened forehead.

"It's time to get up," she replies.

I groan, pulling the covers up to my chin, refusing to get out of my bed. I watch her as she stands up and heads towards the window. She flings the curtain open, causing me to hiss from the sunlight that almost blinds me.

"What the hell, Mom!" Her laughter fills my room, causing a slight grin to pull at my sleep-crusted mouth. I squint my eyes at her as she walks to the bedroom door.

"Get your ass up before your birthday brunch gets cold."

After a few stretches and dramatic yawns, I force myself out of bed. Grabbing a t-shirt and basketball shorts from my dresser, I glance at my phone—it's almost 12:30 p.m. Multiple texts flash across the screen from my friend Blake, my uncle Jesse, and Blake's sister, Beck, all wishing me a happy birthday. Stepping out of my room, the savory smell of various foods surrounds me. My stomach growls as I follow the tempting aroma coming from the kitchen. Breakfast items are spread out across the kitchen table: bacon, scrambled eggs, and buttermilk biscuits with gravy. My mouth instantly waters at the sight of the generous spread before my eyes.

As soon as I sit down, Mom walks over and places a plate in front of me—pancakes shaped like the number 16. Since I was a year old, it's been something she's always done on my birthday. So simple, yet thoughtful. She's collected pictures for every birthday, except my thirteenth. I stare at the pancakes, unable to hide the smirk on my face. The six is disproportionate, giving *Hunchback of Notre Dame* vibes, but I keep that thought to myself.

"I have to say this may be your best creation yet, thank you," I say with a side of humor.

She glances at the pancakes, placing her hands on either hip. I carefully watch as she purses her lips and then responds, "There were a few minor complications with the 6, but I'd say it adds character." I give a slow, exaggerated nod as we both hold back a laugh.

I pick up my fork, ready to take my first bite. "Eh, eh, no, sir! Let me get a picture for—" Before she can finish her sentence, the back door flings open, in walks Beck and Blake. It doesn't surprise either of us, considering they have a habit of barging in the house like they own the place. I guess it doesn't help that they've lived two streets over from us since I was around seven. Plus, Mom has treated them as her own since the first day we met, riding bikes in the street. It was just the two of them and their dad, Eric. Their mom had passed away from an unexplained heart attack less than two years prior. It was too painful for Eric to live in the house where they had once raised their family, so he eventually sold it and moved to our town. It had only been two days since they moved in when we first met, and from that day on, it was always the three of us.

Beck comes up behind me, wrapping her arms around my neck. "Happy birthday, Ez." I give her arm a quick rub, silently thanking her. She then takes a seat beside me, giving a lax smile. Her curly, auburn hair hangs down, gathered to one side like she's always worn it. Her deep blue eyes meet mine before she turns to my mom. For a moment, I am distracted by her presence. She has changed over the years. I always remember the goofy tomboy who tried to keep up with Blake and me. She never wanted to play with dolls, dress up, or wear makeup. She would even flip off the neighborhood girls who lived nearby, because she wanted no part in their "girlie" activities. But now, when I look at Beck, I see she is turning into a woman. She doesn't need the little extra things to make her beautiful. She just *is*, and honestly, always has been in her own way.

I shake my head, catching myself staring longer than I should. Blake sees me and gives my arm a solid punch before sitting down at the table. "Did you not get my texts this morning, asshole?"

I glare at him, rubbing the spot where his fist connected. "Which one?" I ask through gritted teeth. He rubs his stomach dramatically while Mom gives them each a plate piled high with food.

"The one where the three of us are going to the lake for the day, and then having a bonfire at our place tonight. Dad will be down at the station on-call and already said he's good with it, as long as Esther agrees." He states it almost as a question, instantly giving my mom puppy eyes. *Pathetic.*

She cuts her eyes to me and then back to Blake. "If your dad is good with it, then so am I," Mom replies casually.

Blake blows her a quick kiss, thanking her for her generosity—which makes Beck and I roll our eyes in sync. Something we've done since we were kids, anytime Blake did or said something dramatic. He's always bragged that he was my mom's favorite. We just let him talk out of his ass, most days.

"So, what do you think, old man?" he continues.

I keep chewing on my pancake, ignoring his question. Beck interrupts for me. "Old man? You do realize we turn eighteen in four months, right?"

Blake dismisses her comment, replying, "Psh, yeah...but you're older than me."

Beck and I exchange glances, then turn back to him. She scoffs. "By one minute and twenty-two seconds, Blake." The two of them then share their strange, twin-telepathic stare-off before we all, including my mom, burst into ridiculous laughter.

After the birthday brunch, Beck and Blake walk back home to get ready for the lake. I get up to help Mom clean up the kitchen, despite her initial refusal of at least ten times, until she finally gave in. There wasn't much to clean up aside from empty dishes—the twins made sure we left no food behind. So, in a way, I guess they had pitched in, too. Once we get everything cleaned up, we head to the living room. Every year on my birthday, mom and I sit and look through pictures of me from when I was growing up. Mom has always been one to snap photos of most things. She's often talked about how my grandmother loved taking pictures when she was a kid; maybe it's where she found her love for doing the same.

I've tried to picture what my grandmother was like. I never met her or saw a picture of her. Mom only has old photos from when she was growing up, and my grandmother had passed away when mom was in her early twenties. The way mom's face lights up when she speaks of her makes me believe she was a good person. How could she not be? She wasn't Mom's biological parent, but she sacrificed her own life to save my mom. I've often pondered how my mom would have turned out if she had stayed in foster care longer than she did as a kid. I couldn't imagine switching homes constantly and not having stability.

You hear horror stories about people raised in foster care and how they end up as terrible individuals. But then there is her; the woman who gave birth to me, who has loved me unconditionally through all the hell she's been through. We take a seat on the couch, and I watch as she opens the wooden chest, which also serves as a coffee table. Picture albums stack neatly inside the chest. We gather them all up and begin looking through them. I glance over at Mom as she excitedly explains every photo and how she remembers each one as if it were yesterday.

We come across one from when she had me at the hospital, my father and Uncle Jesse standing on either side of her as she holds me in the hospital bed. We both go silent when we see my father's face, his expression cold with no sign of excitement for my arrival. Meanwhile, Jesse has a side smirk, smiling down at my mom. Over the years, I've quietly wondered why she's kept the few photos that include my father. Sometimes I wish I could forget he ever existed; other times, I want to remember exactly who he was. Or maybe it's because I knew that no matter how hard we tried to erase him from our lives, something deeply embedded him in this house and our minds forever.

Mom flips to the next page of photos and laughs through her nose, quickly pulling a picture out from the album. I gently grab it, instantly grinning when I see three goofy kids' faces looking back at me. The photo was taken shortly after meeting Beck and Blake on our street. In the front, Blake and I are sitting on our bikes, smiling so big. Off to the side sits Beck, on her bicycle, lips puffed out and arms crossed, giving us her best evil eye. Blake and I had just told her moments before the picture was taken that she had cooties and couldn't hang with us boys. She got so mad; I knew right then she had a fiery side to her, and it wouldn't be easy to keep her away. It annoyed me at first, but as time passed, she grew on me. And what I mean by when time passed is that the three of us were inseparable just one day after Blake and I swore to keep her cooties away.

After spending nearly an hour looking through all the picture albums, Mom boils some tea on the stove while I go to get ready for the lake. As I step into my room, I quietly close the door and lean my back against it. I close my eyes and breathe slowly through my nose and out of my mouth. It's something that I do pretty often to calm my nerves. It was around the age of fourteen that things began to change for me. I didn't understand at first why my chest would feel so heavy or why my heart seemed like it was trying to force its way out, making my breathing become heavy and rapid, like I couldn't catch my breath. I did my best to battle it on my own. I never wanted to upset my mom or add to her already full plate. She didn't deserve it.

I hid it until I couldn't anymore. So many nights of jerking from my sleep, unable to catch my breath after a nightmare. Every single time, my mother came to my rescue. She held me, rubbed my head, and reminded me that everything would be okay. Only her touch and her voice was able to make it go away. That's when we found out I was having panic attacks. We kept it quiet for a while, but it only got worse. Whenever I had to go to school or tried to go anywhere that wasn't close to home, the panic attacks would take over.

Mom couldn't handle it anymore, and my uncle Jesse recommended I speak with a doctor. So we did just that, without giving too much information about the disappearance of my father, but explaining when my panic attacks happened. It took little for us to realize why I was having them—they diagnosed me with anxiety and PTSD. I was terrified of leaving the house, especially leaving mom home alone. I was worried about my father lurking somewhere, waiting for the perfect opportunity to hurt her—again. The thought of what could happen if I were not there to protect her…and the nightmares only intensified that fear, leaving haunting visuals that still crowd my mind.

What made the situation even tougher was that I couldn't confide in the twins. Mom made me promise to keep what happened on my thirteenth birthday between just the two of us. She insisted it was too risky. That night, we came up with a cover story. We would tell everyone that they separated, that he had stormed out and never returned, and that we had no clue where he had gone. Mom didn't want the police involved, especially given my age and the fact that I had used a knife on my father. It would attract unwanted attention, and she feared that other authorities might step in and take me away from her. The thought of foster care sent chills down her spine—and mine.

So other adjustments had to be made to help with my episodes. Mom pulled me out of 9th grade so I could be homeschooled. That helped a little. The doctor offered medications to help my symptoms. Mom refused them at first, but it only took seeing me fold one more time for her to take me back to the doctor's office for the prescriptions. It started as a very low dose, considering my age. But as I got older, the doses increased. With reliance on medications and attending school from home, things eased up a bit. The nightmares decreased from happening most nights to just a few. The panic attacks mostly stayed away, but the heaviness in my chest always lingered, reminding me it wasn't going anywhere; like a beast hiding in a dark cave, only showing its glowing eyes. I was its prey, its meal to devour when ready.

I rub my hand along my chest, glancing over at my dresser. I quickly walk over and open the top drawer, reaching for the two bottles hidden underneath piles of socks. I throw three pills in my mouth, chewing them up like candy as the taste of bitterness coats my tongue. Once the chalky substance reaches my stomach, the heaviness in my chest gradually eases. It's like a trigger in my brain. Even though the medication hasn't kicked in yet, it's the comfort in knowing I've taken it that calms the beast inside me.

Back in the kitchen, Mom stands by the window with a hot cup of tea in hand, using her favorite butterfly mug. She turns her head to smile, then nods at the tea she poured for me that's waiting on the table. I grab it, breathing in notes of cinnamon and honey. I lean against the counter beside her, taking her in as she gazes out at the woods behind our house. I don't know how I would ever survive without her. I've spent years trying to protect and ensure her safety, but I've never once thought about my survival. What it would mean if I ever lost her. The thought makes my insides turn.

My eyes fall to where her other hand rests along her tiny collarbone. Images of that night flash in my head, and all over again, I can see the dark bruises around her neck, the symmetrical imprint of large hands. For weeks, those bruises lingered on her, and I had to be reminded that it was my father's hands tight around her neck, so close to ending her life. I shake my head as the anxious feeling crawls along my skin. Mom notices my discomfort and places her hand on my arm. "What's wrong, Ezra?" she asks softly.

I bite down hard on my bottom lip as I take in the concern

behind her stare. I let out a breath through my nose. "I'm not going today, I'd rather stay home."

She removes her hand from my arm, shaking her head. "Yes, you are. I won't take no for an answer." She crosses her arms at me, giving me her best serious expression, still holding her cup of tea. It's hard to take her seriously, given how small she appears standing in front of me.

"Why does it matter if I go or not? I don't need to celebrate my birthday, it's just another day." I guzzle down the tea and place it in the sink before turning to walk away.

Mom grabs my arm, causing me to stop in my tracks. I keep my face turned away from her, staring at the floor, waiting for her response. She lets out a gentle huff. "Because you've spent the last three years worrying about me, hardly going anywhere with your friends. You've barely lived, Ezra. And I blame myself for letting you do it for so long. You can't protect me every second of the day. And even if you could, it's not your place to do so. So please, if you can't go for yourself…go for me, please?" Her voice cracks with her last words.

My eyes pinch shut at the desperation in her voice. I slowly turn around, bringing my eyes to hers. She does her best to smile at me while holding back tears. That's all it takes, seeing her like this. As bad as I want to say no and go shut myself in my bedroom, I can't do it to her. "Fine, I'll go…for you." Relief immediately flashes across her face. She quickly sets her tea down and pulls me in for a hug. I close my eyes and lay my forehead on her shoulder as I take in her sweet, comforting scent with hints of lavender and rosemary. She's always smelled the same since I was a small kid.

"I love you, you know that, right?" she mumbles into my chest.

I nod my head against her shoulder. "I love you, too, Mom." She squeezes me a little harder as a silent reply.

A car horn blares outside just as my phone vibrates in my pocket, signaling that Beck and Blake have arrived to pick me up. Mom pats my back as we finally let each other go from our hug. I turn toward the front door just as Mom speaks. "Can you do one thing for me? Your uncle Jesse is stopping by after work tonight. Could you make it back home by 11? He'd really like to see you for your birthday."

"Yeah, of course, Mom." She gives me a quick nod and follows me to the door.

Beck and Blake sit at the end of the driveway, music cranked up way too loud, head-banging. Mom and I exchange a look, probably both thinking the same thing. As I walk toward Beck's car, I can't help but glance back at Mom. "Are you sure you'll be okay?" I ask.

She purses her lips, holding back a smile. "Yes, Ezra, I'll be fine. Now go have some fun with those crazy-ass twins! Jesse and I will see you later tonight."

I nod and climb into the backseat of Beck's car. Just as we pull away, Blake rolls down his window and sticks his head out. "Don't miss me too much, Esther!" he shouts obnoxiously. Beck reaches over and slaps him on the back of the head. I glance at Mom through the window as she walks back into the house, shaking her head at Blake's antics. As we drive away, I watch my house fade behind us.

Taking a deep breath, I finally turn my attention to the twins, who are bantering about nothing important. Beck's blue eyes catch my reflection in the rearview mirror as she looks at me, and I can't help but silently stare back. There was something different about her gaze. And just as I was trying to figure it out, she quickly shifted her focus back to the road, leaving me wondering what she was thinking about.

THREE MINUTES

We park at the end of the quiet, dead-end street where trees form a thick wood line, their leaves rustling gently. The twins quickly spring out of the car to retrieve their items from the trunk. Blake hoists a large blue cooler, while Beck juggles two bags. One small and sleek, the other much larger. Realizing I've only brought myself and my phone, I offer to carry Beck's bags for her. In return, she gives a smile of appreciation.

We then start our trek through the dense, wooded area with tall trees looming overhead. If anyone were to watch us, they might think we are simply vanishing into an endless green forest. But for us, this forest holds memories; we've wandered these paths countless times, memorizing each twist and turn. Starting as curious kids, we explored corners we probably shouldn't have. This particular path is one I'm glad we did. It was our secret trail, leading to something much more than just lines of trees.

After a few minutes of walking along the path, we reach two large, moss-covered logs on either side of the trail, their sturdy shapes pointing toward the small clearing beyond the trees. I still vividly remember the day Blake and I rolled those logs into place. When we were around ten and eleven-years-old, we truly felt we had accomplished something significant, having created the coolest checkpoint on our way to our final destination. Beck had enjoyed watching us struggle to move the logs from their original spots. It didn't help that she nagged us from the tree limb she sat on above us. Every so often, small twigs or crumbled leaves would hit my head, accompanied by giggles and snorts. I learned it was best not to react because it only made her even more amped up. Still, it was hard to hide the smile on my face—until Blake caught it and shoved me for feeding into his twin sister's playful antics.

The memory sticks with me as I step out into the sunlit clearing, the warm rays surrounding me like a comforting blanket. A breeze swirls through the air, carrying the last weeks of summer. In Mavesdale, September marks the end of the season's warmth. I carefully set Beck's bags on the ground, taking a moment to absorb the beauty of this hidden gem we had discovered during our childhood adventures. The trees' vibrant greens sway, their leaves slowly hinting at the golden hues of early fall. The familiarity of it all stirs up years of memories.

After removing our shoes, we stand on the flat ledge, our feet firmly planted on the cool, rough stone as we gaze out at the expansive lake that stretches before us. Its surface shimmers like a sheet of glass, perfectly mirroring the blues of the sky above. Across from us, in the distance, are the western mountains. In the evening, the sunsets here are stunning. The pinks and purples cast over the distant peaks of the mountains, while reflecting on the water. It reminds me of something you'd see in a painting hanging in an art gallery somewhere.

Beck empties her larger bag, pulling out an oversized blanket to lie on the ground. I grab one side to help lay it flat, while Blake sets the cooler down on one corner to anchor it. Next, she pulls out a small Bluetooth speaker.

"I'll take that, ma'am," Blake drawls. He often feels the need to control what we're listening to, whether in a car or in any other situation involving music. That's how he developed his stage name, *DJ Bliz-ake*. And yeah, I know how cringy it sounds—that was the whole point when Beck and I assigned the name to him. He despises us for it, but he holds his chin high as he does.

Once he turns the music up, he yanks his shirt over his head and tosses it carelessly onto the ground, sprinting toward the ledge. He quickly shouts, "First one in has the biggest dick in

Mavesdale!" He then jumps headfirst over the ten-foot ledge, landing smoothly in the water.

Beck and I exchange amused looks as we move closer, looking down at Blake as he floats on the lake, signaling us to come join him. Beck rolls her eyes playfully as she strides back to the blanket where her things are. I trail behind her, slipping my shirt off and removing my phone from my pocket. As I catch up, I can feel her glance over her shoulder, her gaze briefly tracing the contours of my shoulders and chest. A flush rises to my cheeks, but she quickly clears her throat, redirecting her attention back to the items scattered on the blanket.

I watch as her auburn hair flutters in the breeze, catching the sunlight and shimmering in shades of red and brown. She keeps her eyes fixed on the ground, a slight blush creeping onto her cheeks as she pulls her shirt over her head, the fabric clinging briefly before falling away. With a flick of her wrist, she unbuttons her shorts, sliding them down her long, sun-kissed legs. When she stands back up, I let my eyes wander along her body. She wears a dark blue two-piece bathing suit that perfectly showcases her young, womanly curves. My eyes linger on the small birthmark at her lower left hip. What was just a mark to me before now feels more intimate. I catch myself wanting to trace my thumb along it, but the silly thought quickly evaporates as Blake yells for us.

"Ladies first." I gestured toward Beck.

Without a moment's hesitation, she steps confidently to the edge and launches herself into the air, diving in. She deliberately lands just inches from Blake, sending a splash of cool water into his face. He retaliates by showering her with another wave of water.

"Alright, birthday boy, let's see what you've got!" Blake's voice echoes. I turn around, planting my feet firmly on the tip of the ledge and letting my heels hang off just a little. "Oh, here we go, show-off," Blake whines dramatically, though a giggle escapes from Beck beside him. I bite back a smile as I backflip off the ledge, landing feet first into the water, just feet away from the twins.

The lake feels lukewarm against my skin. I lean back into the water, letting the tension that has clung to my muscles slowly melt away. With each moment, I sense the anxiousness that was wrapped tightly around my nerves slowly begin to fade. I needed this today. This place has always been a haven where I can escape my thoughts. Even though it's only minutes from home, I could always come here to create distance from my father. He was hateful most days, or he barely spoke to me at all.

We were never close, at least as far as I remember. Over the years, his drinking worsened, and that's when he started being physically aggressive toward my mom. He was always so angry at the world. Sometimes I wondered if he just hated us. We were always relieved when Uncle Jesse came over. Dad never acted out when he was there, but the tension was visible. I think Jesse suspected something, too. There was no way to hide the smell of alcohol that seeped from my father's pores.

So many times I wanted to call Jesse and tell him everything, but I never did. I often wondered if he already knew, and was trying to shield me from the truth. I was only a kid worrying about things I shouldn't have to. But he's always been kind to me, even though he isn't my father; he filled in some gaps I never got to experience with my own dad. I've always looked up to him. Even with work taking up most of his time, he has done his best to ensure that Mom and I were okay.

After that night on my thirteenth birthday, I went over a year without coming here—or going anywhere, really—aside from still going to school. Unless my uncle Jesse was visiting,

I made a point to be close to home. The threats my father gave before he left never left my mind. I realize that I've missed out on so many things over my teenage years. I've allowed him to haunt me, just as he wanted. My racing mind comes to a halt as something unexpectedly grasps my leg beneath the surface of the water. I instinctively reach down and grab what feels like an arm. Suddenly, Beck bursts from the depths, laughter bubbling out of her. I retaliate, swiftly dunking her head back underwater. When she reemerges, her laughter intermingles with mine.

Beck shakes her head vigorously, her wet curls flying around her face in a wild, playful dance. With a mischievous look in her eyes, she intentionally flings water in my direction, droplets catching the sunlight like tiny diamonds. The familiar scent of her floral shampoo envelops me, sweet and refreshing. As she closes her eyes, I watch her effortlessly comb her fingers through her damp hair, the sunlight making each strand shimmer. She then carefully tucks the curls behind her ears.

Her blue eyes, vibrant and clear, now lock onto mine, studying me with an intensity that feels both exhilarating and unnerving at the same time, as if she's trying to decipher the thoughts swirling in my mind. I find myself caught in a moment of silent contemplation, my gaze shifting back and forth between her captivating eyes. The sun reflects off her thick lashes, holding tiny droplets of water that glisten in the golden light, as if nature itself is highlighting her beauty at this very moment. Something has shifted between us; I can feel it flowing through me, but I haven't quite figured out what it is. I used to see Beck as just my best friend. My protective nature has always been there for her, and I know I care deeply for her. How could I not? We've been in each other's lives since we were kids. But this…this is something different. And I know the answers to it all will reveal themselves sooner rather than later.

03

Back at the twins' place, Blake and I worked together to prepare the fire pit in the dark. We had initially planned to leave the lake much sooner, but Blake, ever the mischief-maker, decided it would be hilarious to scare his sister out of her wits by leaping from the ledge into the blackness. As Beck anxiously paced back and forth, calling out his name in a mixture of annoyance and concern, I tried to calm her nerves, insisting it was probably just another one of his infamous pranks. During this, that asshole had quietly crept up behind us. My instinct kicked in, and without thinking, I threw a punch that caught him square on the lip. He knows me well enough to know I don't do well with surprises. However, the bruise blooming on his mouth made it more amusing to me when he nonchalantly claimed it was worth it to see the stunned expression on Beck's face when he pulled off his scare.

He is always full of surprises. What I also thought was going to be a night with just the three of us, he didn't think to tell me he had invited a few people from high school, including his latest crush, Andrea. Beck was also unaware of it. The only thing that kept me from losing my temper was the thought of Blake having to explain his busted lip to Andrea. I genuinely looked forward to witnessing that awkward conversation.

After we get the fire going well, Blake sprints into the garage, coming back with a clear bottle in his hand. "Alright, dude, it's time for a birthday shot." He gently shoves the bottle into my hand, Tito's vodka bottle that has about a fifth left. I shake my head, giving the bottle back. Drinking has never been something I was fond of. I think witnessing the damage it did to my father made me want to stay clear of it. And maybe sometimes I wondered, since I was a piece of him, that I would one day turn into the monster he was.

Beck eventually joins us by the fire, still wearing her same clothes over her bathing suit. She glances at the bottle in Blake's hand, quickly snatching it. "Where did you get this?" She cuts her eyes at him.

He nonchalantly shrugs his shoulders before responding, "It's from Dad's secret stash in the garage fridge."

She rolls her eyes, shoving the bottle into his chest. "Try not to drink it all."

He gives her a devilish grin, gripping the bottle in one hand. He then dramatically places his other hand over his heart. "I would never do such a thing, dear sister. Ez and I were about to take a shot together."

She glances at me, pressing her lips into a fine line. I run my hand through my hair, letting out a sigh. Blake squints at me as he pops the cap off the vodka. "Dude, it's one fucking shot, just live a little."

Beck's eyes stay on me, waiting for my response. "You don't have to, if you don't want to, Ez," she mumbles calmly. She knows how I feel about alcohol. But after thinking for a moment, I realize I might be overthinking it more than I should. One shot won't hurt anything; maybe it'll even calm my nerves a little before the others arrive.

"Fuck it, one shot. But only if Beck takes one with us." I playfully nudge her arm with mine.

She swirls her tongue around the inside of her cheek, glancing back and forth between us, then snatches the bottle from Blake as she turns to me. "Of course, but you first, birthday boy."

I grab the bottle, clutching it tightly. Without thinking, I turn it up and press it against my lips. The cool liquid flows down my throat, instantly warming me from the inside out.

"Damn, dude, I said a *shot*, not three in one gulp."

I shrug and hand the bottle to Blake. Both twins take a generous gulp from it and immediately break into song, singing me Happy Birthday. *What would I do without these two?*

Andrea and her cousin Tristan arrive shortly afterward. Andrea's friend, Macey, had been planning to come, but something came up, which was fine with me. Andrea is in the same grade as me, and had second period with me in 9th grade before I was pulled out for homeschooling. Tristan was a junior then. I never really spoke to him or cared to. He was big into sports and, honestly, had a cocky mentality. It's been years since I last saw him, and from what Blake has told me, he hasn't changed a bit. I think Blake has only put up with him because he's Andrea's cousin, and they seem to spend a lot of time together.

I watch as they walk up, waiting for Andrea to notice Blake's lip. I look over to Beck, seeing if she's paying attention. Sure enough, she is eyeing them both with her arms crossed. Blake gives Andrea a gentle kiss, wincing a little as he does. She pulls back, looking at him to see what's wrong. Her eyes immediately go to his lip, and her mouth drops. "Blake Evans! What happened to your freaking lip? Wait—are you wearing concealer?" I stifle a laugh at her question.

"Dude, did you dig in my makeup?" Beck chimes in with annoyance in her tone.

He shrugs his shoulders, carelessly running his hands through his short hair. "Listen, I may or may not have pranked the two of them. And in return, startled Ezra so badly that he started flailing his arms like a damn walrus and clipped me in the lip. It's unfortunate, really." He nonchalantly picks at his nails. Beck and I shake our heads while Andrea rolls her eyes, unable to hide her smile and knowing Blake's full of shit.

We all eventually gather around the fire pit. I watch Blake and Tristan compete to see who can shotgun a Coors Light the fastest. Andrea sits directly across from me, while Beck is on my right.

Andrea clears her throat. "So, how have you been, Ezra?" she asks. I look over at her through the smoke.

"I'm doing all right." She clicks her fingernails on the side of her beer can. "So, do you still have—"

Tristan cuts her off, sluggishly plopping down between her and Beck. "Yeah, man, you still having those uh—panic attacks and shit?"

My lips press into a fine line as I make eye contact with him. "They are manageable now." I give my best fake grin. I catch Beck adjusting in her seat from the corner of my eye. Tristan gives a dramatic nod before throwing back another beer and crushing the can.

"It must be weird as fuck being around people, considering you're homeschooled, huh?" A slight smirk pulls at his mouth.

I roll my shoulders to ease the tension. "Again, manageable."

I watch Tristan's mouth quickly open to give me another snarky comment, but Blake cuts him off as he leans behind Andrea with his arms around her shoulders. "Well, guys, Andrea and I are planning to make it official soon, and waiting until after her graduation next year before going all the way." Andrea rolls her eyes while slapping him lightly on the arm. We all let out a joking laugh, knowing that they've already done the deed many times.

Tristan exaggerates a cough. "Oh, speaking of. So, Beck." Everyone goes quiet, wondering where he's going with this. I glance at her as she stiffens in her chair. She turns and looks at Tristan, chewing on the inside of her lip. He takes a sip of his freshly opened beer, then glares at her. "So, how was it?" he croons. Beck keeps her focus on him, looking unbothered. "How was what?"

He takes another gulp, then wipes his mouth with the back of his forearm. "How was it losing your virginity the weekend after graduation?" Blake unintentionally spits beer from his mouth. I look over at Beck without turning my head. I can see the embarrassment in her expression. My heart pounds. Without thinking, I reach down and grab the Tito's vodka from the ground, popping the cap and taking a huge gulp. She graduated a couple of months ago, and I had no idea this ever happened.

Beck watches me before crossing her arms and looking back in his direction. "I don't think it really matters, or even concerns you, Tristan." He lets out a low laugh, throwing one of his hands up. "No, no, you are right. Plus, I've heard enough of it from Davis. He's made sure to express just how tight your—" Everything goes blurry around me. One minute, I'm sitting; the next, I'm across the fire pit, grabbing Tristan's shirt and pulling him up from his seat. He may be a few years older than me and have a bulkier build, but that means nothing when it comes to height. We now stand eye to eye.

I hear Blake beside me, patting me on the shoulder, but I block him out as I focus on the douchebag in front of me. I let out a long breath through my nose. "Beck's personal life doesn't concern you, and never fucking will." I can feel the vodka pumping through me, causing heat to radiate from my face. Tristan throws his hands up and gives a fake laugh. "Whoa, man, I'm just fucking around."

I shove him a little before releasing his shirt. I form fists on either side of me, digging my fingernails into my palms in an attempt to calm my racing heart. I turn to Beck to check on her and find she is wiping at her clothes. I then notice a huge wet spot on the bottom of her shirt and all over her shorts. I look down and see Tristan's beer on the ground beside her chair. I must have knocked it out of his hand when grabbing him, causing it to dump on Beck's lap without realizing.

"Oh, shit. I'm sorry, B." She shakes her head at me, brushing it off. "It's okay, I'll go change." Before I can say anything more, she turns and walks quickly into the house. Blake heads in her direction, but I stop him with my hand. "I'll go check on her. I need to break away for a moment, anyway." Blake gives me a concerning nod, but walks back over, sitting down beside Andrea. As I head toward the house, I hear Blake and Andrea snapping at Tristan.

Once I'm in the garage, I pull out my phone to check the time. It's after ten o'clock already. I send a quick text to my mom, just feeling the need to check in on her since I haven't yet today.

> Me: Hey Mom, are you doing okay?

> Mom: Hey, Ezra, I am. I've been reading a little and cleaning around the house. Uncle Jesse will be here soon. How has your day been? I hope you've had a little fun for your birthday.

> Me: I have. You know Blake and Beck keep me busy.

Mom: It wouldn't be them if not. lol

Me: I'll see you at 11 or before, okay?

Mom: See you then, honey. I love you.

Me: I love you too, Mom.

Relief blankets over me, knowing that Jesse is almost there. I walk in through the garage door that leads to the kitchen, and turn down the hall before stopping at Beck's room. She has the door shut. I hesitate at first, but I have to make sure she's okay before I head home. I lightly knock on her bedroom door. "It's me, Beck." I hear shuffling in her room. "Come in," she answers.

I walk in, quietly shutting the door behind me and leaning up against it. Beck turns and looks at me. She's removed her shirt, still wearing the blue bathing suit underneath. I catch the massive beer stain on her shorts. I pinch my lips together. "Sorry about your clothes, that wasn't meant to happen." She squints at me. "Was any of that supposed to happen?" I ponder which part she's referring to. "I didn't mean to snap…it just happened. No one is allowed to disrespect you like that. Not when I'm around."

She nods, looking down at the floor before giving me a quick smile. I click my tongue on the roof of my mouth. "So…Davis?" She flinches at his name, then lets out a hard sigh. "Yeah, well—I— it just happened, okay?" A weird ping of jealousy surges through me. "Why didn't you tell me?" She brings her eyes to me with a look of guilt. "I just, I don't know." She turns and sits on the edge of her bed. "I guess I was ashamed. Or maybe just scared that you'd look at me differently." She picks at her nails, refusing to look up at me.

"All the other girls at school had lost their virginity, and here I was, graduated and still a virgin." She laughs through her nose. "We went to a party the following weekend to celebrate graduation. I drank way too much, and Davis was there showing me attention, and I-I got lost in it. I regretted it instantly, it happened so fast."

I cross my arms and stay silent, feeling there is more she wants to say. She eventually brings her eyes to mine, and I can see the struggle within them. She bites on her bottom lip, shaking her head. "You know, I always fantasized that it would be you. That you would be my first. Ever since I knew what sex was and what it truly meant, I told myself I'd have that with you. I-I wanted us to be that for each other. Because—well, who else would it be? You were Ezra, the boy down the street, my best friend. You were *my* Ezra, no one else's. But I realized as I got older, you were my brother's best friend, too. And well, it was just a fairy tale I made up in my mind." She pauses and rubs her temples with her fingers.

Something ignites inside of me at her confession; it felt like she had held it in for so long. How did I not know these things? I always thought I knew her more than anyone. But I somehow missed this massive piece. I knew something had recently shifted between us, but I had been so caught up in my own thoughts that I hadn't realized it was so much more.

I lift myself from the door and walk over to her. She stays seated, but observes me. I stand in front of her, grabbing her hands to pull her up. She doesn't resist, and we stand just inches apart while she looks up at me. Her eyes dance across my face in curiosity while my hand trails up and down her arm, goosebumps rising beneath my fingertips. All these years, growing up together, so close to being young adults. It all clicks into place.

Her breathing becomes shallow as I continue to rub her arm lightly. I hesitate for a moment, but the slight buzz I have gives me the push to speak. "Do you still want that with me?" I breathe out. Something sparks in her eyes, and she slowly nods her head. I wet my lips, gently grabbing her with both hands, pulling her even closer. I tilt my head down, my breath against her lips. "Can I kiss you, Beck?" Her lips part, and I watch as she bites down on her bottom lip. "Yes," she whispers.

I place my hand along her jaw, gently pressing my thumb and forefinger underneath her chin. I tilt her head back more to where our eyes meet again. I can see the desire in her gaze, the blues in her eyes like rapid waves ready to crash at any moment. I connect our mouths, first a slow, sensual peck—my chest flutters at the press of our lips. For a moment, I wonder if hers does, too.

Our mouths open in sync and our tongues collide, tasting one another. My eyes squeeze shut as we passionately explore each other's mouths, taking our time like we've waited for this exact moment for so long. The taste of her is something sweet that I want to savor and indulge in. Beck lifts herself on her tiptoes, wrapping her arms around my neck as her fingers find their way into my hair, gently gripping the strands. I wrap my arms around her, pulling her flush to my body—the heat of us both like an inferno.

I pick her up from underneath her thighs, stepping toward the bed, our mouths never parting. She wraps her legs around my waist as I kneel onto the bed, gently placing her underneath me. I pull away, putting my forehead against hers. We both pant, trying to catch our breath like we've just run a mile together. I lift, gazing into her eyes. *Beautiful, always beautiful.*

I trail my hand along the side of her face, letting my fingers find her curls. Her eyes flutter with every touch I give. "You can still be that for me, Beck," I rasp out. A gasp leaves her throat as she searches my eyes, almost like she didn't know whether I had already given myself to someone else. Does she not know that I've touched no one like I'm touching her now? Her hands find my hair, and she twirls dark strands around her fingers. She pulls my head down and kisses me tenderly.

She then pauses for a moment, staring at me like she's mentally noting my features and expression. "I do want you, I always have." She breathes. "Let me do this for you." I search her eyes, giving a slow nod, not knowing exactly what she means but trusting her words. She places her hands along my chest, gesturing for me to let her up. I lie back on the bed, watching her. She reaches beside her bed, grabs her purse, and retrieves something from the inside compartment—a condom.

My eyes scan her as she removes her shorts, slowly sliding them down her legs before she hooks her fingers beneath her bathing suit bottoms, pulling them down, too. My breath catches in my throat at the sight of her lower half bare. I take a deep breath, sit up, and remove my shirt, shorts, and boxers, throwing them beside the bed.

I prop up on my elbows, keeping my stare on her. Beck runs her eyes down my body, stopping between my legs. She sucks her lips into her mouth, biting down on them. My heart pumps viciously as she crawls onto the bed between my legs. I watch every detail and movement she makes. She keeps our eyes connected as she brings the condom to her mouth, ripping it open with her teeth.

She sits back on her knees, leans forward, and takes a deep breath. She gently wraps her hands around my swollen length, causing my breath to hitch from her sudden touch. I'd thought about this moment so many times before, wondering what a woman's touch would feel like—the intensity of it.

Beck brings her other hand down, clutching the condom, her hand trembling. I reach over, wrapping my hand around her wrist, stopping her. Her eyes jolt back and forth between mine. "You don't have to do this, B." She shakes her head, sucking in her breath. "No, I-I want to. It's just that with Davis, I didn't get to do this…it was so fast. I want this to be perfect for you." I rub my thumb along her wrist before letting go. "It's good, Beck, you are good." She gives me a nervous nod.

My lips separate as she slowly slides the condom down my length. She sits up on her knees and scoots closer, climbing over my legs. She then positions herself over my tip, using one hand to hold me in place, and the other gripping my shoulder. She closes her eyes and slowly begins lowering herself down on me. We both gasp at the same time. Pressure builds in my chest and stomach. She pauses for a moment, biting down on her bottom lip.

My hands instinctively grab and hold her hips tight. She lifts and lowers again, sliding down further onto me. The feel of warmth shoots through me. I squeeze my eyes shut and quickly open them, not wanting to miss even a second of this with her. I can see the battle of pleasure, and perhaps even discomfort, in her expression. "Are you okay?" I whisper. She nods anxiously. "I'm okay. I just need a moment."

She squeezes her eyes shut, then opens them quickly to make eye contact. Then, with a final drop of her hips, she fills herself with all of me. My grip tightens on her hips as we both catch our breath. The feel of her tightness around me makes my vision blur. She rocks her hips in a slow rhythm, her nails digging into my shoulders, surely leaving marks as she continues her addictive pattern.

A pleasure I've never experienced before takes over me completely. I feel the pressure building quickly—nothing like when I've touched myself. I can barely focus with every nerve in my body reacting to her being so close. I try so hard to hold back, wanting the feeling of this moment to last forever.

My thumb runs along her birthmark on her hip. Mesmerized by how stunning she looks, my hand runs up her stomach. I trace my fingers around her bathing suit top, and her nipples harden beneath my touch—moans and heavy breathing flow from our mouths. The air is thick with lust. "Beck, I-I can't last much longer," I grit out. She sucks in her bottom lip, rolling her head back as she continues to ride me into submission. "It's okay, Ezra, let it go. It's supposed to be like this." Her voice is reassuring and sweet like honey.

She stops momentarily, grabbing my hands and placing them around her waist. She presses her hands over mine, motioning for me to take the lead. I grasp around her waist, her skin like silk. I start slow, but pick up the pace, lifting her slightly and dropping her back down onto me. Everything goes dark around me, and we both let out a muffled moan. A heavy release shoots out of me as I feel her pulsing around my length.

I pull her down onto my chest as we both try to catch our breath. I once thought I truly knew Beck on a deeper level. We grew up together and spent countless days and hours together. But this, this is different. A feeling of predatory instincts clouds my senses. *I love her. I've always loved her.*

The sounds of a siren approach outside, followed by multiple air horns. Beck jolts up from my chest, pulling off of me. I quickly sit up, yanking the condom off and tossing it in the small trash can beside her bed. Pulling my phone from my shorts pocket, I slip my boxers back on and then my shorts. Before I can check the time, a door slams hard, and within seconds, Blake bursts into the room, panting hard.

His eyes were initially concerned, but he instantly became shocked when he saw Beck and me. "Dude, what the fuck!" he yells. Beck throws the cover over her lower half. Blake shakes his head, trying to understand what he just walked into. I look down at my phone, seeing that it is 11:01. *Fuck, I'm late.* I quickly turn back to Blake, and his mouth opens. "It's your house, Ez. It's—it's on *fire*. Dad just drove by, heading there now." My heart sinks in my chest. I look at Beck, her expression full of fear and worry.

Wasting no more time, I sprint out of her room, knocking Blake to the side. I hear him and her shouting for me, but I keep running as fast as I can. My mind races, running through different horrible scenarios repeatedly. *They got out. They're safe outside while they tame the fire.* I repeat it aloud, speaking it into the air. I finally blink, and I'm already one street away from my house. I see the smoke rising across the sky, and the smell of burned wood fills the air, making my eyes sting. Thick air presses against my bare chest.

I try to catch my breath as I approach my yard. Multiple fire trucks line the streets and front yard. I spot Jesse's pickup truck sitting near the mailbox, unscathed. My eyes freeze on the house, the home I grew up in, in deadly flames. My heart lurches, trying to rip from my exhausted chest. I glance at my phone in a panic. *11:03.* From the corner of my eye, I spot an ambulance, and relief sparks within me. I sprint over, hoping to see my mom and Jesse there, unharmed. Two paramedics discussing something turn and look at me, shaking their heads in confusion.

I whip around, unable to focus, turning in circles. *Where are they? There's no way…* I look back towards the house just as one of the living room windows bursts out with roaring flames. A firefighter comes out from the side of the house, his uniform covered in black smoke. He quickly looks my way and runs towards me. He then pulls his helmet and face shield off. It's Eric, the twins' dad.

"Where are they?! Are they okay?" I yell amongst the loud noises around us. Eric runs his gloved hand through his sweaty hair, shaking his head. "They weren't outside when we got here. The neighbors called as soon as they noticed the fire. W-we tried getting in through the back door, but the fire is out of control. We're going to try going through—" Before he can finish his sentence, I jolt towards the front door. Eric attempts to grab my arm, but I move too quickly.

"Ezra, you can't go in there like that, you won't make it!" Eric yells, but I ignore him. I refuse to let them die. I should have been here. I should have never left. I grab the doorknob of the front door without thinking. The handle burns my fingers and palm, making me snatch my hand back. I quickly brace myself and kick the door as hard as I can. The door instantly rips from the hinges, bowing inward.

An avalanche of smoke and heat pours from the busted-down door. I bring my arm up over my face, trying to shield it as best I can as I move forward. I begin searching, screaming their names. To my right, toward the living room and kitchen, there is nothing left—everything's consumed by raging fire. I trek toward the hallway, trying my best not to breathe in the smoke, holding my breath as long as I can, then taking small breaths in between to keep from passing out.

My lungs feel like they could collapse at any moment, as much as I try to keep the smoke out, it devours me wholly. I check everywhere I can see through the fire and black smoke. The eerie sound of everything melting and crumbling around me causes my heart rate to skyrocket. I try to ignore the feeling of my chest cavity tightening as pain runs through my side into my leg.

I reach my mom's room and notice the door is shut, smoke billowing from underneath it. I hear Eric and other firefighters shouting from the front door. There's no time left; they have to be inside. They're okay; they just need my help. I kick the bedroom door open. Flames burst out, and I raise my right arm to shield my face. The force of the fire pushes me back, knocking me onto the floor. Immediately, the right side of my body burns and stings with raw pain. I bite down hard on my tongue, tasting blood.

I grab my chest, unable to breathe any longer. I glance at my right arm, the flesh melted away, seared skin peeling back in places. I grit my teeth, trying to fight through the agony. My lungs are giving out. I take short breaths, holding on as long as I can. I tilt my head, looking through the door into my mom's room. I squint my eyes, trying to see past the hellfire that surrounds me.

My strained eyes catch sight of something just feet away: two charred bodies lie motionless, barely recognizable, but I know it's them. They are holding each other as if trying to shield themselves from the flames, but it's obvious it's too late. I try to cry out, I try to scream, but there's no air left in me—only smoke and fire. A sharp pain grips my chest. I'm suffocating and will die in this house, along with my mom and Jesse.

As my vision fades into darkness, muffled voices approach, their words swirling around me. Something yanks at my right arm, sending a sharp jolt of pain through my veins. The voices surround me, but only fragments of sound reach my slipping consciousness. I feel my heart working hard, its beat weak and faltering, each pulse a reminder of my life slipping away. The searing shadow of death draws near, and a shiver of resignation sweeps over me—I have earned this fate. I did this. I killed us all.

04

59...58...57...I count down in my head. My eyes squeeze together, fighting through the creeping sting but focusing on the pain building against me. I force my eyes open, staring back at myself in the bathroom mirror. Beads of sweat cling to the tips of my damp hair as heat travels through me at a slow, agonizing speed. I pull my eyes down to where I hold the Zippo's flame against my skin. The tang of burning, melted flesh fills the air. A familiar scent I've grown accustomed to over the years.

My hand trembles as I grip the lighter, the faded skull design visible beneath my fingers. *33...32...31...*I try to stay focused as my other hand presses against the countertop, bracing myself for the final seconds. I hold my breath, grinding my teeth together. Their black, charred faces flash into my mind, their bodies holding each other. I imagine the pain they endured during those last moments, when they knew they were about to die.

Low, muffled groans escape my lips as I bite my tongue, the

metallic taste flooding my mouth. This is nothing; their pain was far worse. I did this. I deserve to feel this. *3...2...1...* The timer on my phone rings. I let go of the Zippo, dropping it into the sink and grasping the counter tightly, my knuckles turning white. I bow my head to catch my breath, sweat dripping from the ends of my hair. I glance at my side where the skin is bubbly and oozing watery blood that trails down onto my stomach. Jolts like lightning run up my side, causing me to tense.

I breathe heavily through my nose, the sound echoing softly in the room's stillness. My gaze drifts back to the mirror. The reflection staring back at me reveals a face etched with defeat and exhaustion, shadows clinging to my features. I shake my head, dislodging a wave of frustration, then swiftly shut off the timer on my phone. My fingers curl around the cool metal of the Zippo. I squeeze it tightly in my hand, feeling the ridges press into my palm before I finally set it down on the counter with a soft clink.

I wince as I crouch to pull off my boxers. Standing again, I glower at my reflection—my battered body, young yet brutally scarred. I flex my right arm, eyes tracing the damage, lingering on the fire tattoos that snake along my arm and other parts of my body. They're entwined with faded remnants of old burns, representing the very thing that changed me. These scars are a reminder of all I've lost and everything I will never deserve.

My thoughts drift back to that night. I was so certain I was going to die; after all, it felt like my time. I should have perished along with my family in that house. But Eric took that from me. I don't hold it against him anymore. I resented him at first, but as I grew older, I came to understand why he did it. And as time continued, I realized that dying in that fire would have been the easy way out for me. This is my punishment: living, but dead inside.

I step into the shower and turn on the water, letting the ice-cold liquid shock my body. I twist it all the way to hot, shift to the side, and press my hands against the shower wall. My wound screams in protest as the water grows hotter against my scorched skin. I clamp my lips shut, stifling a soft gasp as the steam beats against the flayed skin.

Once I'm done, I pull out the first-aid kit I keep stored in the bathroom cabinet. I take out the antibiotic cream, large gauze, and bandage wrap. First, I lather on the antibiotic cream, applying a generous amount. I don't remember exactly when I started hurting myself this way. It was many months after the fire, and after I had completely healed from the burns.

My mental state was all over the place, and the panic attacks were worse than ever. The nightmares I had once managed to control resurfaced with a vengeance. For a while, I would wake up soaked in sweat and shaking, expecting my mom to be sitting at the edge of my bed, ready to comfort me as she used to. Instead, I faced an unseen ghost. Yet, some nights, I would wake partially, feeling the touch of familiar fingers brushing my face. I know it was just my imagination, but those were the only nights I could sleep peacefully.

The voices returned, and the guilt was a silent killer. I couldn't shake it. I needed a new way to silence them while also paying for what I had caused. I started slowly at first; I couldn't concentrate or handle the pain initially. First, I did ten seconds, then gradually increased the duration. It was a learning process. It had become a painful addiction to the point where I wasn't giving my skin enough time to heal before the next burn. This had led to a nasty skin infection.

I discovered that in the intervals between burns, it was crucial to allow my body ample time to recover from the wounds. In the past, my skin would heal within a couple of weeks, but now the healing process takes a month or longer. Some areas of my skin are now too scarred and damaged to repair fully. The nerve endings have become permanently numbed, while others are overly sensitive, reacting sharply to the slightest touch.

The most challenging aspect was concealing the truth from Eric and the twins. I kept my secret for quite some time, carefully avoiding any situation where I might need to take off my shirt. I gravitated towards darker fabrics, the deep hues shielding what hid beneath. They simply accepted my silence, believing it was my way of hiding the deepest scars left by the fire. Yet, beneath the surface, I could sense their concern, the weight of unspoken questions hanging heavily in the air, even as they respected my boundaries and refrained from prying. It was a delicate dance of pretense, leaving a lingering tension between us that I couldn't shake.

I should have known Blake would eventually piece it all together. A part of me felt relief that it was him, not Beck, who uncovered the truth. Even though it pained him, he swore he would never tell a soul, and I held him to that dying promise. Things had been tumultuous between Beck and me ever since the night of the fire. I had shattered our bond, and she was caught in the aftermath of my reckless actions. The thought of revealing my demons to her constantly gnawed at my insides. I could never let her know my secret, it would break her in ways I could never forgive myself for. But in the end, no matter how much I try to avoid it, that's what I do—I *hurt* the ones I love.

05

Past—Five Weeks After The Fire.

I saunter down the street from the twins' house, grimacing as the fabric of my clothes rubs against the bandages all over my body. Five long weeks have passed since the fire. During those weeks, I stayed in the hospital recovering from second- and third-degree burns. Multiple areas required immediate skin grafts, which they sourced from my inner thighs for the repairs.

I annihilated the right side of my body. The doctor's guess was it happened when I knocked down the bedroom door and threw my right arm up to shield myself from the flames that burst through. The only good thing was that it protected my face. Somehow, it was unscathed, while I now have permanent scars from the top of my neck, down my right side and stomach, stopping just before my belly button. My entire right arm, including my hand, was damaged. I had thought I had died in the fire. I didn't even realize I was in intensive care until the following evening.

As soon as I opened my eyes to the sound of the hospital

monitor beeping, everything began to both unravel and come together. Eric and the twins stood by my bed, their faces etched with horror. I was in a state of hysteria, overwhelmed by a mix of pain and dread. Because of the wounds on my right arm and side, they could not use restraints, opting instead for heavy sedatives. After that, the days seemed to blur together. I recall them checking in regularly and sitting by my bedside, but it was Beck I remembered the most. She was always there, right by my side.

They released me just yesterday, and advised me to take it easy since I still have many months to recover. Eric insisted I shouldn't leave the house or engage in any heavy activities in the meantime. Despite his concerns, I felt compelled to do this. I need to see what's left behind. The twins offered to come for support, but I refused their offer. I needed to do this alone.

I stand in the driveway, my heart heavy as I look at the charred remains before me. The remnants of my home are nothing but an abandoned wasteland, reduced to gray ashes and debris. Scorched beams of wood lie scattered, while fragments of the walls still stand. Bright yellow caution tape flutters gently in the breeze, marking the perimeter where the house once stood. The crisp fall air, tinged with the scent of wet earth, mingles with the faintest hint of lingering smoke. It's clear that at some point, rain had washed over part of the wreckage, blurring the edges of what remains, almost like nature itself mourned the loss alongside me. I take a deep breath as I walk toward the devastation. My heart pounds with each step, the soles of my shoes are already coated in fine black particles as I sift through the debris. I scan the area, hoping to find something salvageable, but my search comes up with nothing.

Now, I stand where my bedroom once was, flooded with memories of my final moments here. I gaze toward the spot where the window used to be, recalling my mom perched on the edge of my bed, her finger brushing my forehead to sweep away stray strands of hair. I glance over and spot the box spring from my bed. My eyes dart around, searching for the knife. I rush over, kicking through the rubble. Not caring about my bandages, I dig with my hands. The knife was in its same spot, wedged between the mattress and the box springs; it should've fallen between them during the fire. Whatever was left of it, but I find nothing.

Anger surges through me as I try to process the chaos surrounding me. There's not a single item left to remind me of my mother. My uncle had come to visit for my birthday, and I wasn't even here. Three Minutes changed everything. They both died for nothing. A wave of heat rises in me, and I let out a loud cry that echoes in the open space. I grab the box spring and hurl it as far as I can, forgetting about the pain that throbs through my body. My hands ball into tight, trembling fists as I attempt to catch my breath. Raising my hands, I stare at the black soot clinging to my nail beds.

With my head hanging low in silent defeat, I make my way to the spot where I last saw them—where their lifeless bodies clung to one another. The image is etched in my mind, sharp and haunting. My heart crumbles in my chest as a rush of overwhelming emotions floods my thoughts. I collapse hard onto my knees, running my hands through the black death that surrounds me.

A flood of questions swirls within me, each one clawing at my insides with relentless urgency. *How did this tragedy unfold? Why was the bedroom door shut? Did they die quickly? Or was it a slow, painful death being claimed by the flames?* The reports claim a catastrophic gas leak started the fire. Yet, answers slip through my fingers like smoke. The examiner couldn't uncover the exact truth behind their deaths; all that remained were charred remnants, both unrecognizable. There is no evidence to piece together the shattered puzzle of that night. All the questions I so desperately need answered perished along with my mom and Jesse.

My hands clasp together in front of me as I close my eyes, falling forward and resting my forehead against them. The horrible smell of burned plastic and wood singes my nostrils. I imagine their last moments alive. They must have been so scared. What haunts me most is how they were found holding each other—like they knew they were going to die, with no choice but to accept it and be there for each other.

I never got to say goodbye to either of them. My last interaction with my mom was just a brief text exchange, right before I became too wrapped up in being buzzed and losing my virginity to my childhood best friend, just two streets away from home. Meanwhile, she and Jesse were tortured in flames. The weight of that truth hits me like a ton of bricks, and a sob escapes my lips as an unbearable ache tightens around my throat. I chew on my bottom lip, desperately trying to steady my trembling features. I loathe myself for all of this. I'll never truly heal or find it in my heart to forgive myself for what happened.

A cool breeze brushes against the back of my neck, sending a ripple of goosebumps down my spine. I tilt my head to the left, drawn by a flash of vibrant color that catches my eye. I quickly blink away the fresh tears, trying to refocus my vision. Everything around me feels dreary and gray today, including the sky. A short distance away, a butterfly sits, its colors striking and full of life. I watch in awe as it gracefully flutters its wings.

I push myself to my feet, brushing away the debris clinging to my arms and pants. The bandages on my right arm and hand are now smudged with black. As I draw closer, I discover it's a monarch butterfly. Its wings blaze a vibrant orange, reminiscent of flames, with a striking black outline that highlights the delicate white spots at the tips. I kneel slowly, just a foot away, captivated by its beauty. Thoughts of my mother flood my mind. She adored these butterflies and what they represented. A wave of memories washes over me as I continue to gaze at the butterfly.

Mom and I walk through her flowers in the backyard. I make sure to listen as she names each flower, brushing her fingers against the silky petals. As a six-year-old, I couldn't care less about the flowers and their names, but seeing her light up when she talks about them makes me happy. Today has been a good birthday so far. The sun is shining, and it's warm outside. Dad didn't come home last night, but that's okay. I like it better when it's just my mom and me here, or when my uncle Jesse stops by for a visit, anyway.

"Ezra! Come here, look!" Mom shouts. "Isn't it beautiful?" I stand beside Mom, glancing at the butterfly sitting on a blue flower. "It's a monarch butterfly. It will migrate soon with its other friends. It's actually a little early this time of year."

I watch as Mom gently places her finger near the flower it sits on. "What are you doing?" I ask.

"Shhh, just watch, honey." We both sit quietly, never taking our eyes off the butterfly. For what feels like forever, it crawls onto my mom's hand, gently flapping its wings. Mom lets out a soft gasp. "You know…after you were born, the nurses brought you over for me to hold you for the first time. You were a tiny little thing then. I held you so close to my chest, just amazed at how cute you were. You were the calmest baby, barely even cried when you were born."

My eyes light up. "Really?"

She smiles and nods at me. "It was a beautiful day, too, like today. I rocked you in my arms, looking out the window. The sky was a bright blue, with not a cloud in sight. And suddenly, there it was." I stay quiet for a moment, waiting for her to continue. She laughs through her nose. "A monarch butterfly. It flew onto the window and stayed there for a good while. It was so beautiful, like you. I knew little about them at the time, but when we were released from the hospital, I researched them.

"They symbolize a new life being born, strength, and so much more. And I knew right then that you were special. My little resilient butterfly." She lightly taps the tip of my nose with her free pointer finger. "Some even say that it means a loved one who has passed is visiting to say hello." Mom wraps her arm around me and puts her other hand in the air. The butterfly clings on a moment longer before flying away. We both stood silently and watched it until we could no longer see it.

I shake my head, fighting back the new tears that beg to fall. I refocus on the butterfly. My eyes catch a glimpse of something shiny beneath it. I crouch down, carefully extending my hand near the butterfly. Almost immediately, it clings to the tips of my fingers—so delicate, yet so resilient. I lift my arm higher and watch as the butterfly flutters gracefully off toward the woods.

Returning my gaze to the shiny object, I bend down and pick it up, brushing off the dirt as best I can. My heart sinks when I see what it is—my father's Zippo lighter. I turn it over in my hand, recalling the skull design on the front. He always carried it with him. My thoughts drift back to the night he left. I have no way of knowing whether he took it with him, everything happened so quickly. Maybe Mom discovered it after he was gone and tucked it away somewhere safe. What bothers me most is *where* I found it. It wasn't in a dresser or stored away somewhere. Its location suggests it was lying on the floor near the main bathroom entrance. Unless my mom had taken it out, or perhaps she had given it to my uncle at some point, and he had it with him that night.

My thoughts whirl in a chaotic storm of confusion. I slowly pull the silver lid back, flicking the wheel with my thumb.

Mesmerized, I gaze into the flickering glow. I extend my left palm above the flame, its radiance illuminating my skin. As I lower my hand closer, the warmth envelops me, similar to the searing touch of fire against flesh. But soon after, a sharp, creeping pain snatches at my wrist, urging me to jerk the Zippo away. I draw in several shaky breaths, the air feeling thin in my chest, and with a decisive clink, I snap the lid shut.

I flex my hand, looking at the red burn on my palm that has formed. No matter how hard my body tries to heal, this injury has become a part of me. The fire and pain will always linger in my life. They reside within me now, and I was never meant to escape them. I raise my gaze toward the woods, where a gnawing feeling tugging at my chest tells me he's out there somewhere, watching. He promised me that our time wasn't over. I know the truth will eventually come to light, and I'll likely have to confront that truth—confront him.

06

Present—Eleven Years Later

"Ya know, you could have taken tonight off. I'm capable of running this place myself," Blake rants while wiping down barstools. I saunter over, turning on the *open* sign hanging to the left of the entrance. I peek out the window, noticing vehicles pulling in just like they always do at opening time. I turn back to Blake. "When did I say you couldn't? And what else would I be doing?"

He shrugs his shoulders. "Fuck, I don't know. It's your birthday, man. You could take your bike on a scenic joyride or something."

I shake my head in annoyance, walking behind the bar. "I take a scenic route every time I come into town. I'm a grown-ass man, I don't need advice on where or how I spend my time. You, of all people, know today is not a fucking celebration for me." I flare my nostrils, feeling my face heat up. Blake opens his mouth, just as the front door creaks open and customers flood in. He looks toward the door before meeting me behind the bar. He rubs the back of his neck and sighs.

"I'm sorry, Ez, I didn't mean—I just wish you'd for once think about yourself, after all this time." His concerned stare lingers on me for a moment before he shakes it off and turns his attention to the approaching customers. I push open the double doors leading to the back, quickly flexing my hands at my sides. I know he means well; he always does. But I wish they'd stop worrying about me. I've been this way for so long. They need to understand this is who I am, and always will be. *Broken.*

I walk through the storage area where the alcoholic beverages are stored before entering the small office. I flip on the switch, sit at the desk, and take a deep breath. Reaching into my pocket, I pull out the skull Zippo lighter, push the lid back, and flick it with my thumb. My eyes flicker over the flame before I repeat the motion, again and again. My gaze falls on the sticky note attached to the side of the computer monitor. I grab it with my free hand and read the small print.

Inventory looks good for next week. I updated everything in the database yesterday.

- Beck

I turned on the computer monitor, pulling up the inventory software and skimming through it. Since I offered Beck the job of managing inventory, she has consistently stayed on top of everything, ensuring I never have to remind her of what needs to be done. I knew she would excel at it, even when she fought me on it for months. She begged and pleaded for me to let her bartend and for Blake to handle the inventory side of things, but I couldn't allow it. With the pervs who come in here, I would end up snapping someone's fucking neck if they even looked at her wrong.

This was the safer option, one where I could have her involved while keeping her safe. That, and I wouldn't be facing multiple assault charges because of buzzed customers unable to keep their limp dicks in their pants while drinking. It's been a little over five years since I bought this place with the money I inherited from my uncle Jesse. Back then as a twenty-two-year-old I didn't know what I was doing, but I managed with help from the twins and their dad, Eric.

I was heading back home when I saw the for-sale sign; I passed by this place often on my way into town. It was the only bar around Mavesdale, and for those living near the mountains and in our small town, it was a popular spot. The owner had reached his sixties and was ready to retire from the bar business. I had never considered it as a career or even stepped foot in this bar before. Honestly, I never really thought about what I was doing with my useless life.

The owner led me through the bar, his pace brisk as he pointed out various features and explained the ins and outs of the business. I could sense his reluctance; it was likely clear to him that I was a novice in this world. Yet, as he spoke, I began to absorb everything—the flickering lights overhead, the polished wooden bar top that gleamed under the dim lights, and the eclectic mix of décor that added a unique character to the space. By the end of his tour, something sparked within me—a feeling I hadn't expected. It was as though my heart, despite its weaknesses, was instinctively guiding my vision for this place.

The process of becoming an owner, I discovered, was surprisingly straightforward in Mavesdale. The local laws and requirements were clear, giving a direct path to ownership without unnecessary complications. And just like that, sixty-five days later, I stood proudly as the primary owner of a bar I had named Monarch Haven.

After discussing various business models with the twins and deciding on their pay, I made them co-owners of the bar, each holding a 5% stake. What they didn't know was that if anything were to happen to me, they would split full ownership. It was a safety net I needed to establish. Regardless of what life throws at me, I wanted to leave them something meaningful. It was the least I could do. After all, I've been a burden in their lives.

Over the next month, we dedicated ourselves to a small amount of remodeling and repainting the bar, turning it into a space that felt like our own. I particularly appreciated Beck's keen eye for detail and her ability to create a warm, inviting space. Her feminine touch was clear in every corner, from the carefully chosen color palette to the cozy seating arrangements that encouraged conversation.

Honestly, as young adults, we turned this place into something I take great pride in. Though I'm not someone who drinks alcohol, having the ability to oversee others' consumption under my watch gave me a sense of purpose. This endeavor allowed me to maintain a certain level of control—something I've always craved in various aspects of my life. Deep down, I know this drive comes from my obsession with order and stability, and through the bar, I found a way to channel some of that compulsion.

In my younger years, I felt powerless over many aspects of my life: my father's uncontrollable drinking and rage; the fire that shattered everything; and the tragic loss it brought. The scars on my body are a nagging reminder to the world, echoing the storm in my mind that gnaws at me like an unforgiving disease. The weight of those memories still drags me down, leaving me feeling weighed down and trapped. While the fire is no longer externally visible, it smolders within me, setting aflame every nerve.

Over the years, I've found ways to manage that pain, gaining a small degree of control in certain areas. But it will never be enough. I'll never be enough for anyone, which is why I choose to be alone. No one deserves to endure the hell I carry inside. It's a pain that only I should bear. I have the twins and this bar, and for now, that's enough to keep me company amidst my misery.

My phone vibrates in my pocket, jerking me from my thoughts. I quickly pull it out to check it.

Blake: Can you take over while I run to the bathroom? The Cajun chicken sandwich I ate for dinner is fighting back with a vengeance.

I let out a heavy sigh, sliding my phone back in my pocket while massaging the bridge of my nose. I love Blake, but there are times I'd like to wring his fucking neck. I quickly turn the computer off and head back out to the bar area. The crowd is just as expected on a Friday afternoon. I quickly scan the room while washing my hands. Every barstool is full and surrounded by chattering, including the dark green sofa nestled in the corner. It was Beck's idea to have the couch in here, and it's usually the first to go, especially when women stop by to socialize and have a drink.

Two out of three booths are occupied, while others stand around the jukebox picking through songs. A man and a woman sway back and forth to the music, snickering in each other's ears. Most faces are familiar or regulars who come almost every weekend. Some tourists occasionally pass through when visiting the mountains.

Since owning this place for all these years, I've caught onto different patterns and habits of humans. A lot of them spend their free time here, almost like they count down the hours until they clock out from work—just to come here to spend their hard-earned money on alcohol, poisoning their livers on repeat. It's depressing, if you really think about it. Who am I to judge, though? I don't even drink, and my life is an unraveling hellfire of depression.

The front door to the bar creaks open faintly, muffled by the music and loud talking. In walks a guy I've never seen before. He stands tall, appears to be reasonably fit, but is more slender. He steps inside the door and moves to the side, revealing someone walking behind him. She stops right inside the door, scanning the room with a slight smile on her face.

She's a tiny little thing, maybe around 5'5, which is short considering I'm 6'5. Her wavy, blonde locks rest wildly around her face, bangs reaching right below her brow. I pull my eyes away from her, looking back at the jackass who didn't even have the decency to open the door for her. He smirks down at her, flicking his fingers toward the one empty booth. She returns a soft smile and follows behind him as they sit down.

I pull my attention back as customers order new drinks and request refills. A few moments pass, and from the corner of my eye, I see Jackass approaching the bar by himself. I close another customer's tab and turn my attention to him.

"What can I get you?" I ask as I throw a hand towel over my shoulder.

He glances at the drink menu, tapping his fingers repetitively on the wooden bar. He then clicks his tongue. "I'll have a Jack and Coke." I give a slight nod—typical choice for newcomers. I wait patiently, thinking he's ordering something for the girl he's with, but he continues tapping his fingers, watching others at the bar.

"Will that be it?"

He shakes his head, as if I've snapped him out of a silent daze. He then laughs through his nose. "Oh, right. Yeah, my girl will have the same as me." He points back at the booth where she's sitting. "It's her 21st birthday." I nod as I open a new tab on the screen. That's an unusual drink choice for a lady, but it's not the first time I've seen it. Everyone has their own preferences. The words *his girl* ring in my mind.

I clear my throat. "Got it, I'll need to see IDs."

He squints, leaning in closer. A small snort escapes from his nose. "Seriously, dude?" he replies.

I rest my palms on the bar and give him a calm, hard stare. "Do I look like I'm joking?"

He pulls his head back slightly. "Aw, dude, I'm just messing with you." He quickly turns his head to the right and whistles. I glance over at her just as she shifts her focus to the bar. He waves his hand to call her over.

I watch carefully as she grabs her purse and approaches the bar. She places her bag on the counter, and they exchange quiet words. Both turn to face me while retrieving their IDs. He's the first to pull his out and hand it over. I nod as I quickly glance at it. Scottie, age twenty-four. *Who the hell names their kid Scottie? I silently disapprove inside my mind.*

I go to hand back his ID, and he pauses as he grabs it. I notice him scanning my hand, his eyes traveling up my covered arm to my neck. "Gnarly ass flame tattoos, dude! Holy shit, are those scars?" *If this motherfucker calls me dude one more time.* I flick my eyes at her; she peeks at my hand, then quickly looks back down, fidgeting with her ID before gesturing for me to take it.

I glance at her photo, then at her name—Raina Adele Hope. Such a unique name. She's twenty-one today, born on September 7th. We share a birthday. I hope hers actually means something to her, at least. I give her a slight nod with a quick, tight-lipped smile. As I hand her ID back, her fingers graze mine, making me wince. She quickly looks up at me, her expression unreadable. I notice the faint freckles that scatter across the bridge of her nose and cheeks. Her eyes are vibrant, shimmering with different shades of green. Her pupils flick back and forth between mine. For a moment, I wonder if she sees the fire burning me alive behind them.

My thoughts are quickly interrupted by Jackass. "So is

your whole body scarred up like that? Was it a bear attack or something?" I notice her nudging him with her elbow. He shrugs in response, still examining my hand. Heat rises around my neck, burning me from the inside out. I slowly push up the sleeves of my hoodie, revealing more scars and tattoos running up my right arm.

His eyes widen at the sight of it—something I'm used to when someone new notices my scars for the first time. I roll my shoulders, place my hands firmly on the counter, and lean forward. I leave my face unreadable. "Do you always ask strangers stupid ass questions that do not concern you?" My teeth clench as he pulls back from my response. He opens his mouth to respond, but I walk off to prepare their drinks, not caring to hear another word come out of his mouth.

I make Dipshit his Jack and Coke, while deciding to make the girl something different to prove a point. Once the drinks are ready, I slide his across the bar, refusing to hand it directly to him. I then turn to her, reaching out with her drink. "Not sure if you've had one before, but it's called a lemon drop."

I watch as Scottie pulls a confused look. "Didn't I order her the same drink as me?"

I press my lips together. "You did, but she doesn't look like a Jack and Coke kind of girl," I say nonchalantly.

He lets out an exaggerated huff, snatching his drink up and holding it close to her. "Here, taste it." I watch as she presses her glossed lips to the glass, and he slightly tilts it up. My eyes follow her throat as it lightly bobs.

She pulls back, using her free hand to cover her mouth. Her nose instantly scrunches from the taste. "Scottie, that is God awful."

I can't help but let my sly grin of satisfaction tug at my lips. I stay silent as we both watch her take a sip of the drink I prepared for her. She pulls her lips away, coated in liquid. She licks away the remains, closing her eyes for a moment, as if savoring the flavor. "Mmm, this is really good," she hums. Her voice is delicate, yet full of life.

I clear my throat. "It's on the house. Happy Birthday."

She smiles softly at me. "Oh, thank you…" She pauses.

"Ezra. My name's Ezra." Her beautiful eyes seem to light up.

"Well, thank you, Ezra." I give her a quick nod as they walk back to their booth. She looks back at me, pulling her bottom lip in and gently biting it before offering a quick, innocent smile.

"Are you staring at that hot chick's ass?" Blake chimes in from beside me, jerking my attention toward him. I relax my shoulders, grabbing the hand towel still slung across my right one, and toss it into the towel bin under the sink.

"It took you long enough in there. Did everything go okay?"

He pats his stomach. "I'm feeling brand new now, brother." I shake my head at him in a joking manner. "Now imagine if I hadn't been here." Blake shrugs off my response and walks away to check on customers.

I glance up at the clock over the entrance door—it's nearly 7:30 p.m. I pull out my phone and check my notifications. I hadn't realized Beck had texted around twenty minutes ago, letting me know she was stopping by. She should be here any moment. I close my messaging app and open my home security camera feed. My phone constantly alerts me to any movement at all hours, both inside and outside. Still, I have a habit of checking it during times I'm away, even without alerts. Usually, when I do, it's because of wildlife near the house or on the property. Maybe I'm paranoid, searching for something or someone that will never appear. You can never be sure, though.

I hear the double doors to the back swing open, and I slightly tilt my head. Beck steps through, her presence effortlessly commanding attention. Regulars perched at the bar shout out, "Hey," to her, while smiling and waving. She always brings positive energy to this place.

She places a container down in front of me and then turns, wrapping her arms around my neck. My hands naturally enclose around her. Breathing her in, I catch that same comforting scent—her scent. Glancing to my left, I see the birthday girl watching us with a hint of curiosity. I quickly shift my attention back to Beck. "Happy Birthday, Ez!" she exclaims as we release each other. She looks as stunning as ever, even in her simple outfit. Tapping her fingers on the container, she adds, "I would have dropped this off at your place this morning, but someone didn't pick up their phone."

I smile at her as I reach for the container, already knowing what awaits me inside. Gently, I lift the lid to reveal two pancakes shaped like a 2 and a 7, accompanied by a small lidded container of syrup and a plastic fork. I force my gaze back to hers, offering my best fake smile.

After the accident, Beck started the tradition of making birthday pancakes for me each year. I understand the good intentions behind her thoughtful gesture, but instead of feeling warmth or love from the memories of my mother, all I feel is a wave of nausea that triggers the darkest parts of me. And it's like all over again, we are burning in that damned house.

I can't bring myself to tell Beck how this affects me; it would shatter her. So, I silently bite my tongue until the metallic taste stings my palate. I open the small container of syrup and watch it slowly drizzle over the pancakes like molten lava. I grasp the plastic fork, shifting it in my hands before taking a bite and forcing my expression to remain neutral. But my mind plays tricks on me, and the texture reminds me of soot, lingering like a residue stuck beneath my nails. But now it's lodged in my throat, making it hard to swallow, clinging to my insides. Yet, I push through, determined to finish every bite.

The smell of burning flesh seeps into my deepest being, hungrily ripping at my lungs. My burning eyes are wide open, scanning, searching for something. But a black, sticky fog surrounds me, tightening around my chest with each heavy breath I take. I urgently scoot forward, keeping my arms stretched out, unable to see the path in front of me. Heat stabs and tears at my skin as I walk through the thick smoke.

Without warning, my hands crash into an unseen surface. It's not a wall, but an intangible barrier that feels like an open space, blocking me from passing through. The dense air around me hums with a strange energy, and I sense that whatever lies beyond this barrier is urgent and vital. Desperation swells through my veins as I lean into it, pushing with every ounce of my body weight. I can feel the resistance pressing back against me, solid yet elusive. Panic grows like cancer against my nerves. I pound against the surface repeatedly, my palms stinging with each impact, my breath coming in ragged gasps.

A faint cry comes from the other side, and I freeze, straining to listen closely. For a moment, all I can hear is the crackling of the fire. Then, another sound breaks through—a sob that lingers in the air, yet falls short. I wave my hands in front of me, attempting to clear the fog that clouds my vision. As I dig into my eyes to sharpen my focus, the sting begins to dissipate. When I finally reopen them, the air ahead appears clearer. I glance around, observing the relentless destruction brought on by the fire and smoke. Lifting my hands to feel my way, I encounter the familiar, transparent barrier, but I notice movement just beyond it. I squint, trying to hone in on the figure that suddenly materializes just a few feet away. My eyes widen in realization—it's my mom.

My heart thuds hard in my chest as I dig my fingers into the invisible wall keeping me from her. She has her back turned to me, her head slightly tilted down. I go to speak as a burning lump forms in my throat. "Mom...are you okay? I'm...I'm here...I made it." I keep my eyes on her backside.

A strange sound comes from her, almost like a painful gasp. "You're too late, Ezra." Her voice is clear and emotionless. My heart sinks. I push and bang, trying to break through the barrier. Her shoulders jerk, causing me to freeze. She then slowly turns around, her breaths uneven and short. My mouth drops open at the sight of her. One side of her face is melted and burned, her jaw exposed, while muscle and flesh protrude through where the skin is missing.

My whole body is shaking as I take in what is left of my beautiful mother. My eyes move down, realizing what she is holding in her hands. Pancakes—the same pancakes from my 16th birthday. "Why did you let me die?" she whimpers out.

I shake my head in horror. "Mom, no, I...I'm here. But I can't... get to you.. See?" I quickly bang my hands and throw myself towards the barrier as hard as I can.

She shakes her head at an unnerving speed. "YOU DID THIS... YOU DID THIS!" she screams over and over. My hands fly into *my hair as I press my palms over my ears, trying to block out her painful cries.*

I squeeze my eyes shut and drop to my knees, gripping my hair tightly as I feel thick strands rip from my scalp. Her cries grow louder, making my eardrums throb. Suddenly, a loud popping noise breaks the air, and her wailing stops abruptly. I jerk my head back up and open my eyes. A trail of burning red fire circles around her, trapping her within it. She stands motionless, her blueish-green eyes looking through me.

My jaw clicks as I watch the fire trail up her legs; she doesn't move or react. There's a haunting gleam in her eye that makes my gut churn. I draw my right fist back and throw every bit of power I have into the invisible shield—the sound of bones cracking and popping as I punch over and over. A loud yell protrudes from my mouth, filled with anguish and fear.

She crumbles to the floor, her stare still on me as her body quickly turns to ash while it travels up her brittle body. "NOOOO!" I plead. Out of nowhere, something moves to the right of where my mom lies. I squint my tear-soaked eyes, blinking away the tears. A tall, dark figure stands in the corner, its form resembling that of a large man. The only thing visible is the glowing, reddish-orange eyes. I turn my eyes back to Mom, who is now nothing but bone and ash. From the corner of my eye, the figure inhumanely jerks its head, and a demonic laughter stings the air.

"You are next, boy. You'll burn in hell, too," the figure growls.

A hot sensation strikes my heart. I slam my hand into my chest, digging my fingers into my skin. It moves at a rapid speed, and the feel of hot lava dissolves my insides. I clench my teeth together, trying to control the growing pain. Every nerve in my body ignites like a lit match. I lift my arms in front of me to see there's a red glow under my skin. My breathing turns into pants as I battle the agony growing around me. My hands shake profusely in front of me, and my fingers become distorted as fire shoots from my fingertips. I'm burning alive from the inside out. My head falls back as I accept my fate. Fire travels up my throat, forcing my mouth to fly open. I cry out as everything around me turns to flames.

I wake up gasping for air, my throat feeling dry and sore while my body is engulfed in an intense heat. Sweat trickles down the side of my face, stinging my eyes and blurring my vision. I grasp the damp sheet tightly, trying to catch my breath, but the heat continues to sear my sensitive skin. Without wasting another moment, I stumble out of bed and head to the bathroom, ready to shock my body with a blast of ice-cold water.

Once I'm out of the shower, I re-bandage my side; the recent burns are healing decently, considering. I make myself a large cup of coffee and sit down in the living room, turning the lamp on beside the couch. It's just shortly after seven in the morning, and it's still dark outside. I sit for a moment in silence, running my hand through my wet hair and trying to decipher the nightmare I just had. They're different each time, but very much similar in ways.

Sometimes my uncle Jesse appears in my nightmares alongside my mom, but most of the time, the focus is solely on her. Each dream seems to end with someone burning alive, and just before I wake up, a dark figure emerges, lurking in the shadows and fixating on me. After all these years of night terrors, that figure has never shown its face. My thoughts often drift to my father, even though there is no evidence that anyone started the fire; I'm still haunted by it.

So much so, that I've outfitted the entire property with cameras, including the bar. Maybe my paranoia is getting the better of me. I can't help but wonder whether the strange figure in my dreams is something I've conjured up in my mind or is a representation of my father. Either way, I refuse to take any chances. Many nights over the years, I've woken up to see a dark shape outside my bedroom door or heard sounds that hinted someone was lurking nearby. Yet every time, there's nothing in the surveillance footage. The night that man left on my 13th birthday, he left behind a deep-seated fear in me I still can't shake.

He doesn't exist in Mavesdale or anywhere else that I know of. When the house burned down, he was named as the owner on the deed, yet they were unable to locate him. So as his heir, I was left with the burden, but at just sixteen, I felt powerless to act. By the time I turned eighteen, Eric stepped in to help me sell the land and the remnants of the property to a developer. I wanted to sever all ties with that place. Starting anew was challenging enough, especially having to live with Eric and the twins just two streets away from my past nightmare.

Despite all the tragedies woven through my life, they didn't leave me in a financial bind. Between the proceeds from the house and my uncle's belongings, I managed. I had no idea he left everything to my mom and me in his will. While it caught me off guard, it strangely made sense, considering he was always there for us and had no kids of his own. We were his family.

Just a couple of months after turning eighteen, I moved into the mountains to my uncle's cabin. It was nice to get away from that neighborhood in some ways, but for a long time, I felt like I was invading his space, even though he was gone. Because of that, I left his bedroom untouched and turned the guest bedroom into my own. I've made changes throughout the house, but I refuse to go into his room. Maybe someday that'll change, but considering it's been nearly nine years, I highly doubt it.

It's peaceful here. I've always loved this cabin and its location. The nearest neighbor is about half a mile down the mountain. I've gotten used to being alone here, except for the occasional visits from the twins and their dad. Girls I've slept with over the years were never allowed here; I either went to their place or booked a hotel room for a night in town. It was always clear what I wanted, and they agreed it would just be a good time with no strings attached. I don't date or get involved in relationships. It's as simple as that.

After what happened between Beck and me, I promised I would never allow myself or any woman to be in that position again. I knew I wasn't capable of being what someone truly needed. How could I be? Everything I touch seems to fall apart or wither away. The last thing I ever wanted was to drag someone else down with me. This is my *hell* to burn in, no one else's.

I can tell Beck still struggles with my decision, and maybe that's because I didn't fully explain myself or my reasoning. We've never sat down and talked about everything, it just kind of happened, and was pushed aside as we tried living our lives like everything was normal. Believe me, I wanted it to work; I wanted to be that for *her*. She was the one who deserved the fucking world. I loved her, and she loved me. But it was inevitable. After the fire, I couldn't shake the haunting images and emotions that surged through me—to the point it almost pained me to look at her in any other way but my best friend. Despite my efforts to protect her heart, I ended up breaking it instead. It feels like I'm damned if I do and damned if I don't.

I take a generous gulp from my coffee, propping my feet up on the small wooden coffee table as I pull up the surveillance at the bar. I skim through footage before pulling up the videos from the other night. I fast forward through, reaching around closing time. I zoom in on the booth where the new girl, Raina, and her jackass boyfriend sit. Both of them were snickering about something. They eventually get up and make their way to the bar to close out the tab. I focus on her as she stands waiting, watching as she scans over me multiple times.

I've watched this footage at least five or six times since that night, and I'm still unsure of what her expression meant. Was she intrigued with what she saw? Or was she disgusted by my hideous scars? As she goes to leave, she casually says, "Oh, and happy birthday, Ezra." Although I can't hear it in the footage, I still remember the way her delicate voice caressed my scarred skin, each word sending tingles up my arms.

I switch to the outside cameras, pulling up right as they walk out the front door. They stop in front of what looks like a silver Chevrolet truck; it's Dipshit's, I presume. She gently leans up against his driver's side door as they seem to carry on a conversation of some sort. I fast-forward a bit more and stop once I see him inching closer to her. His back is to the camera, and his body keeps her almost entirely hidden. But I watch closely as he pushes up against her, slowly sliding both hands through her blonde locks. Now they're kissing each other. It's a slow, sensual kiss. Despite that, after watching it multiple times, I still can't help but *feel* something. What that feeling is, I'm unsure.

The same thoughts keep racing through my mind. *Does she enjoy the way his hands feel tangled in her hair, while his body presses against her? Does she get butterflies when their lips touch? When he fucks her, does she arch her back from pleasure?* I shake my head, pulling out my Zippo lighter and flicking it back and forth absently. Finally, their kiss breaks apart, and I let out a sigh of relief. My eyes follow her as she walks around the truck and gets in. Yet again, Fuck Nuts fails to open the door for her. Is he even aware of his surroundings? I roll my eyes as I watch them drive off into the distance, aggressively flicking my lighter a few more times before tucking it back into my pocket. My fingers comb through my hair, pushing the damp strands from my face. It's a shame, really. She was such a pretty little thing; too bad I'll never see her again.

The elevator lets out a beep as the doors gradually slide open, pulling me back from my deep thoughts. I step out onto the eighth floor of the apartment complex before glancing left and right, making sure no one is around. Continuing to the end of the hallway, I reach the last door on the left. After a quick look over my shoulder, I slip inside and head up the stairs. Three flights later, I enter the four-digit code and listen for the satisfying click that signals the door is unlocked. I finally push open the door that leads to the roof.

The air is pleasantly warm up here. I take off my bike helmet and hoodie, setting them down by the four-foot railing. The night sky is a deep blue, dotted with stars hanging above. After pausing to gaze upward and inhale deeply, I shift my attention to our small town below. Most of it is cloaked in darkness, with only a handful of streetlights casting a soft glow. I often venture up here after hours to gather my thoughts. This apartment complex, the tallest building in town, provides a badass view of the distant mountains at sunset.

I still remember when this place was first built; a time that coincided with some of my darkest days. It was just a couple of months after I moved into my uncle's house. I was at the local grocery store to meet a guy about buying my crotch rocket. We had been in touch for about a week, and I finally decided I wanted to take the plunge. I just needed to take it for a spin around town before fully committing to the purchase. As I rode past the complex that I had seen countless times before, I looked up at the roof while sitting at a stop sign. Suddenly, a random thought entered my mind: I wonder what the mountains would look like from up there. So now here I am, so many years later, still coming here.

I pull out a cigarette and place it between my lips, reach for my Zippo, flick it on, and inhale deeply, focusing on the crackling of the tobacco. I blow out the smoke, watching it swirl and expand in the night air as my thoughts drift off again. I think about the first night I came here and made it on this very roof. At first, it felt so exhilarating to be up so high, away from everyone and everything. It was like I could clear my head of all the negative thoughts and emotions that plagued me. But as soon as I let my walls down, the voices rushed in like a haunting storm.

My heart raced wildly in my chest, each beat uneven and frantic. I held onto it tightly, wishing I could somehow tear open my chest and silence the pounding that persisted. Gradually, I edged closer, gripping the railing with white knuckles as I gazed down at the sidewalk meeting the road below. I imagined my body sprawled out—bloody and contorted—while people rushed by, their screams echoing in the air. The thought of simply letting go and finally feeling free flashed through my mind, tempting me in a fleeting moment before I took a step closer to the brink. It wasn't until I found myself climbing over the railing that I realized just how deep into these thoughts I'd descended.

My shoes hung slightly off the five-inch ledge while my hands were behind my back, gripping the railing. I slowly leaned, pulling some of my weight forward against the railing. The cold breeze bristled against my hair, causing me to close my eyes. The voices in my head whispered sweet venom in my ears. *Let go... let go.* I allowed my fingers to slip slowly as I prepared to end everything—all the pain, the grief, the constant fire that burned me internally. I was ready to claim death as my own. Because all this time, I had been walking this Earth only existing. Numb, while feeling everything at the same time. Nothing made sense, while everything did. I wanted to *die.*

I pulled harder, feeling my shoulders stretch as they silently protested, my arms shaking behind me. *Just let go, Ezra,* I kept repeating in my mind. A distressed gasp caught in my throat. I squeezed my eyes shut, forcing back tears that threatened to spill as I bit down on my bottom lip. My grip was slipping and sweat began to pool in my palms, making it harder to hold on.

I took a deep breath, preparing to finally let go. Suddenly, a voice echoed in my mind so clearly that I whipped my head around, convinced someone was on the roof with me. But then it hit me—it was my mom. I wasn't sure if it was just my subconscious or if I was losing my grip on reality. Yet hearing her say my name struck a chord deep in my chest. *What am I doing? What about Beck and Blake?* If I go through with this, it means my mom and Jesse would have died for nothing. More importantly, I don't deserve an easy way out. I need to live and face the consequences of my mistakes. I won't live for myself; I'll live for my mom and the twins, all while carrying the weight of all the pain I've caused.

I took one last look down, and a wave of queasiness swept over me. The sheer drop below made me dizzy, but I was thankful it was night; no one could see me on the verge of ending it all. Just as I prepared to pull myself back, the railing I clung to suddenly creaked loudly. My attention snapped to the side as I noticed the metal bending under my weight. Before I could react, it let out a piercing screech and lurched forward, pushing me along with it. In an instant, my right hand slipped from the railing, leaving me dangling off the edge of the roof.

I gritted my teeth against the sharp pain in my left shoulder blade, a reminder of the strain from carrying my weight all at once. I fought to keep my composure and resisted the urge to look down. Steadying myself, I used my right hand to grip the ledge and turned to confront the roof. Quickly scanning the railing, I felt a surge of relief to find it was merely a section that had bowed outward. Exhaling slowly, I mentally prepared myself. I reached as far as I could with my right arm, grasping the bottom of the railing. With careful movements, I let go with my left hand and repositioned my grip, securing it further along where the railing remained intact.

My whole body was shaking from hanging on for so long. I knew I couldn't hold much longer, and it would take every ounce of strength I had left to pull myself up to safety. Taking a few deep breaths, I braced myself as best as I could. In one swift motion, I gritted my teeth and used my upper body to haul myself up. Once I made it over the railing, I collapsed onto my back, panting like there was no tomorrow. I clinched my left shoulder hard, sure that I tore my rotator cuff. A tingling sensation raced up my legs and arms as I lay there, staring up at the stars in disgust. For hours, I remained on the roof, lost in thought.

What a foolish fucking thing I had done—almost done.

A car horn blares somewhere below, pulling me from my harsh memory. I glance at my cigarette; a long ash clings to the end, ready to fall any moment. I let out an aggravated sigh, taking a long hit before flicking off the cherry and smothering it with my shoe. I flick my eyes over to where the railing still bows forward. Before I left that night, I did my best to fix it. It's not leaning as severely as it was, but it will need to be replaced to be secure again. At this point, I doubt it'll ever be repaired—which leaves it as another reminder of the fuck up I am.

I instinctively grab my left shoulder, it had never fully healed from that night. I take one last look over the town before grabbing my hoodie and pulling it on. With a quick motion, I run my fingers through my hair to sweep it back from my face. I pick up my bike helmet and slide it over my head, adjusting it. I always make sure to wear it when I come here. The last thing I want is to draw unwanted attention or bump into someone I know, especially a customer from the bar.

Once I'm back at the elevator, I stand by patiently, hands tucked in my hoodie pockets to ensure no one catches a glimpse of my right hand, its scars and tattoos that would give away too much. I really don't want to run into someone I'd rather avoid. Finally, the elevator dings open, and I step inside. I watch the floor numbers descend, stopping at the third level. I shuffle to the far left, leaning against the wall and railing to make room for the oncomer. As the doors slide open, an older man walks in, and I catch the sound of a woman's laughter mingling with a deep voice from the hall.

As the older man steps into the elevator, the laughter from the woman down the hall transforms. I look down the right side of the hall to see her struggling to enter what I assume is her room. A guy stands right behind her, grabbing her shoulders and spinning her around just as she shouts for him to stop. Now that she's facing him, my eyes widen in shock. *Holy fuck, that's…* Before I can finish my thought, I push past the older man in the elevator and rush down the hall. In moments, I grab Douchebag from behind and slam him against the wall next to the door, pinning him there with my elbow. I quickly glance over at her to make sure she's okay. "What the hell, dude?!" he yells, trying to shove my elbow away from his throat. Frustrated, I pull my elbow back and deliver a sharp jab to his nose before wrapping my hand around his neck. I snarl at him while he raises his hands in a gesture of surrender. What a *pussy*.

I could easily cut off his air supply without a second thought, but I shake off the idea and refocus on her. A sudden gasp escapes her lips, and her hands come together to cover her delicate jaw. Our eyes meet through my helmet; her expression reveals a mix of fear and… perhaps a flicker of curiosity. The sight of her diminished a fraction of the anger surging within me. She is just as beautiful as I remembered her. I reach my right hand out to her, but quickly refrain. I exhale softly through my nose. "Did he hurt you?"

She bites her bottom lip, holding it between her top teeth as she shakes her head slowly. The jerk lets out a scoff in response to my question. "Dude, we were just messing around!"

I roll my eyes, keeping my gaze fixed on her. Frustrated, I let out a groan. "Do you ever just shut the fuck up?" I notice her eyes shift to my hand again. She studies it for a moment, and suddenly, I can see a realization dawn in her expression. Her hand flies to her mouth.

"Ezra?"

Frustration bubbles up inside me as my hand betrays my identity. Raina clearly recognizes me. I clench my hand and release vomit-mouth Scottie, who glances between Raina and me in confusion. "Wait, who the hell is…Ez—oh…wait…the *bartender*?!" he exclaims, suddenly aware. Touching his nose, he winces and pulls his hand back to reveal blood. "You busted my nose, dude!"

I merely shrug, lifting my elbow to check for a stain. "You've got blood on my favorite hoodie," I reply, shaking my head. I then reach over, grab his shirt, and wipe the sleeve of my hoodie. "You're lucky it's black," I add with a casual tone. He just stares at me in disbelief.

Raina hasn't taken her eyes off me, and now her expression is impossible to read. I can't tell if she's pissed at me or pleased to see me. She tilts her head and clicks her tongue before asking, "What are you doing here?"

Fuck, that part. I quickly respond, "Just visiting a friend. I was about to leave—until I thought I was witnessing a woman being assaulted." I glare at Scottie behind my helmet, hoping he can still feel it. "Anyway, I'll let you two carry on with whatever this is." I give Raina one last look before turning to head back to the elevator. As the doors slide open, I peek back at her, deliberately ignoring Scottie and his bloodied nose. "Oh, and Raina, try keeping your boy toy under control." She bites down on her bottom lip, almost like she's holding back a smile. Scottie scoffs, but says nothing. *He's smarter than I thought.*

Once the doors close in the elevator, I rest against the wall. What are the odds of this? She lives here, and for how long? I recall glancing at her ID at the bar. I would have noticed if her address was here. Now I've really made a lasting first impression by assaulting her punk boyfriend. Great. Just when I thought our paths would never cross again. Here she is, living in the very place I visit from time to time. Did I make a mental note of her room number? Yes, yes, I fucking did. So what? Because I already know, no matter how hard I try to stay away from this girl, that I will find myself here again or will run into her somewhere in town. It's inevitable. And there's this nagging sense that Raina Adele Hope is the one person who will make me lose the grip on what I've so desperately held onto for years—my control.

"So, let me get this straight," Blake begins, a curious look in his eyes. "You just *happened* to be in the elevator of this girl's building, minding your own business, when it stopped on her floor?" I nod, bracing myself for where this is headed. "And then you find yourself standing in front of her door with your elbow in her boyfriend's neck?" He sets a glass mug down on the bar, drying his hands with a towel. I stay quiet, knowing he's not done yet. "Ya know, I've thought of you as a lot of things, Ez, but a creepy stalker wasn't one of them." There it is. I pinch the bridge of my nose and let out a displeased sigh.

He assists a few customers near the bar before strolling over to where I'm restocking glasses. He nudges my arm and smirks. "So, did you tell your crush that the very building she lives in is the same one you almost went skydiving off of?" He lowers his voice, leaning in closer. "Without a parachute, mind you." Sometimes I question why I spill personal information to him that I really should keep under wraps. I guess it's because I know he genuinely cares and is looking out for me. He never pressures me or tells me what to do. He listens, judges me for a moment, and then cracks a dumbass joke to lighten the mood, brushing off his worry. And he knows that if he ever spills my dark secrets to Beck or anyone else, I would beat the ever-living shit out of him.

With an annoyed shake of my head, I shoot him a glare, trying to burn through his charming, blue eyes. "Yes, Blake. I also confessed my undying love for her," I say, my tone dripping with sarcasm.

"Holy shit…did you just crack a joke, Mr. Ezra Gray Stone?" He dramatically places his hand over his chest, his mouth wide open. "You're not so *gray* after all…" I choose to avoid drawing attention to his childish theatrics.

"So…who are we confessing our love to?" Blake and I both look toward the double doors. *Fuck, Beck.* I glance back at Blake, who suddenly has his back turned to me, talking to customers sitting by the bar. *Fucker.*

I quickly turn back to Beck, forcing a tight smile. "Oh, it's nothing, just your brother running his mouth as usual."

She gives me a knowing nod and steps in for a hug. I pull her close, inhaling her familiar scent. She lets out a soft breath through her nose at the contact. "I've missed you, you know?" Her voice is so soothing. My hand gently cradles the back of her head, feeling her silky curls wrap around my fingers.

"Yeah, I've missed you too, B." I clear my throat, releasing her from my hold.

She steps back slightly, still keeping her hands around me as she gazes up. I glance down at her, feeling my heart race a bit beneath my chest. She tilts her head and gently brushes the hair off my forehead. "Your hair's longer than usual…I like it like this." Out of habit, I sweep it back with my fingers and chuckle softly.

"Oh, really? Maybe I'll keep it this way then." Beck gives me an easy smile, her eyes drifting over my shoulder.

Blake suddenly appears behind me, giving my shoulders a friendly pat. "We really need to hit the lake soon…before it gets too chilly." He then turns to Beck, pulling her into a quick hug before playfully digging his elbow into the top of her head. She snaps back with a solid punch to his chest, their usual twin banter on full display. I glance between them, noting how to most people they look identical. While I can see the similarities in their features and mannerisms, I also catch the finer details: Beck's hair is curlier with an auburn hue, while Blake's is predominantly straight and medium-toned brown. One striking feature they share, though, is their deep blue eyes, a trait Eric always claimed they inherited from their mother.

I've always wished I had my mom's eyes, but instead, I ended up with my father's—deep, rich amber hues. In the light, they shine like fire, much like the flames that have engulfed my life. It's almost comical how ironic it all is. Mom frequently complimented my eyes, often saying they resembled Uncle Jesse's. In a way, she was right, but there were times I suspected she was just trying to brush aside the thought of me inheriting my father's wicked gaze.

The door chimes as more customers stroll in. Blake walks away, ready to take more drink orders, but glances back over his shoulder. "You two pick a day, and I'm in." Beck runs her fingers through her hair, tucking it behind her ears.

"How about next Thursday?" I suggest.

She pulls out her phone, swiping through her calendar. "Yeah…that works." Her gentle smile sends a chill down my arms.

"I'll have a lemon drop, please," a familiar, angelic voice sounds from behind me. The hairs on the back of my neck stand as I turn around. There she stands, elbows relaxed on top of the bar. Her golden, blonde locks lay delicately around the frame of her face.

Her green eyes find me, holding my gaze. A playful grin pulls at her glossed lips right before Blake steps into my view of her.

"I'm going to need you to take over. I need a quick restroom break," Blake chimes with amusement laced into his words. Aggravation coils under my skin as I look back at Beck, giving her a nod of confirmation for our lake plans.

I make my way to the bar, keeping my expression neutral. After quickly washing my hands and drying them with a towel, I take my place directly in front of Raina, the bar counter separating us. "I didn't know you'd be here," she says, setting her purse down on the counter.

I had a hunch she wasn't being entirely truthful, though. I bite the inside of my cheek as I study her for a moment. "Well, since I own this place, I'm here most of the time."

Curiosity dances around in her eyes. "Oh, good to know," she replies, tapping her fingernails lightly against the bar top.

I clear my throat, changing the subject quickly. "I overheard that you'd like a lemon drop…correct?" She gives a slight nod, her eyes moving to something behind me. I begin preparing her drink when a hand runs along my shoulder blade. I tilt my head back, finding Beck standing beside me. Her attention goes to Raina, her expression holding something I can't quite grasp.

She quickly brings her eyes back to me. "I'm going to head home. Dad's wanting to make popcorn and watch a movie together."

The smile she gives reaches her eyes. She chose to stay there after Blake moved out years ago, she didn't want Eric living alone. And I love that about her. I set the glass down, placing my hand near her lower back, grazing my fingers along her arch. I smile back. "Tell Eric I said hello."

She reaches behind, placing her hand over mine and giving it a light squeeze before walking off. I refocus on preparing the drink, choosing not to look back at Raina. Once her drink is ready, I place it in front of her and glance back at her. She gently chews on her bottom lip. I watch as she reaches for the drink. "I see your girlfriend is here a lot, too," she murmurs nonchalantly. I pause for a moment; I can see why it may have looked that way to her. There has been confusion here before, and questions about what Beck and I really are. I've tried not to draw too much attention to it, knowing how touchy it is for her and, well, me.

I grab a rag, wiping up the small mess from prepping Raina's drink. "She's not my girlfriend. She's…a close friend."

Raina clicks her tongue, running her finger on the rim of her drink. I watch intently as she brings her finger to her mouth, licking off the sugar residue. A slight smile tugged at her lips. "Noted."

Since we are on this subject, I chime back at her. "Why isn't your little boyfriend here with you?"

She pauses, letting out a quiet laugh before taking a small sip of her drink. "He's not my boyfriend. We just…hang out sometimes."

So they're just fuck buddies, I presume. My face heats a little at the random thought. "Interesting, so I was right then? He's a boy toy?"

She slants her stunning, green eyes at me, tucking her hair back on one side. A testing smirk appears. "Something like that." She gulps down the rest of her drink, sliding it in my direction. "He would be here tonight, but some guy randomly elbowed him in the face recently, and well, he's nursing a black eye." Her eyes flick up to mine.

I slightly grimace at her comment before I reach for her empty glass. "Damn, only one? I was hoping for two." She gives an annoyed eye roll, but her expression is playful. "How did you two end up meeting?" I inquire.

Raina licks her lips, clearly amused. "You seem to have quite a few questions for someone who pretends to be uninterested."

I give a slight shrug in response to her remark. "I'm just trying to connect with a customer; it's part of my job," I explain.

She leans in closer, nodding thoughtfully. "Fair enough… since we're connecting and all, I work as a vet tech at the local animal clinic. Scottie brought his cat in for a wellness checkup, and after about five minutes of checking Fluffy's vitals, he handed me a torn piece of paper with his number on it."

I can't help but laugh at that. Of course, he's a cat owner. And really, what grown ass man names his fucking feline *Fluffy*? Shaking my head, I redirect my attention back to her. "Why doesn't your ID show the address of your apartment complex?"

She tilts her head slightly. "You're giving off some stalker vibes there," she replies.

I run my fingers through my hair, trying to keep my cool. "No, I'm just observant," I counter, hoping she'll elaborate.

"I just moved here about five months ago after finishing college," she explains, "and I might have procrastinated on updating my address. I'm still waiting for the new one to come in the mail."

I nod in understanding. "What made you choose Mavesdale of all places?"

She turns as she glances around for a moment. "I spent quite some time looking for the right place, then the job just sort of…fell in my lap. They were short-staffed, and honestly, who wouldn't want to live just minutes from the mountains? It felt like a win-win for my personal life and career." That makes sense. A playful smile tugs at her lips. "If I had known there was a grumpy bar owner around, I might have thought twice." I tilt my head in mock offense as she turns back toward me, glancing over her shoulder. "I'll have one more of those, please," she calls out, then grabs her purse and heads over to the jukebox.

I watch for a second longer, noticing her sift through the song choices. I observe her from behind. Her outfit is simple, but it suits her. She wears a fitted burgundy leather jacket and jeans that fit perfectly around her plump a—

"Did I give you enough time to win her over?" My thoughts are cut short.

"Stop fucking doing that," I snap at Blake, who snuck up behind me *yet again*.

"Whoa, buddy, my bad." He throws his hands up. "I was just playing my part as your wingman. I could at least get a simple thank you." I purposely bump into him as I reach for a new glass to prepare her next drink. He smirks, walking off to check the other customers sitting near the bar.

I stare at the side of his face for a moment. For close to twenty years, I've put up with his shit. I can only be thankful that Beck isn't a duplicate of him. Which sounds absurd, considering they are twins. They most definitely come as a packaged deal. But where Blake is obnoxiously annoying at times, Beck is centered and calm. I will say, they level each other perfectly. Blake is just, Blake. Where I am serious about most things, he finds a way to be unbothered. He often reminds me that life isn't meant to be so serious, so say fuck it and crack a joke.

I shake my head as I finish Raina's second drink. My eyes drift back to her, standing by the jukebox. *What the hell is wrong with me?* I've only had a few random conversations with this girl, yet I can't shake the feeling that I want to have just one more—or maybe even more. *Abso-fucking-lutely not, Ezra. Get your act together.* Frustrated with myself, I sweep my hair out of my face.

"Uh, there goes Gavin on his shit…" Blake chimes beside me. I flick my attention back to Raina, watching as Gavin goes up behind her at the jukebox. We've had issues with him in the past, saying inappropriate things to Beck when he's gotten a good buzz and his dick spoke before his mouth. He was warned, or shall I say threatened. I also cut his drink limit down, and that seemed to help. There hasn't been a problem since. I don't take kindly to disrespect, especially when it's toward a woman. I may seem quiet and to myself to most, but if you willingly push me, you will see a side I try to keep buried away.

I focus intently on him, my gaze burning through the back of his head. Blake steps right up beside me. "Just stay calm, Ez. He might just be waiting to pick a song." As Blake's words hang in the air, I see Gavin's left hand trailing along Raina's lower back, his palm resting exactly where her arch lies beneath her jacket. A wildfire of anger sets off within me. I barely catch Blake's frustrated grunt of "*Ah fuuuuuck*," behind me as I stride towards them. The only thing I can feel is rage boiling over, threatening to spill out. Raina has already yanked his hand away from her back, pointing a tiny finger in his face.

In an instant, I find myself right behind Gavin. I swiftly grab the back of his shirt and kick the back of his right knee, sending him tumbling to the floor while still holding onto his shirt. Coming around and crouching down, I press my knee into his ribcage, leaning my weight into it. He lets out a loud groan from the pressure. "Wha-what the hell, man?" he exclaims. I flash my teeth at him, then hoist him up with one arm, guiding him to the door by his shirt and giving his shoulder a firm shove with my free hand.

Once we're outside, I spin him around and release his shirt, ensuring we're close enough for him to sense the anger radiating from me. I exhale sharply through my nose, tasting the blood from where I bit my tongue. "What did I tell you, Gavin?" I demand.

He throws his hands up in confusion. "Man, I was just—"

I step forward, cutting him off. "You're banned from coming here for a month, and when you do come back, your drink ration is getting slashed even further until you learn to keep your thoughts—and your hands—to yourself. Do you get me?" I can see the frustration flickering in his eyes, the struggle between saying what he really thinks and following my orders to leave quietly. As expected, he chooses to comply, giving me a brief nod. I keep my gaze on him until he drives off in his truck.

As I walk back through the front door, the room falls silent. The only sound is the music playing in the background. I lift my chin, spotting Raina by the bar, arms crossed, clutching the drink I made for her. I scan the room, noticing how everyone quickly resumes their conversations as if nothing had happened. Blake is behind the bar, shaking his head and giving me a knowing look as I step back behind the counter. "Feeling better?" he asks casually.

I shrug. "Not really. Honestly, I would have preferred using my fist…but I refrained."

Raina sets her now-empty glass down on the counter with a clink. "What was that?" she blurts out, her green eyes looking much greener than before. I catch myself staring at them longer than I should. Blinking, I manage to keep my expression neutral and pull my gaze away.

"I don't tolerate that kind of behavior in my bar, and this wasn't his first time being warned." I glance at her, noticing her chewing on the inside of her lip.

"And what kind of behavior is that?" she asks.

I lean forward, bracing my hands on the counter. "It's the kind where a grown man disrespects a woman." She locks eyes with me for a moment, then her gaze travels up and down my neck. My scars and flame tattoos stand out clearly in the shirt I'm wearing today. I watch her eyes trace them like a road map until they meet mine again. She scrunches her tiny nose, and I can see her freckles bunch together on the bridge. A flutter hits my stomach; for a brief moment, I want to count each freckle, tapping my finger gently on each one. I grip the counter tightly, trying to rein in my thoughts.

I clear my throat and ask her, "What's that look for?"

She offers a slight smile, reaching into her purse. "Honestly, I find it…kinda hot," she replies. I squint at her, a grin breaking through my usually composed demeanor. She pulls out a crumpled receipt and rummages around for a pen at the bottom of her bag. As she scribbles something down, I watch intently. Finally, she slides the wrinkled piece of paper across the bar toward me. I glance down, reading the number she's written. "Since you already know where I live, I thought you might as well have my number," she says. I fall silent, unsure of how to react and uncertain about what she's expecting from me.

She catches my concerned expression and chuckles softly. "You know, I could really use my own personal bodyguard… Scottie isn't doing such a great job, anyway."

As she brushes her fingers through her bangs, she grabs her purse and turns to head out. I furrow my brows. "Wait, are you okay to drive?"

She pauses, glancing back over her shoulder, a playful smile lighting up her face. "I've only had two drinks, and sobered up pretty fast after that little show you put on for me." I tighten my lips, and she lets out a light laugh. "Goodnight, Ezra." I give a quick nod, watching her until she disappears through the door. Quickly, I pull out my phone and check the cameras. I see her getting into a small silver SUV.

"Pretty stalker-ish of you, Ez…" I close my eyes and slide my phone back into my jeans pocket, trying to shake off the image of giving Blake a good throat punch. He lets out a dramatic sigh beside me. "Your game is slipping, brother. You know…usually it's the guy who hands out their number."

I whip my head around to glare at him. "Do you ever just shut the hell up?" I grind out, frustration tightening my nerves. His expression remains unfazed as he walks away, chuckling under his breath. *Bastard.*

I snatch the receipt Raina left on the bar, carefully scanning her neat handwriting and committing her number to memory. Folding the paper, I tuck it into my pocket and run my fingers through my hair. I replay tonight's events, along with our few other interactions, trying to untangle why she would want me to have her number. This certainly wasn't my intention. I noticed her glancing at my scars, and she witnessed how easily I can lose my temper. I thought I had done everything possible to give her the impression that this had been nothing more than a conversation with a customer, that I was not keen on complicating it. Yet, despite that, there's an undeniable intrigue within me. I've seen her studying me, still choosing to engage, even after I assaulted her precious Scottie.

I can't shake the feeling that she came here tonight hoping to find me. Just the thought kindles a warmth within me, stirring something deep and unexpected. But along with that spark comes a wave of frustration. I'm caught in a whirlwind of conflicting emotions; I want to see her again, but every rational thought in my mind urges me to keep my distance. This isn't like my past encounters—I've always been upfront with other women, setting boundaries from the very start, and I've successfully kept my personal life private, even from the twins.

But there's something about her that makes it impossible to maintain that distance. She's different…there's an intensity in her gaze, a determination that hints at a stubborn streak beneath her seemingly calm exterior. It's both alluring and unnerving. As I wrestle with these thoughts, the weight of the situation presses down on me, leaving me to wonder what it is about her that has so thoroughly upended my carefully constructed walls. Why her? What is it about this girl that drives me to question everything I've kept control of? I can't help but feel overwhelmed by the mix of attraction and caution. *Fuck me.*

10

My sweaty palm grips the bathroom counter as I steady myself, feeling the familiar ache of the scars on my right hand with each deliberate stroke. I take my time, glancing down at the image on my phone from the bar footage. Although the quality isn't perfect, it's just enough to fuel my desperation. My eyelids flutter as I focus on the sight of her, zoomed in where she's sitting gracefully at the bar. I can't help but notice the way she bites her bottom lip, a playful grin lingering on her face, her green eyes sparkling with curiosity. I savor the way her bangs frame her arched brows, brushing softly against her long lashes.

I grip my dick harder, picking up my movements. My mouth falls open as my eyes squeeze shut. I picture her sitting at the bar facing me as I approach her. She has that playful look in her eyes. Once I'm standing in front of her, I grab her thighs, spreading them wide as I move between her legs. The blue dress she's in rides up her smooth thighs, revealing thin, lace panties. I imagine my large hands gripping her petite face while my thumbs graze across the faded freckles along her cheeks.

I gently wrap my left hand around her neck, feeling how small it is beneath my grip. Her pulse quickens under my palm, not from fear, but from excitement. *Desire.* I lean in closer, guiding her back against the bar. Her pink-tinted lips part slightly as her green eyes lock onto mine. I slide my hand away from her neck, slowly tracing down between her breasts where her nipples tent the delicate fabric of her dress. Taking my right hand, I glide it up her thigh, revealing more of her enticing form.

I gaze at the white lace panties between her legs. Sliding my fingers up, I run my thumb over the fabric where her center aches for me. A helpless moan leaves her mouth, the sound causing me to bite down hard on my bottom lip. I eagerly pull my hand back, rubbing my thumb along the tips of my fingers, feeling the warm wetness that clings to them, letting me know just how much she needs my touch. She watches me intently as I bring my thumb up, grazing it along my tongue. Her delicious scent clings to my taste buds.

A rush of pressure surges through my stomach, drawing me closer to a state of pure ecstasy. I lock eyes with Raina, her gaze urging me to touch her once more. I kneel before her, gently resting her legs on my shoulders. She steadies herself, gripping the sides of the bar chair. I let my fingers glide around the lace trim, pulling it aside to reveal her center. A deep groan escapes my lips, the craving to taste her intensifying rapidly.

I move closer, wrapping my arm around her thigh and gripping it with my hand. Keeping her panties tugged to the side, I hesitate no longer, running my tongue along her sensitive spot. A desperate gasp leaves her. I grip her tighter, slowly circling her throbbing clit with my tongue. She breathes out my name. So much want, so much *need* behind each letter. And the way my name sounds on her tongue causes my dick to grow harder. I continue caressing her with my mouth, taking notes of the way her body reacts to my touch.

I can feel my release inching closer, growing stronger. I move my hand down her thigh, pressing my thumb right above where she aches for me. I make small, sensual circles that match the rhythm of my tongue. Raina's hands instantly find their way into my hair, gripping and tugging. I growl into her center, bringing my eyes up to meet hers. I study her as I bring her to her undoing. She watches me closely, her eyes finding mine. Her lashes flutter with each pleasurable plunge of my tongue. Our moans mix, sounding so appetizing together.

I can't hold off any longer—my eyes fly open as I come back to reality. I reposition my grip on the counter, bringing my gaze back to her image on my phone. I stroke and tug, imagining Raina's undoing. In seconds, my head falls forward as my cum shoots into the sink. My heart pounds against my chest as I regain my full vision. I grab a tissue from the counter, wiping the tip of my dick off before tucking it back into my briefs. I annoyingly shift my eyes to the mess I left in the sink. Slightly ashamed of myself, I turn the faucet on high and watch the evidence wash down the drain.

I look up in the mirror at myself, watching as sweat droplets trail down the side of my face. This isn't one of my proudest moments. It's been months since I've had any form of sexual encounters with a woman, and since these last few weeks, I haven't been able to get this girl off my damned mind. It doesn't help that my dick has a mind of its own. I tried to think of anyone else but her. I tried to picture myself touching another woman, but my dick rejected it, until *her*. Hopefully, now that I've satisfied it, I can move on and add it to my collection of failures.

I turn to the side and lift my arm to take a look at my recent, self-inflicted wounds. They've healed well enough that I no longer need bandages, at least for now. As I take a moment to focus on myself, I notice the dark circles under my eyes, a telltale sign of the little sleep I've managed to get. Last night's dreams were relentless, the same as always, but this time there was a new face—Raina's. It scared the hell out of me. I needed to clear my head somehow. I considered burning myself, but held back since I'm meeting the twins at the lake this afternoon. So, I had to find a different way to cope this time.

I turn the faucet on, letting the ice-cold water fill my palms. I lean down, cupping the water and splashing it on my face. Its coldness washes away some of the tiredness from my eyes, but it doesn't take away the mental exhaustion I feel, which isn't anything new in my life. I quickly grab the towel hanging over the shower door and pat my face dry. I let a deep sigh leave my restless body before I exit the bathroom and prepare for the day.

After getting to town, I filled up my bike's tank. I still have about an hour to kill before meeting the twins at the lake. I now sit in the small parking lot directly across from Raina's apartment. I know damn well I shouldn't be here, but here I fucking am. It's not like I drove out of the way; I had to pass through town, regardless. But I haven't quite figured out why I'm sitting here staring directly at Raina's room. *Very stalk-ish of you, Ezra.*

I slide my bike helmet up to my brow and let it rest there as I dig into my jeans pocket for my cigarettes. I pull one out, tuck it between my lips, and light it with my Zippo. I inhale the smoke, feeling it wrap around my lungs deliciously. I exhale a large cloud while my eyes stay trained on Raina's room. I can't help but wonder whether she's home or at work. I haven't thought about driving by the local vet's office where she works. I know she owns a small silver SUV, but I'm not sure of the model yet.

It didn't occur to me that she could also be with Scottie; what if he's in her room right now? The thought of it makes my heart pound in my chest. She's too good for him. She's witty and strong-minded. She needs a man who will protect her at all costs and match her feisty spirit. Scottie should stay the fuck away from her and go snuggle his precious Fluff—

"Ezra?" A delicate voice sounds from behind me. I turn my head, finding Raina standing just feet away from me.

Her hair is up with pieces framing her face, her bangs slightly parted in the middle. She is even more stunning with her hair like this, allowing me to appreciate the contours of her face. She stands with her keys in one hand and her other clutching her purse on her shoulder. Her lavender scrubs indicate she has been at work. The color complements her light green eyes. I can see why Douchebag Scottie took his shot the first time he saw her— she is not hard on the eyes.

I keep my expression neutral as I take another drag from my cigarette, quickly blowing out the smoke to respond. "It's me, in the flesh." She slants her eyes at me before turning and hitting the lock button on her car. I take notes of the vehicle she drives, a Chevrolet Equinox. She moves closer to me, eyeing my bike and the cigarette snug between my lips. Before I can respond, she quickly plucks it from my mouth, placing it between her fingers.

I remain quiet, observing her as she stares off into the distance, taking a small puff. The cherry barely crackles before she exhales, a look of discomfort flashing across her face. She quickly hands it back to me, and a grin spreads across my lips. "I would never picture you as a smoker."

I watch her rummage through her purse, pulling out some hand sanitizer. "I'm not…but I've always wanted to give it a try."

I pause, hoping she'll continue, but she falls silent.

"And…?" I press her gently. Her nose scrunches up in response.

"It tastes terrible, actually." I let out a chuckle, taking another hit before flicking the cherry into the parking lot.

She tilts her head and looks at me. "It suits you, though," she comments. I raise an eyebrow, unsure.

"What do you mean by that?"

She shrugs lightly. "I don't know, you give off that bad guy look. The tattoos…with the mysterious vibes."

I give an understanding nod. "Do you think I'm a bad guy?"

She studies me for a moment before replying. "No…I think some of it is a shield that you've put up in front of people, maybe because you've been through things. But deep down, I believe you care a lot for people, especially those close to you." I glance away, chewing the inside of my lip. Raina quickly clears her throat to change the topic. "So are you here visiting a friend again?"

I casually slip my Zippo back into my pocket, trying to brush off her earlier comment. My face goes blank, my defenses snapping back into place. "Yeah, something like that. I'm heading to meet the twins from work. We have a little private spot by the lake."

She gives a nod. "Sounds cool. Maybe you could take me there sometime?"

I quickly refocus on her. "I'm not sure how Scottie would feel about that."

She rolls her eyes. "Scottie doesn't get to dictate what I do."

I hold back a smirk. "Point taken." I pull my helmet down over my head, lowering the visor.

Raina glances toward her apartment. "Alright, I should get going…my lunch break is almost over."

She gives me a quick smile before walking away, glancing back over her shoulder. "Oh, and I'm still waiting for you to text me," she reminds me. I say nothing as I start up my bike. My eyes follow her as she crosses the street and heads into her apartment. I find myself staring at her room, waiting for a sign that she's settled in and safe. After a few minutes, I finally catch a glimpse of her at the sliding doors that lead to her small balcony. She locks eyes with me for a moment before disappearing from my view.

As I drive away, Raina's words replay in my mind, leaving a lingering feeling I can't shake. I've always been pretty good at hiding my emotions, but somehow it feels like she can see right through me. But how? I hardly know her, and she knows little about me except that I run the bar and have a bit of a temper. There's a part of me that wants to keep my distance, yet I also feel a strong urge to keep her close and protect her from the world. It's a struggle to shield myself from how she affects me. And curiosity keeps getting the better of me. There's just something about her—she's like a gentle rainstorm, calm on the surface but capable of unleashing a torrent beneath. She could be the very thing that holds the power to extinguish the fiery inferno smoldering deep inside me, and that thought terrifies the fuck out of me.

11

I gaze out at the mass lake, tuning in to the twins' playful debate over who will take charge of the music on the Bluetooth speaker. I chuckle softly at their silly bickering. No matter how much time passes, some things remain the same. Glancing up at the sky I notice the overcast, but overall, it's a perfect day to be here. Before long, the chilly days will set in, and the mountains will be blanketed in snow.

I pull my phone from my swim shorts and quickly scan the surveillance feeds from the bar and the house. As I scroll through my contacts, my thumb stops on Raina's name. I had saved her number after I got home that night from the bar; my restless mind wouldn't let me do anything else. I convinced myself there were good reasons to keep it. But honestly, that doesn't matter much now. I know exactly where she lives and works. If I wanted to find her, I'm pretty sure I could track her down with little effort. Unless she's somewhere with *him*.

Beck settles down next to me with a dramatic sigh—I can only assume Blake won the battle. "You are lucky to be an only child," she teases.

"I'm pretty sure I put up with your brother just as much as you do." I glance over at her and give a playful nudge.

She leans back on her hands, arms stretched out behind her, and looks up at the sky for a moment before tilting her head and flashing me a knowing smile. "Yeah…you are right. We're both screwed."

A large hand grips my shoulder, and soon after, Blake crouches down between us. "You guys just can't help but say my name, can you?" he teases with a grin.

Beck rolls her eyes at him. "Can't resist," she replies dryly, her voice dripping with sarcasm. Blake nods proudly and straightens up, rolling his shoulders as he scoots backwards. I can already tell what he's planning. Beck and I exchange a knowing glance. With a playful wink, Blake takes off, sprinting toward us. Just as we shift apart, he dashes in between us, performs a front flip off the ledge, and gives us both the middle finger on his way down to the water. Classic Blake.

"The water feels amazing…bring your asses down here!" he yells from below.

Beck shouts back, "Be there in a minute!"

I look down at Blake floating on his back, catching him rolling his eyes. "I'm going to make a lap to the other side…you both better be in the water when I make it back!" Beck and I both snicker at his demands. Things then get quiet for a moment as we both stare out at the place that made some of our best childhood memories. This has always been a safe place for me, somewhere close to what home used to be, but far enough to escape the hell I endured.

I hear Beck take a deep breath next to me, running her fingers through her auburn hair. "I don't think I'll ever get tired of this place…even after all this time."

I nod in agreement. "Yeah…I feel the same."

She lets out a soft laugh. "I still picture us as kids here…and you…before everything changed."

I shift slightly at her words, pulling out my Zippo from my pocket and flicking the lid back and forth with my thumb. "I'm still me, Beck."

We lapse into silence for a moment, and I see her turn a bit to face me. "Are you really, though? Sometimes I feel like I hardly know you anymore…ever since that night…with us." I can hear the hurt in her voice, and it breaks something in me. I never wanted things to turn out this way. I never meant to make her feel like this. All I ever wanted was to keep her safe—from me.

Frustration wells up inside me as I snap the lid shut on my Zippo. "I'm not sixteen anymore, B...everything changed after that night, and you know it."

I notice her biting her bottom lip while she nervously rubs her arm. "Like how you felt about me?" She clears her throat, taking a moment to gather her words. "I thought our moment was something special...I wanted it to be special for us, so badly. But then everything fell apart right after. I spent months questioning everything. But then we gave it another shot, and the way you looked at me that night made me believe it was all just a huge mistake between us."

I can't believe how many years have gone by, and she's still felt this way. And it's my fault. I never took the time to fully explain myself to her. Back then, I was just a teenager, grappling with grief and all the sudden changes in my life. And as time went on, I turned into a shadow of my former self. I buried my fears and pain, thinking I was shielding those I loved. But in reality, I ended up hurting someone I truly care about.

I scoot closer to her, resting my right hand on her leg. She glances down, studying the mix of scars and tattoos that decorate my skin. For a moment, I see her hesitate, but then she softly places her hand over mine, her fingers gently brushing my wrist. I flinch a little at the sensitivity around the scarred areas she touches, but I don't pull away. "Beck…I never meant to hurt you, and maybe it was selfish of me to think you understood why things happened the way they did." I run my free hand through my hair, my thoughts tangled. "That first night with you was unforgettable…I wanted that for us, too—I craved more than just that moment with you. But then it all fell apart. The fire…losing my mom and uncle. I fought so damn hard to push it all aside, to separate those memories, but you have to understand. While we were sharing something beautiful, my family was trapped in that burning house." A tear slips from the corner of her sapphire eyes, but she quickly wipes it away, giving a slow nod.

"Please know…it's not your fault. It's just awful how everything turned out because…I know things between us could be different if not for that. But no matter how hard I try to move on…I can't, and I'm really fucking sorry that you got caught in all of it." I take a deep breath and give her leg a gentle squeeze. When she meets my gaze, her watery eyes search mine. "Beck, believe me when I say this…I love you so damn much. I want nothing more than for you to be happy…even though that happiness can never come from me."

She quickly looks away, nodding in acceptance, understanding the weight of my words. Then she squeezes my hand back and asks, "Are you happy…Ezra?"

I shift my focus back to the lake, noticing Blake making his way back from his lap. "Yeah…as much as I can be," I reply, lying just a bit. I feel her eyes on me as we both process the conversation that we've needed to have for so long.

"Well, I love you, too…and I want you to be happy as well." Looking back at her, I manage a genuine smile. I slide my hand from beneath hers and rest it on top of hers, giving it a gentle squeeze.

"Holy shit, check out how huge this thing is!" Blake yells from below. Beck and I quickly reposition ourselves, releasing each other's hands. Peering over the edge, we get a view of Blake's bare ass surfacing from the water as he floats face down. It takes all my willpower not to get up and find a rock to toss at him. Beck and I exchange glances, unable to suppress the laughter bubbling up inside us. Leave it to dumbass Blake to lighten the mood.

Finally, Beck stands up, brushing off her legs. "Are you getting in?" she asks.

"Yeah…I just need a smoke real quick. I'll see you down there." She smiles before diving in. I close my eyes and take a long, deep breath, feeling the tension in my shoulders ease. It's as if we've both been holding on to so much for too long, and all we needed was that conversation. I can't help but feel guilty for leaving her in the dark for so long. But I truly hope that the tension that hung between us is finally behind us now.

Thump…thump…thump. My heart pounds as I sit on my bike across from the driveway, gazing at a house that feels unfamiliar. Everywhere around me is swallowed by the night. Through the open blinds, I watch a man and a woman in the living room, engaged in conversation. They're likely sharing stories about their day at work or chatting about their weekend plans. I watch as the woman rests her head on his shoulder, radiating contentment. He gently places his hand on her stomach, rubbing in small circles, and I realize with a squint that she has a small, round belly—she's pregnant. Just then, a young boy dashes into the living room, plopping down next to the man who I assume is his father. The boy wraps his arms tightly around the man's neck, and the man reciprocates with a squeeze. They embody the ideal family that everyone dreams of being a part of.

There's a persistent ache in my chest that I just can't shake off. Growing up, I struggled to feel my father's affection; I can hardly remember a simple hug from him. Instead, my memories are filled with his lectures, his yelling, and the many times he wasn't around. Some moments from my childhood seem fuzzy and dreamlike, almost like they're slipping away from me. It's as if my mind is trying to shield certain parts of me from the traumas I faced as a kid.

My mom was always there, doing her best to fill the gaps in my childhood. Meanwhile, my uncle Jesse, though often busy with work, made a genuine effort to be a positive male role model in my life whenever he could. At times, it seemed he was caught in a tug-of-war between not wanting to overstep my father and trying to compensate for his younger brother's mistakes. Yet I still wonder what he truly knew about my father and the dynamics in our house. For years, I've been trying to piece together the countless unanswered questions that lingered after the fire.

I crack my neck, trying to shake off the tension as I focus on the cheerful family in front of me and the house that feels so foreign. Do they have any idea about the history beneath the very ground their home stands on? Do they know that once, another family lived here, broken and scarred? Then one fateful day, everything went up in flames, claiming two lives and leaving behind a teenager with his world reduced to ashes? I clench my fist and press it against my anxious chest, feeling anger surge through my veins. Staring at this home and the happy family inside only serves as a harsh reminder that the history here has been erased, built over, and forgotten. I'm the only one who carries the weight of guilt and the sting of pain. I never knew that loss could live deep inside your bones, like a starving ache that slowly eats away at your bone matter. I've only learned to live with it and accept it as my punishment.

So deep in my thoughts, I hadn't realized my heavy breathing and the fast beating of my heart. *Fuck, not right now.* I press my fist hard into my chest, trying to steady my breathing. *In through your nose and breathe out through your mouth, Ezra.* My mom's soothing words whisper through me. I repeat her words to myself over and over. I begin to feel slightly light-headed while a sudden flow of fear pokes at my nerves. My hand grips where my heart panics beneath my chest cavity, while my left hand grips my right shoulder, my fingers digging into the tense muscle hidden under fabric. "Hey! Can I help you?" A male voice sounds from my left. I jerk my attention back to the house, seeing the man from inside walking across the yard toward me. *Shit.* I throw my hand up, waving it in the air, before quickly turning my bike on. I can't imagine what's running through his head: a random male sitting across from his house at nighttime. I can only be thankful my helmet is on, hiding my identity.

Before he reaches the street, I speed off into the night. My blurred vision worsens as I struggle to focus on the darkened streets ahead. Panic surges through me, and in my haste, I forget to turn on my headlights. My breathing grows heavy inside my bike helmet, thickening the air around me. It feels like I'm trapped within a wall, gasping for air. I weave down several roads, desperate to put as much distance as possible between myself and that house. My vision starts to fade, and a tingling numbness creeps into my right arm. Just ahead, I catch sight of a small patch of woods, and a flicker of relief sparks in my chest. I steer the bike into the grass by the trees, but as I try to park, I tumble off, letting the bike crash onto the ground beside me. I scramble on all fours before yanking off my helmet and tossing it aside. Sharp tingles race through my arms and hands as I lower my head between my arms. I grasp the grass beneath me, craving the feeling of the earth. The cool, damp blades soothe my fingers as I work to regain control of my body.

I make an effort to focus on happy thoughts and memories that bring me a sense of safety and calm. I envision my mom with her infectious smile and hear her warm voice in my mind.

I think of the twins and their irritating banter. Then, I picture her—Raina. Gradually, my heart finds its rhythm, and I anchor my attention on that. The tingling in my limbs starts to fade as I ground myself once more. Finally, my breathing begins to slow. *In through your nose and breathe out through your mouth, Ezra.*

I roll onto my back, placing my palms over my chest as I gaze up at the sky where flickering stars are scattered like tiny diamonds. The crescent moon shines brighter than ever. I try to soak in the night's stillness and the sounds of crickets and the whispers of the forest as exhaustion seeps into my bones. With a flick of my wrist, I pull out my Zippo and a cigarette from my pocket. Closing my eyes, I take a deep drag of the addictive smoke. My eyelids grow heavy; it wouldn't take much for me to drift off right here in this damned grass. Those episodes drain every ounce of energy from me, proving just how weak I truly am. I mask my pain every day, but it always finds a way to break me down. And before I know it, I'm that scared little boy again, yearning for my mom's reassurance to quiet the voices in my head. But she's long gone, leaving me to battle this constant fight-or-flight state of mind on my own.

My eyes glaze over as I take a long drag from my cigarette, watching the cherry glow a vibrant red, alive with intensity. I lift my shirt, tracing my fingers along the scars I've etched into my skin over the years. Slowly, I pull the cigarette from my lips and roll it between my fingers, not even glancing at it. I guide it to my side, my fingertips gliding over the tender scarred surface. With a gentle touch, I press the glowing cherry against my skin, a sharp hiss escaping my lips as I quickly pull it away, feeling a slight burn tingle through me. I close my eyes for a brief moment, then open them again, refocusing on the dark sky above.

Again, I press the glowing tip of the lit cigarette against my side, savoring the familiar sting as I twist it back and forth, using my skin as an ashtray. I keep at it until the cherry fizzles out completely. After letting out a heavy sigh, I brush away the ash from the small burn and tug my shirt down to cover it. I push myself up off the ground and search for my bike helmet, running my fingers through my hair to slick it back before putting it on. Turning my gaze toward my bike, it dawns on me that I had accidentally laid it over. My thoughts have been so scattered that I completely forgot it was still running.

I pick it back up, swinging my leg over the seat. I tighten my grip on the handles, feeling the rubber under my callused palms. My head droops between my shoulders in defeat. I can't shake the feeling of foolishness for going there. I had avoided it all these years, and even though I knew what the outcome would be, I still decided to leave the lake and go by there. It was in the back of my mind the entire time at the lake. The conversation Beck and I had didn't help the situation, either. The events of tonight have revealed exactly who I am—a human built of thin, cracked glass. A fragmented window that's ready to burst into flames from the inside out. It proves me to be the very person I've tried so hard to conceal—*a broken one.*

<h1>13</h1>

Past—Five Months After The Fire

Tonight marks the first time Beck and I have been alone in the house since I moved in. Eric is working a late shift at the fire department, and Blake is spending the night at Andrea's since her parents are out of town for the weekend. I've done my best to settle in here, given everything that's happened. For months, things have remained quiet. It feels like everyone is tiptoeing around me, careful not to say the wrong thing or draw attention to my difficult situation. I can't blame them, though. How can anyone know how to respond when someone is going through shitty times? It's uncomfortable for everyone. Honestly, I feel guilty that they have to deal with my baggage, which has followed me here. My circumstances are quite unusual. I'm genuinely grateful to the twins' dad for allowing me to have a place to call home. *Home.* Just saying that word makes my stomach turn. As long as I've known this place and family, it will never truly be that for me.

My train of thought is interrupted as Beck steps into the

kitchen. "What are you making?" she asks, leaning her elbows on the counter.

I set the wooden spoon down next to the stove. "I'm making my mom's chicken alfredo," I reply. She tilts her head slightly, a smile playing on her lips. I laugh at her expression. "It doesn't compare to hers, but it's edible."

She inches closer, eyeing my culinary creation bubbling away. "You'll have to let me know how it turns out," she says, her curiosity evident.

I clear my throat, feeling a bit nervous. "Well…I actually made enough for two…I thought since it's just us tonight, we could enjoy dinner together and maybe watch something?" I glance back at her, catching a look of surprise on her face. She then tucks a strand of hair behind her ear.

"Oh! I'd love that," she replies. A wave of relief washes over me, calming my racing heartbeat.

Things have felt off since that night, and I struggle to find the right words to explain to her how I feel or why we've built this fragile wall between us. Where do I even start? With all that has happened all at once, my mind hasn't fully processed it all or figured out how to cope. I've tried my best to shove it all down and keep it to myself, but some feelings just won't stay buried. And the nightmares come and go as they please—some nights are worse than others, waking everyone in the house. During those tough nights, it's Beck who has sat by my side. I suppose it's just her instinct to nurture as a female. Sometimes I've jolted awake and, for a short moment, thought she was my mom. Yet, there are also nights I can't make sense of, where I can't tell if I'm dreaming or losing grip on reality. Maybe both sometimes.

I don't want things to be awkward between us, and tonight I'm attempting to set things right—not for my sake, but for hers. She truly deserves that. I can't ignore that I miss her; I long for the way things used to be and the feelings she pulled from me that day before everything went crashing downhill. The real question is whether those feelings can turn into something more, and if I can let go of how things unfolded that night. As anxious as it makes me, this is me trying to figure it out. Tonight is my chance.

I carry the prepared plates over to the couch where Beck is flipping through channels on the TV. I set her dish down on the coffee table and take a seat beside her with my plate. As she glances at our meals, a smile spreads across her face. "This looks really good, Ez," she compliments.

I take a deep breath through my nose, nodding in appreciation. "I hope you think it tastes as good as it looks." I watch her closely for a moment as she twirls the pasta around her fork and brings it to her mouth. Her eyes flutter shut for an instant as she savors the first bite. Raising her hand to cover her mouth, she turns to me with wide eyes.

"Holy shit, this is amazing!"

I can't help but smile. "Really?" I ask, wanting to hear her confirmation.

She nods enthusiastically. "Really!"

I take a quick bite, savoring the nostalgic flavor that floods me with memories. "So, did Esther teach you how to make it?" she asks.

Wiping my mouth, I respond, "Not exactly. After you know… my father left…spending a lot of time at home…my mom and I would cook together in the kitchen. I watched her closely and took notes. Eventually, I got to where I could whip up decent meals for her. She deserved that, you know? And she always loved it when I made her chicken alfredo." I notice Beck set her fork down and turn toward me. Her hair is pulled back into a high, messy bun with loose curls framing her face. She's dressed simply in fitted, black sweatpants and a light pink tank top. I can tell she's glossed her lips, but that's about it. I've always admired how she stays true to herself, never trying to impress anyone or get all dressed up. She's beautiful just as she is.

She places her hand on my left arm. "Thank you for sharing a piece of her with me. It really means a lot, Ez."

I raise my right hand and gently cover hers. "Of course. I know she was important to you and Blake, as well."

For a brief moment, she looks away, pulling her hand back to rub her palms together. "She filled in the gaps that our mother left behind…when she didn't have to. I've always loved her for that," she confesses. Her words strike a chord within me. I've always known my mom held significance for them, but I never really considered how much she and Blake missed having a mother around for most of their lives. At least I had sixteen years of my mom's love before she was taken from me.

I take a moment to study Beck. For someone who grew up without her mother, she has always been such a remarkable person. She's strong, caring, and brimming with love. I've had the privilege of knowing and loving her since I was seven. I've watched her remain the same Beck while blossoming into the incredible young woman she is today. More than anything, I want to be what she deserves. I may not have it all figured out—we're just teenagers trying to navigate life—but I want to make the effort.

As she reaches for her fork to take another bite, I quickly interlace my fingers with hers. She turns her head to look at me, her stunning, blue eyes reflecting a mix of confusion and something deeper. Without hesitating, I gently grasp her face, drawing her nearer. Our lips meet instantly, and the sensation sends shivers down my neck. Letting my tongue slide past her lips, I feel us both hungry for this connection. This moment is perfect—I've missed the taste of her lips ever since that night. And I can sense that we've both craved this for months. My mind stays focused, her name on the tip of my tongue as I lose myself in the sweetness of our kiss. Beck…my beautiful Beck.

I trace my hand from her jaw down to her chest, gently pushing her back against the armrest of the couch while keeping our lips locked together. She doesn't pull away; instead, she lets me guide the moment. I plant soft kisses on her lips, then along her jawline, gradually working my way down to her neck. My tongue glides over her smooth skin as I place purposeful kisses. A soft gasp escapes her as her pulse quickens beneath my lips. Pausing for a moment, I take her in. She looks up at me, biting her bottom lip, sending butterflies fluttering in my stomach.

I scoot back on the couch, gently lifting her legs and resting them across the cushions. Taking a deep breath, I stand up quickly, reaching into my sweats to pull out a condom I placed there for if we reached this moment tonight. As I hold it up, Beck's eyes light up with anticipation, and although she doesn't say a word, her gaze clearly reveals her desires. I slowly slide off my sweats and boxers, leaving them tossed on the floor beside the couch. Her eyes roam over my lower half, taking in the sight of me as I watch her tongue glide along her top lip. When her gaze lands on my inner thighs, where scars from the skin grafting are visible, a wave of nerves washes over me. Still, I keep my cool, reminding myself that my body has changed since then. I need to reveal these parts of myself to her, gradually. For a short moment, I catch a hint of sadness in her expression, but she quickly masks it.

Her eyes stay on me as I grip the condom in my hand and

climb on the couch above her. I lock my fingers around the seam of her sweats, slowly sliding them off her hips and down her legs. My eyes scan over the blue cotton panties that hug her hip bones. I run my thumb over the birthmark that kisses her lower stomach, before tugging down her panties. She stays silent, only the sounds of our heavy breathing and my pounding heart surrounding us.

I ease myself between her legs, taking notes of the small amount of room provided on the couch. I then tear the corner of the condom with my teeth, picturing the way Beck did it our first time. I gently roll the condom on, focusing on her. I bite down on my lips, preparing myself. In the back of my mind, I repeat. *You are in control, Ezra…you are in control.* Finally, I position myself. Even with the condom I can feel her wet entrance graze across my sensitive tip. I shut my eyes for just a moment to gather my thoughts, thrusting forward and immersing her completely. We both let out a breathy moan, savoring the sensations that envelop us.

I continue a slow, meaningful rhythm, taking in the way her eyes shutter when I fill her completely. My thoughts go back to that night, the way her hips moved with me inside her. *How can something feel this good?* I bring my mouth to hers, wanting to taste her lips again. She quickly weaves her fingers through my hair as our tongues lap one another. *This.* Kissing her feels so intimate. And I never want to take it for granted. I pick up speed just a little, unable to hold back the groans that fall from my mouth. Beck pulls back from our kiss, taking my right hand and placing it against her breast. I flinch slightly at the sensation of her skin brushing against my scarred hand. She quickly withdraws her hand, concern filling her eyes. I almost catch her lips forming the words *I'm sorry.* I shake my head and focus on how her breasts sit beneath the fabric. Gently, I squeeze and run my thumb over the peak of her nipple. Small, needy moans escape her lips.

I can feel pressure building in my lower stomach as I continue sliding in and out of her. I could feel this way with her forever. How could it be better than this with anyone but her? My mouth falls open as I pick up my pace. Beck's eyes slam shut as she grips the armrest on either side of her head. I can feel my undoing reaching its peak—until a loud buzzing interrupts my thoughts. I jerk my head toward the coffee table, seeing an incoming call on Beck's phone. My eyes catch the time at the top of the screen…11:00 p.m. Panic and fear slam into my chest all at once. I shut my eyes tight, desperately trying to regain my composure, but the crackling of fire and piercing screams echo in my ears while my skin feels like it's on fire. Voices tear through my thoughts, brimming with bitter fury. *You did this! It's all your fault!* My insides blaze with a searing heat, my blood feels like molten lava, scorching everything in its path. Guilt and shame cut into me like shards of glass, and thick black smoke fills my lungs, suffocating me slowly.

"Ezra! What's wrong?" My eyes snap open at the sudden voice, blinking furiously to clear my vision. The sound of my heavy panting fills the room as I take in my surroundings. I slowly realize that I'm in the living room. A sharp pain shoots through my right arm, and my blurry gaze lands on a small hand gripping it tightly. It's Beck, lying beneath me, her expression mortified. Sweat trickles down my temple as I glance back at her hand, her nails digging into my scars. My chest feels heavy, making it hard to breathe. I quickly jerk away from her grasp, tumbling off the couch and landing on the floor. Panic sets in as I scramble to my feet and stagger toward the bathroom, using the walls for support.

I throw the bathroom door open and collapse onto the cold tile on all fours. Desperately, I crawl to the toilet, barely lifting the lid before I start to vomit uncontrollably. I heave and retch until there's nothing left inside but a hollow emptiness and overwhelming dread. Exhaustion washes over me, and I slide down from the toilet, lying flat on the floor. It takes every ounce of strength I have to reach up and slam the door shut. Curling into a fetal position, I feel the chill of the tile against my bare thigh. A faint, pained whimper escapes my lips, and I can't hold back the hot tears streaming from my eyes.

A light tap on the door interrupts the silence, followed by Beck's concerned voice. "Ezra…are you…are you okay?" I can tell she's been crying. I try to respond, opening my wobbly mouth to form words, but nothing comes out; just the loud voices in my head drown me out. *MURDERER!! YOU KILLED THEM!* I slam my eyes shut, clasping my hands over my ears, my fingernails digging into my scalp and surely drawing blood. I bite down hard, sharp pains shooting through my jaw from the force. I did this. I caused all of this chaos, all for what? Just to get my dick wet? It cost two lives. My bottom lip quivers at the realization. *I hate myself…I hate every part of me.*

14

I powered down the work computer after finalizing our monthly bar profit margins, feeling a sense of relief as I wrap up another cycle of figures. As always, Beck has ensured that our inventory operations ran as smoothly as possible. Her attention to detail has always played a crucial role in making my part of the job manageable, and I genuinely appreciate her for that. Beck's ability to handle chaotic situations with such calmness is a trait that sets her apart—something I've found difficult to envision in my role with Blake, considering he's always hated math. He thrives in the lively atmosphere of the bar, where his outgoing personality is well-suited to engaging with customers and managing the fast-paced environment. I believe he's exactly where he wants to be. Together, we've created a balance that keeps this place running smoothly.

I walk through the double doors that lead out to the bar and spot Blake off to the side, mixing up some drinks. He glances over his shoulder and asks, "You done for the night?" I nod in response. He fills a metal shaker, turning back to me with a raised eyebrow. "Have you talked to Beck today?"

I crack my neck, watching him work on another drink. "No, not since yesterday at the lake."

A wry smile creeps across his face as he shakes his head. "So, I guess you two had *the talk*, huh?"

I lean against the counter, crossing my arms. "Yeah, something like that."

Blake lets out a scoff. "A man of few words...So now that that's out of the way, when do you plan on telling B about her?" He motions toward the bar area behind him. I quickly turn my head in the direction he's looking. *There she is.* Raina is sitting in the same booth from the first night I laid eyes on her. My gaze shifts to the person seated directly across from her, and my brows furrow as a wave of heat rushes over me. I never thought I'd have to see Dipshit again.

I trail behind Blake as he distributes the drinks he mixed at the bar. "How long have they been here?" I ask, curiosity creeping in.

He chuckles softly, "Honestly, I'm not sure...maybe around thirty minutes. I figured you'd caught them on the cameras." I brush aside his comment and fix my gaze on her, silently wishing she'd look up and see the irritation etched on my face, but she remains oblivious. My hands flex at my sides, tension building inside me. In a moment of impatience, I pull out my phone and find her contact.

> Me: Why did you bring him here?

I glance up from my phone, focusing intently on her. She takes a sip of her drink while listening to Dipshit ramble on. Moments later, she sets her drink down and reaches for something beside her. I watch as she pulls out her phone, a fleeting look of confusion crossing her face before it shifts to a broad grin. I see her fingers dancing across the screen, and in just a few seconds, my phone vibrates in my hand.

> Raina: So this is what it takes for you to reach out to me?

> Me: I guess so…are you going to answer my question?

> Raina: I wasn't aware that I couldn't? I mean this is the only bar around here…and who are you to tell me I can't?

> Me: Ouch. I mean…this is my bar.

> Raina: And? So what…are you going to kick us out?

> Me: No…unless you want a replay of last time you were here. I'd hate for poor Scottie to get wounded again.

I look up from my phone just in time to see him walking toward the bar. I step forward, anticipating that he'll order a drink. But instead, he doesn't spare me a glance, breezing right past me to where Blake stands behind the bar. Blake glances over at me, his lips pressed tight in surprise. I turn to Raina, who is biting her bottom lip, clearly trying to hold back a smile.

> Raina: Do you blame him?…you literally blacked his eye for no reason.

> Me: No, it was for a good reason.

> Raina: Which was…?

> Me: He should have never put his hands on you without your consent.

Raina: So touching is wrong, but stalking is acceptable?

Me: Wtf is that supposed to mean?

Raina: Nothing…So I'll make a deal with you.

Me: A deal?

Raina: I won't bring him back here if you take me to your little lake spot you told me about.

Me: Wow…so you're bribing me?

Raina: It's your choice…I know Scottie would gladly take me wherever without bribery…

Me: Fine…when?

Raina: This Sunday or Monday…it's the only days I have off this month.

Me: Monday. I'll pick you up.

Raina: Can you give me a time? Or should I catch you stalking me in the parking lot across from my apartment again?

Me: 4 p.m. And wear a bathing suit just in case.

Raina: It's a date. See you then.

Me: This is not a date.

Raina: Right…OKAY…grumpy.

Me: Have a good night with dipshit.

I turn my attention toward her as she slips her phone back into her purse. For a moment, her green eyes catch the light in my direction with something intriguing, but then she quickly averts her gaze, focusing on Scottie as he approaches the table with drinks. A heavy sigh escapes my lips. I'm relieved that I won't have to deal with that fucker after tonight.

Blake leans against the bar counter beside me. "Damn, Ez, she really has you wrapped around her finger, eh?"

I roll my eyes at his careless remark. "Excuse me?" I snap back, my irritation bubbling up.

He chuckles softly, tilting his head. "I've known you since we were kids, remember? You don't think I can tell when something's bothering you?" I glare at the side of Blake's head, hating it when he's right. I fall silent, doing my best to avoid looking in Raina's direction. Just her presence stirs something within me. After all these years of keeping it together, managing my emotions around others, this tiny, feisty blonde seems to break down my defenses. Now I've agreed to take her to our special place—the one I share with the twins. All I can think about is Beck. How the hell am I supposed to bring this up to her? I know Blake will keep my secrets, but eventually B will find out. And the last thing I want to do is throw more fuel on the fire of the mess we're working to get past.

I step into the elevator and press the *3* for Raina's floor. As I pull out my phone to send her a quick text letting her know I'm here, I can't help but pace back and forth inside the empty elevator. I'm relieved to be alone, especially after spending the last few days second-guessing today's plans. I didn't take the time to really think things through before diving in headfirst. It was a hasty choice, driven by my own selfishness. Now, I know that if I tried to back out, she'd find a way to get under my skin. It's pretty wild even to say that, especially since I hardly know her. But there's just something about her that drives me fucking mad.

The elevator chimes as the doors slide open. I take a deep breath and step out, making my way toward her room. With each step, my heart races as I get closer. I pause in front of the door, fist clenched and ready to knock, but I hold back and decide to wait instead. I've already sent her a text letting her know I've arrived. Moving away from the door, I lean against the wall beside it. I pull off my helmet and let my head rest against the wall as I take a moment to collect my thoughts.

A couple of minutes pass before I hear footsteps approaching from the other side of the door. Moments later, it swings open, revealing Raina. She barely glances my way before shock floods her expression, quickly followed by a startled shriek. In a blink, she swings her fist toward me. Reacting instantly, I drop my helmet, seize her wrist, and pull her around, pushing her back against the wall with my other hand. I stand directly in front of her, gripping her delicate wrist and pinning it above her head. I look down, breathing heavily. She leans her head against the wall, her gaze drifting to where my hand holds her wrist captive, and then to the other pressing against her collarbone. Tilting her head, she meets my eyes, her lashes fluttering softly like fragile butterfly wings. The shock that once painted her face has faded to…something else. I focus on the rapid beating of her heart beneath my palm before inhaling deeply. She smells so sweet.

I run my tongue along my top teeth. "Careful, Raina…you could really hurt someone with that," I murmur, glancing at her clenched fist.

She gasps lightly, irritation creeping into her voice. "What happened to consent before touching?" she retorts.

My eyes wander over her tiny freckles. She's adorably scrappy, and being this close to her feels dangerous. I quickly shake the thought. "That was *before* you attempted to punch me," I reply, releasing her as I step back and retrieve my helmet from the floor.

She brings her arm in front of her, rubbing her wrist where my hand had been. "Well…I didn't know it was you. Maybe next time, give me a heads-up if you're waiting by my door," she says, her cheeks flushed as she meets my gaze again.

I keep my expression neutral. "Noted."

Once we're back at my bike, I hop on quickly while Raina stands beside me, gripping her small backpack tightly. I push my hair back from my face with my free hand. "Get on," I demand politely. She glances at the limited space behind me and, without hesitation, climbs aboard. I turn slightly to look back at her. "Here…put this on." I hand her my helmet.

"What about you?" she asks.

"I'll be fine…It's not far from here." I glance back, waiting for her to get it on.

She slides it on and clears her throat. "So, how do I look?"

I tilt my head back to see her better. I chuckle. "It's a bit big for your small frame…but it suits you." Then I focus ahead, put up the kickstand, and start the bike.

Raina's hands glide across my leather jacket, gently wrapping around where my stomach meets my sides. I inhale sharply, relieved that the roar of the bike drowns out any sound I might make that she could hear. Even though there's fabric between us, I can't ignore the sensitivity of my scars, especially on my left side, where the wounds I inflicted on myself are newly healed. I roll my shoulders, gripping the handles even tighter. I've never let a woman ride with me before, not even Beck. It's not that she's ever asked; it just never happened. But having Raina so close, holding onto me, awakens emotions I can't quite put my finger on. I crack my neck, pushing those feelings aside and adding them to my growing collection of unresolved thoughts. With a twist of the throttle, I take off.

As we arrive, I park in our usual spot at the dead-end of the street. I deliberately avoid driving down my old street or the one where Beck and Eric live, unsure if she's home. The last thing I need is for her to see me passing by with a girl on the back of my bike, especially if she has an inkling of where we might be headed. It shouldn't matter, given our recent conversation and the mutual understanding that we should remain friends, just as we always have, and nothing more. But it feels like I'm reopening an old wound. And while I'm accustomed to that, I can't bring myself to hurt Beck again or put her in a position where she feels betrayed. I care about her too much. It's just too soon, even if we both recognize that eventually we have to accept moving on and exploring other connections.

Not me, though. I've resigned myself to being alone for the rest of my life. A truth I've come to accept long ago. There are hints at why I haven't pursued a serious relationship after a few casual encounters. Still, even if I wanted to, none of my experiences with other women has inspired me to take that leap. Yet here I am. Since that first night I saw Raina, I haven't engaged with anyone else. But whatever this is between us, I refuse to let it go any further. I can't drag her down with me. Something tells me that if I were to reach that point with her, I wouldn't be able to control myself. She's already shown she can break through my defenses without even trying. So this is strictly a *I don't know what the fuck it is* situationship. All I know is it's one I feel possessively protective of.

As we dismount from the bike, Raina pulls off my helmet and holds it tightly in front of her. I notice her scanning the woods beside us. "Is that where we're headed?" she asks. I nod and start walking toward the trees, with her following closely behind. "Are you planning to kill me and dump my body somewhere?" I abruptly turn to face her, meeting her eyes. She's wearing a playful smile, clearly joking. I roll my eyes and keep moving, choosing not to respond. As we walk, I share a bit about how we stumbled upon our secret spot, careful not to divulge too much. I need to keep this place just as it is, without revealing too much of my past. The more she learns, the greater the chance my secrets and past horrors will resurface, driving her away for good. The mere thought of losing the chance to even know her at all fucks with my head.

We finally step into the clearing, and I take a moment to

soak in this place that has held a special meaning for me since childhood. It's not as warm as it was when the twins and I visited on Thursday, but there's still enough warmth for a potential swim. My eyes drift to her as she scans the surroundings, and I can see the excitement lighting up her face. She follows me over to the ledge where we gaze out at the lake, her eyes fixating on the distant mountains. "I'm not sure what I expected, but this view is absolutely stunning," she remarks. I nod in agreement. It truly is a beautiful haven.

I decide to settle down, letting my legs dangle over the edge. I glance up at Raina, extending my left hand to help her. With a smile, she kicks off her shoes and sets them aside before slipping her small hand into mine. I hold it gently as she sits beside me. I hear a soft giggle escape her lips, and I turn to her. "What's so funny?" I ask.

She scrunches her nose and tilts her head towards me. "As mysterious and grumpy as you try to be…you have a gentleman's side to you."

I shrug at her half-hearted compliment. "I suppose my mother raised me right." She flashes me a quick smile and turns her gaze back to the lake. For a moment, silence envelops us, broken only by the chirping of birds and the gentle rustling of leaves and branches.

"So, do you live in town?" Raina asks brightly.

"Not quite," I reply, gesturing toward the mountains.

"Oh, that's nice! Did you buy a house out that way?"

I shake my head. "No. My uncle left me his place."

Out of the corner of my eye, I see her tuck a strand of hair behind her ear. I expect her to dig deeper, but she stays quiet, and I'm relieved. Curious, I decide to turn the tables a bit and ask her something. "Do you have any family nearby?"

I notice her swinging her feet back and forth. "No, I was raised by my aunt…she lives about seven hours away."

That surprises me. I push a little more. "What happened to your parents?"

She bites her lip, absentmindedly pulling at a bit of grass that has grown through a crack in the rocks. "My mom passed away giving birth to me, and I don't know anything about my dad… nobody does. My mom's parents were around, but they've both been gone for years. So it's just me and my aunt," she admits.

The information she shares makes me want to reach out and comfort her. From what I've seen, she appears so content and happy with her life. Yet I can't help but wonder whether she harbors questions about her father or her mother's passing. My mind warns me to hold back, but a small part of my charred heart urges me to respond physically, just as my mom always did for me. I gently brush her wrist with my hand, catching her attention. "I'm sorry," I say softly. It may not mean much, but it's my way of showing that I hear her. She glances down at where my hand touches her wrist, then looks back up at me, her eyes sparkling with a reassuring smile. "It's okay…really. My aunt has always been there for me." I pull my hand back, immediately regretting the gesture, yet longing to feel her soft skin against mine once more.

I clear my throat and ask, "What was your mother's name?"

Raina lets out a soft sigh, her smile brightening. "Adele," she replies. *Now it makes sense where her middle name comes from.* It's a lovely name, but it doesn't compare to her first name— Raina. She exhales deeply, stands up, and brushes off the back of her jeans.

"What are you doing?" I inquire.

She looks down at me, a playful glint in her eyes. "Getting in the water, duh." I watch as she peels off her thin mauve pullover, revealing the top of her bathing suit underneath. In one fluid motion, she unbuttons her jeans and slides them down her waist and hips. With a toss, she flings them aside with her backpack and top. My gaze travels over her figure, and I notice her one-piece bathing suit, a rich magenta that hugs her frame perfectly. It fits snug, cut low at the chest to reveal just a small amount of tasteful cleavage. My eyes dance down to her waist, where a small cutout sits right above her belly button, partially hidden beneath the fabric. In that moment, I realize how delicate her frame is. And I can't help but think about how easy it would be to lift her up and have her straddle my lap.

"Are you just going to gawk, or are you getting in with me?" Raina taunts, a playful laugh escaping her perfect lips. I glance down, feeling a rush of adrenaline. I crack my neck, the sound almost satisfying, before finally standing up. I shift my leather jacket to the side, the cool fabric sliding off my arms. I then peel off my jeans, turning back to face her. Raina stands there, arms crossed, a playful challenge etched on her face. Her gaze quickly flits upward, almost like she's scrutinizing me. I can feel her eyes wandering along the lines of my neck, tracing the path down my arm to where my sleeve ends, revealing the tapestry of scars and tattoos.

As my gaze locks with her striking, green eyes, I notice the spark of curiosity igniting. It's a refreshing change. Throughout my years, I've encountered many reactions to my scars. Some people react with palpable disgust, unable to mask their shock. Others avert their gaze like I'm some sort of contagion, refusing to get too close. As a teenager, their reactions stung. But as I grew older, I learned to push those feelings aside, burying them deep alongside the other ghosts from my past.

This situation is different with her. She doesn't seem repulsed or uneasy around them. Instead, her eyes reveal a deeper fascination, as if she's imagining the stories behind each scar and tattoo. Most women I've interacted with tend to avoid looking at them or drawing attention to them, including Beck. Honestly, I've always appreciated that; I never wanted to discuss them. I've accepted their existence, but it's easier to pretend they don't exist in the company of others. With her, though, it's different. I don't feel uncomfortable or like I need to cover them up. There's a part of me that wants to take off my shirt and let her explore every inch of the turmoil that's marked my body. But doing that would reveal something deeper—the self-inflicted wounds that never truly heal.

I quickly snap out of my thoughts, a small grin forming on my lips. "Are you just going to gawk, or are we getting in the water?" I notice her jerk a little, as if I've broken some kind of spell. Instead of firing back with a witty comeback as I expect, she turns back towards the ledge, peering down.

She fidgets with her fingers, as if bracing herself for the jump. "When you jump, make sure to—" My words die as she leaps off the ledge mid-sentence. I step to the edge to look down, and Raina surfaces from the water with a shriek.

"Oh my gosh…the water is chilly!"

I brace myself, wishing I had smoked a cigarette before agreeing to get in. I push the craving aside, and dive in. As I sink beneath the surface, the water grows colder the deeper I go. For a brief moment, I hear nothing—not even the voices in my mind. If I could hold my breath longer, I would linger down here a little while more. It's peaceful. Eventually, I swim back up, gasping for air. Raina floats just a few feet away, staring at me. "Did you get lost down there?" she teases.

I wipe my face with my hand. "Was I really under that long?"

She shifts a bit closer, pursing her lips. "I didn't keep track, but it felt like ages."

I squint at her, tilting my head. "Were you worried about me,

Raina?" I murmur.

She splashes a bit of water at me. "Maybe…does that bother you?" I glide closer, closing the gap between us. Her wet, blonde hair sticks to her face and droplets run down her cheeks, kissing her freckles along the way. She's captivating to watch.

"Does it bother you…that I think about you when you're not near me?" I confess, letting my thoughts spill out. She inhales sharply before biting her bottom lip and shaking her head. I can't help but notice how her bottom lip pouts slightly. Slowly, I run my index finger along it. She doesn't pull away; instead, she shifts her gaze between my eyes, allowing me to feel the softness of her lips.

Everything around us falls silent, the only sound piercing the stillness is the heavy rhythm of our breathing. I find myself imagining what it would be like to feel her lips pressed against mine, and for a short moment, I wonder if she's thought about it, too. My daydream is abruptly interrupted when Raina's tongue brushes against my finger, causing me to jerk it back instinctively, jolting me back to reality. "I-I'm sorry…I didn't mean to," she stammers. Her cheeks flush pink as she looks away, embarrassment evident on her face. What the hell am I doing? I know better than this. Frustrated, I sweep my damp hair back from my forehead and turn my gaze away from her.

"I need a smoke," I mutter, swimming toward the small area where we usually climb. Glancing over my shoulder, I gesture for her to follow. She remains silent, but obediently comes along.

As we reach the top, I head straight for my stuff lying on the ground. I dig into my pockets for my Zippo and a cigarette, quickly lighting it and savoring the smoke as it fills my lungs before I exhale. The anxiety I felt starts to fade, replaced by a sense of relief. I turn my attention back to her, and I notice she's absorbed in her phone—she might be texting Dipshit right now.

I take another drag and push the thought aside. "Let's dry off a bit, then I can get you home before dark," I suggest. She nods, nervously chewing on the inside of her cheek.

"I'm sorry," she suddenly blurts out. I focus on her again, shaking my head.

"No...I'm sorry. I shouldn't have done that."

She brushes her hair back, staring down at the ground. "Why?" she asks.

I take a deep breath, feeling frustration build. "What do you mean why, Raina? For one, I don't date...plus, whatever this is... it won't work," I snap, and immediately I can see the impact of my words in her eyes. Damn it. It wasn't that serious, and instead I let it spiral. I reach out, ready to apologize again for being an idiot. Suddenly, Raina's head snaps toward the trail.

"Ezra...?" a familiar voice calls beside me. My heart races, and the hair on my neck stands on end. I turn to look, trying to keep my expression neutral.

"Beck..."

16

Beck glances between Raina and me as she approaches. I do my best to stay composed, even though I'm a whirlwind of emotions inside. I step forward, reaching out for a hug, trying to avoid soaking her with my wet clothes. But she quickly pulls away, looking up at me. "What are you doing here?" I ask, pressing for answers.

She shoots a wary glance at Raina, then back to me. "I was on my way home from Blake's and saw your bike. I tried calling and texting you multiple times, but you didn't respond…it worried me, so I wanted to check on you." *Damn.* My phone's in my jeans pocket, and I haven't even bothered to look at it since arriving.

I notice Raina stepping up beside me, extending her hand toward Beck. "I've seen you at the bar, but I wanted to introduce myself. I'm Raina," she says with a friendly grin.

Beck hesitates, her body language telling me she's trying to keep her cool. She crosses her arms and forces a tight smile instead of shaking Raina's hand. "Yeah, I know who you are," Beck replies, her tone flat.

Raina quickly retracts her hand, tucking her damp hair behind her ears. "Right…" she says, a hint of uncertainty in her voice. Turning slightly, she looks up at me, "I'm going to grab my things…it's probably time to take me home before it gets dark." I press my lips into a thin line and nod in agreement. Returning my gaze to Beck, I try to convey my apology through my expression. I see a mix of anger and hurt in her blue eyes. I shouldn't have brought Raina here without at least giving Beck a heads-up. It looks like I've been sneaky, and the timing couldn't be worse, considering I was just here with her and Blake, having a heart-to-heart. We'll need to sort this out later, but not here, not now.

The walk back along the trail is eerily quiet; even the forest creatures have gone silent, amplifying the tension in the air. Beck has deliberately kept her distance ahead of Raina and me the entire way. When we finally step out of the woods, I feel a sense of relief wash over me, like I can breathe again. Beck doesn't look back as she heads straight to her car. I pause at my bike and tell Raina to hang back for a moment. I rush over to Beck's car just in time to catch the door before she slams it shut. She doesn't even acknowledge my presence, crossing her arms and resting against the headrest.

I lay my head against my hand, gripping the door and let out a heavy sigh. "Beck…just look at me, please." She hesitates for a moment, then finally meets my gaze, remaining silent. "I'm sorry…I should have talked this through with you. It's complicated…and it doesn't mean anything—" I'm cut off by her scoff.

"It doesn't *mean anything*? Seriously, Ezra?" She turns her attention away for a moment, staring off at Raina by the bike. Shaking her head slowly, she pinches the bridge of her nose. "I knew it…I saw the way you looked at her, the way you reacted when she first came to the bar." Her eyes lock back onto mine.

"And now this…don't lie to me. I know you well enough to see that if you're investing this much energy into something, it's way more than just complicated. Bringing her here just proves how wrong you are."

I straighten my posture, focusing entirely on her. "I know how this looks, and I'm sorry. You're right…you've known me long enough to realize that this won't lead anywhere," I admit.

She chuckles dryly, running her fingers through her hair and flipping it to one side. "It's already gone somewhere. You've never pursued anyone…not even me." The last words slip out almost as a whisper. Anger simmers beneath my skin.

"That's not true, Beck. You know I tried, what I wanted for us…Don't throw that in my face."

Frustration flashes across her expression. "Yeah! That was like eleven years ago…then you gave up on us."

I shake my head at her response. I thought we had already discussed this days ago, that she understood my choice and the reasons behind it. I open my mouth to respond, but she raises her hand, signaling for me to stop. "Don't…just don't." She grabs her keys, slots them into the ignition, and grips the steering wheel tightly. "I've known for a long time that chapter was closed for us. I guess I just needed to hear it from you. When we talked the other day, I sensed there might be a chance for you to eventually fall for someone and actually try to be happy. Even if you say this is nothing…it still hurts not to be…her." She glances toward Raina, but quickly looks back at me, fighting back tears. All I want to do is lean down and hold her, but I know she'll see it as pity and not genuine comfort. "I meant it when I said I want you to be happy, Ez. I just need some time to process everything… okay?" I breathe deeply and nod in understanding. She starts the car and waits for me to shut the door. I linger for a moment longer, but finally close the door and step back, allowing her to drive away.

This isn't easy for me. I never wanted to put her in this position, but it's too late now. She needs her space, and as much as I hate it, I know that's what she requires. And I'll respect that. I run my hands through my hair, tugging at the roots in frustration. My anxiety is through the roof, and I'm torn between wanting a cigarette and feeling like I want to set myself on fire. When I reach the bike, Raina watches me, chewing on her lip. The same lips I caressed with my finger in the lake. I bite down on my tongue and turn my attention to my bike. "Are you okay?" Raina asks, concern lacing her voice.

I swing my leg over the bike, keeping my gaze straight ahead. "Just get on the bike," I say flatly. She follows my command. The evening chill has set in against our clothes that are still slightly damp. I glance back at Raina, offering my leather jacket for extra warmth, but she shakes her head, declining the offer.

We stand in the elevator, both of us silent since the lake. I can tell Raina would have preferred to walk in alone, but she knows I'm not letting her do that. An eternity seems to stretch on until the elevator finally dings and the doors slide open. Raina makes a beeline for the exit, clearly eager to escape me. "Wait," I mutter, catching the doors to keep them from closing again. She halts and sighs, glancing back at me. Even when she's trying to look angry, she's still cute. I can't blame her, though; I really messed up. I dragged her into the middle of something without meaning to, between someone she doesn't even have the context of. I press my lips together, making a choice that I suspect will haunt me later. "Can I show you something?" I ask.

Her brows knit together. "What? Where?" she presses.

"Just trust me...I'll show you."

She studies me for a moment, clutching her backpack then glancing over her shoulder toward her room. "Okay," she replies flatly. Reluctantly, she steps back onto the elevator with me. I shift back, allowing the doors to close, and press the button for the eighth floor. I expect a barrage of questions, but she remains quiet. Once we reach the eighth floor, I look around to ensure we're alone. Raina stays right behind me as I approach the door leading to the roof. I can see the confusion written all over her pretty face as I open the door to the stairs. Holding it open, I gesture for her to go ahead. Once I close the door behind us, Raina turns to me, her expression a mix of curiosity and concern. "Where are you taking me? What do these stairs lead to? Isn't there only eight floors?"

There's the questions she was harboring. I can't help but laugh. I step past her and head up the stairs, glancing over my shoulder. "Just come on...you can fire off all your concerns once we get there." She rolls her eyes, but follows me up the stairs.

I approach the door, typing in the code. I hear the lock click, indicating it's now unlocked. "How do you know the code? Did you work here or something?" she presses.

I pause. "No, Raina, I've never worked here. It took me maybe five tries to get the code right." I push open the rooftop door, holding it for her as she steps outside, her expression filled with awe. The sun is just about to dip behind the mountains, and I'm grateful we made it in time. The view is nothing short of breathtaking. Instead of taking it in, my gaze is drawn to Raina's profile. A smile plays at the corners of her lips. She shoots me a sideways glance, arms crossed.

"So this is the friend you were visiting?" *Shit.* I forgot I mentioned that when I found out she lived here. She looks at me, clearly waiting for an answer. I give a slight nod. She steps closer to the railing, her eyes scanning the mountains and the town below. Her hair, now fully dry, is wavier than usual, and her messy bangs rest softly on her brow as she takes in the view. She adds her own charm to the breathtaking scenery.

"Oh, my gosh…how did this happen?" She edges closer, prodding at the loose, bent railing. My heart drops.

"No! Get away from that!" I shout, more forcefully than I meant to. Flashbacks crash through my mind. I'm back there, dangling off the side of the building, seconds away from falling to my death. My fingers slip as I struggle to hold on tighter.

"Ezra…I-I can barely breathe!" A muffled voice gnaws at my conscience. The scent of sweet vanilla wraps around me. "Ezra… please…let go." Her voice is so near, shaking with concern. My eyes snap open, and for a moment, everything is a blur. When my vision clears, reality sinks in. I look down and see that I have Raina pinned against me, my arms firmly wrapped around her chest. She fights to break free, using every ounce of her strength. *What the hell am I doing?* I quickly step back from the railing, pulling her with me before letting go. She leans forward, hands resting on her knees as she tries to catch her breath. After a moment, she straightens up, turning to fix her gaze on me.

"Damn it, Raina…I'm sorry…I-I didn't mean to." I tug at my hair in frustration, turning away from her.

"What the hell was that?" she demands, her tone making it hard to tell if she's scared, angry, or maybe both. I scramble for a quick response, trying to keep my composure.

"I thought you were going to fall," I say, still facing away from her.

She lets out a sharp scoff. "No, Ezra, it was more than that."

I rub my jaw, taking a few deep breaths before turning to face her. I adopt a blank expression. "It was nothing." I brush past her, yanking off my jacket as I suddenly feel uncomfortably hot. She stays silent, probably burning a well-deserved hole in my back with her stare. I plop down on the roof, lying back as I pull out a smoke and light it quickly, snapping my Zippo shut and tucking it into my pocket. I close my eyes, loathing myself for how today has unfolded, once again proving why I'm better off *alone*.

I can hear Raina shuffling toward me, her sweet scent wafting through the air. I inhale deeply, opening my eyes to find her standing above me with her arms crossed. She licks the corner of her mouth and raises an eyebrow. "Consent before touching, huh?" she quips.

I tilt my head to meet her gaze for a moment before looking away toward the sky. Suddenly, she kicks my leg, jolting my attention. "What the fuck, Raina!" I groan in surprise.

She gasps, covering her mouth with her hands. "Oh no! I'm so sorry…It's just that I asked you a question, and when you didn't reply, I thought you didn't hear me," she retorts, sarcasm dripping from her words. Deep down, she knows I heard her. She's such a firecracker sometimes.

"Fair point," I concede, not wanting to dive into the darker parts of my thoughts with her. Maybe it's dishonest, or maybe I just genuinely thought she might fall. I decide to stick to my original excuse. "I thought you were going to fall."

She stares down at me for a moment, maybe planning to kick me again. I won't stop her if so—I deserve it. Instead, she huffs and throws her backpack to the side, lying down beside me. Her arm gently brushes against mine, causing me to tense up a little. I hear a long breath escape her lips. "Can you tell me what's going on with the Beck girl? I deserve that…at least," she admits. I take a long drag from my cigarette, resting my hand back on my stomach. She's right. I brought her into this mess, I can at least give her the basics of the truth. Raina's fingers gently brush against the top of my hand, and I avert my eyes. "What are you doing?" The feel of her soft fingertips gliding across my scars causes my teeth to clench, but not in a bad way. I watch as she smoothly laces her fingers around the cigarette, pulling it from mine. My eyes follow her hand as she brings it to her mouth, the cherry glows and sizzles as she takes a hit from it, blowing smoke into the night air. She doesn't choke or cough this time. I'm impressed. She quickly gestures for me to take it back. I laugh.

"So I'm a bad influence now, too, huh?"

She turns her head toward me. "Basically," she jokes. I expect her to look away, but she continues looking at me. She wants answers.

I look back up at the sky, preparing my thoughts. "I met Beck and her brother, Blake, when I was seven-years-old. We were basically neighbors and grew up together…we've always been close. Things shifted between her and I as we got older…I just didn't know exactly what it was. I always knew she was strong… and beautiful." I glance over at Raina. She stays quiet, lost in the stars as I share pieces of something I've never shared with anyone else. I clear my throat, bracing myself for what I'm about to say. "On my 16th birthday…something happened between us and our friendship. We, uh, had sex. It wasn't her first time…but… it was for me. Long story short, feelings got involved, and other things happened in the mix…We wanted it to work, but it just couldn't…and she's battled with that for a long time…So did I…but I had to accept that it couldn't be anything more than a friendship." I sit up, propping my legs up. I flick the cherry off the remnants of the cigarette, smashing it with my shoe. I lie back down, waiting for Raina to throw questions my way with the information I just shared.

"Do you love her?" she asks gently.

"I do, and always will," I respond immediately.

She takes a deep breath, considering her next words. "So, have you been with anyone else since her?"

I turn my head slightly, surprised by her question, though I suppose it's a fair one. "Raina... I'm twenty-seven," I reply. She looks at me intently, nervously chewing on the inside of her cheek. I can't help but remember how soft her lips felt. "If you really must know...I'm well experienced in fucking."

Her eyes widen in surprise, but she quickly shifts her gaze back to the sky. She lifts her hands, resting them against her chest. "I don't blame Beck for feeling some type of way...you are pretty easy on the eyes," she murmurs under her breath.

I chuckle at her comment. "Right...until you notice these," I say, raising my arm to flaunt one of my biggest letdowns.

"Honestly, I find them strangely attractive," she says instead.

I bring my attention back to her. *Does she mean that?* I open my mouth to respond, but she clears her throat and speaks first. "Do they hurt?"

I'm assuming she's referring to my scars. "Yeah, some places are overly sensitive, while others are almost numb to the touch." I wait, expecting her to ask how I got them. Surely she's wondered since meeting me. She stays silent, but I see her fidgeting with her fingers on her chest. "Are you not going to ask me how I got them?"

She quickly sits up, wrapping her arms around her legs. She looks back at me, her expression filled with concern. "I already know..."

I furrow my brows. "What do you mean?"

She lets out a deep exhale. "Before I committed to moving here, I wanted to make sure I was moving to a safe place, like crime-free, and all. The only thing that came up was about a sixteen-year-old who survived a house fire and lost his mom and uncle to that same fire on his birthday...on our birthday. And the first time I met you at the bar, Scottie had asked you about y-your scars…I knew it was you. You were him."

I sit up, trying to grasp the realization that she's known this dark part of me this entire time. "Why didn't you say anything?" I press.

She shrugs her shoulders. "It wasn't my place to…and I won't pry and ask for details…You can tell me when you feel comfortable to…or you never have to tell me at all." She shifts her gaze to me. "I guess…I'm just happy you survived," she admits. I look forward, biting my tongue. *Would she think differently of me if I told her I wanted to die in that fire with them? That living is worse than being dead?* She catches my attention, pulling her phone out from her backpack. "It's getting late, I have work in the morning." I nod, grabbing my jacket and standing up. She does the same, grabbing her bag. We stand facing each other. She's so small compared to me; she has to crane her neck to meet my eyes. "Well…today was interesting…Maybe we can do it again sometime," she says playfully.

I give her a tight smile. "Yeah…maybe so."

My phone vibrates in my pocket. I pull it out to check it. Blake has texted multiple times.

Blake: You have royally fucked up, brother.

Blake: Can't wait for the juicy deets
of your recent fuck ups:)

I roll my eyes at his texts.

Me: Fuck you, Blake

Blake: I love you too, buddy.

I shake my head, sliding my phone back in my pocket. Raina heads toward the door leading back to the stairs. I follow behind her, trying to process everything that's happened today. I hate to admit that maybe I enjoyed myself for a change, despite my *fuck ups*, as Blake calls them. He doesn't even know about my episode, so I might just have to leave that part out to avoid his commentary. I have enough shit on my plate as it is. One being that Beck despises me currently, the second being me trying to ignore the fact that this tiny little human walking in front of me is causing a problem with my mental state. I clearly am losing control, and while I don't fucking like it, she's like a drug I want to keep trying to see if I'm addicted to her or not.

17

"How's Beck doing?" I ask Blake as we restock the bar, gearing up for the weekend crowd.

He glances my way. "Uh, she's good." It's been over two weeks since I last saw or spoke to her at the dead-end street that we park at for the lake. She's even made a point to swing by work when I'm not around. Blake narrows his eyes as he breaks down the empty liquor boxes.

"What?" I ask.

"Why don't you just ask her yourself?" he suggests.

"Because when Beck says she needs space...you give her space."

He nods in agreement. "Yeah, you've got a point. Anyway, I think she's been occupied with that new guy at the fire department," he adds.

I raise an eyebrow. "What guy?"

Blake chuckles. "Jenson. Apparently, Dad tried to set them up when he first started at the station, but she wasn't interested." He pauses, finishing up with the last box. "Well, they had dinner together recently, and now she's letting him take her out of town this weekend for some concert or something. I'd say that's progress…Beck's had her little flings over the years, but nothing quite like this."

I nod thoughtfully. "Have you met him?" I press.

Blake shakes his head. "Dad really likes him…so much that he wants me to come over for dinner soon to meet him." Clearing his throat, he adds, "He even asked if you'd want to join." I shoot him a perplexed glance.

"Why would I go?"

Blake tilts his head at me. "Because your opinion matters to him…me…and B."

I let out a long sigh. "Fine. Just let me know when."

I shift my focus back to my task, though a sense of anxiety lingers. But I know this is a good thing. She's moving on and exploring options, and she deserves every bit of happiness. I would never want her to feel like she has to spend her life alone, unlike my own choice to remain single and detached. When I was younger, I was selfish with her in ways. If I couldn't have her, then no one could. I think a lot of that came from not understanding my feelings. It took me some time to accept what had to be, and realize it was okay to let her go because someone out there could give her what I couldn't. Whoever she ends up with will be incredibly lucky to have her. I try to picture this Jenson guy. I feel a little at ease that Eric seems to like him and has gotten to know him more on a personal level at the station. I can only hope this guy understands that if he ever hurts Beck, he'll have Blake and me to deal with.

My phone vibrates on the bar counter. Blake glances at the screen, and a smirk instantly forms. I quickly walk over, snatching it from the counter.

Raina: Are you busy? And do you own an actual vehicle…or just your bike?

Me: Not exactly…I'm finishing up things at the bar…and yes, I do…my uncle's truck. Why?

I watch as the three little dots appear and vanish, waiting for her reply. Since the lake and the rooftop, I've only seen her once when she swung by one evening after work for a drink. We've stayed in touch, checking in with each other regularly. And maybe I've kept tabs on her in other ways—like driving past her work and apartment nearly every day to see if her SUV was there.

Raina: I need your help with something… could you drive your truck here? PLEASE.

Me: Is everything okay? That's a random request…

Raina: Coming from the man of few words and answers…can you or can you not?…I mean, I'm sure Scottie is off work now…I could call him.

Me: Don't fucking bribe me by mentioning dipshit's name…

Raina: Well, did it work?

Me: I'll run home real quick, then be there. Give me like 45 minutes.

Raina: THANK YOU

I slide my phone into my pocket, trying to figure out what she needs my help with and why I have to take my truck. Maybe she wants me to move some furniture for her. I rub my jaw in frustration, irritated that she chose to bring up Scottie's name, fully aware of my thoughts about him. She knows just how to push my buttons, and does it without hesitation. *God.* Maybe that's part of what draws me to her. As much as I want to deny her requests to prove a point, I can't ignore the selfish part of me that craves her proximity. I'm aware she'll never truly be mine, yet the thought of her drifting away stirs something within me that I can't quite shake off.

I find Blake leaning against the counter, his posture relaxed yet intense, eyes sparkling with a mischievous gleam that betrays his dramatic amusement. I feel the weight of his blue eyes on me, a mix of teasing and understanding. I bite down hard on my tongue, savoring the taste of restraint as I prepare to respond, but before I can utter a single damn word, he raises his hand. "No need to explain, brother," he interrupts, a knowing grin stretching across his face. "She's got you good." I can feel my heart rate quicken, and I shut my eyes briefly, trying to block out the reality of what he just said. The truth hangs heavy in the air, and I know that no matter what excuse I might give in this moment, my actions tell a different story. The evidence is written all over my face. After all these years of masking my feelings, this one has been by far the hardest. I take a deep breath, desperately trying to compose myself, the urge to deny it all bubbling just beneath the surface. But deep down, I realize that I'm not ready to confront this truth—not now, and maybe never.

18

I knock three times on Raina's apartment door after sending a quick text to let her know I've arrived. I can hear some shuffling and movement from the other side, and I feel a surge of anticipation. Finally, the door swings open, revealing Raina on the other side. She's wearing beige scrubs, and her hair's up in a messy bun with tousled bangs brushing against her brows. Her lightly freckled cheeks are slightly flushed. She greets me with a tight smile, stepping aside to let me in. As I enter, I take a moment to survey my surroundings. We walk through a narrow hallway, and to the left, I spot the kitchen where a small bar counter sits with chairs neatly tucked underneath. Directly across is the living room, with the small balcony just beyond it. The decor strikes me as Mediterranean in style, with an earthy feel. Plants are arranged on either side of the balcony doors. The setup is simple, but welcoming.

I lean against the bar area, crossing my arms. I glance around; everything seems in order. Maybe she needs help moving some bedroom furniture. "So, what do you need help with?" I ask.

Raina walks toward the living room, resting her hands on the back of the couch. Something feels off about her, but I can't pinpoint why. She bites down on her lips, clearly hesitating, before saying, "Okay…don't freak out." I open my mouth to respond, but then I hear scratching noises that make me pause. I listen closely, hearing the scratches again, accompanied by little thumps. My gaze shifts past Raina to a larger hall leading to what I assume is her bedroom and a bathroom.

"What is that, Raina?" She gives me a nervous smile and turns toward the hall. I keep my mouth shut and watch her as she approaches a door to the left of the hall, and opens it. She crouches down, grabbing something. She slowly turns back around and walks toward the living room. *You've got to be fucking kidding me.* My jaw tightens as I make eye contact with a cat. It doesn't look to be full grown yet. Its orange-brown fur has faded stripes all over. I stay silent, bringing my gaze back to Raina. I don't know what her plan is, or what involvement she thinks I'm having with this furry creature. I wait, curious for what she has to say.

She now stands directly in front of me, and I look down at her. The smell of warm vanilla fills the air around us. She holds the cat pressed up against her chest, and I hear light purrs coming from it. Raina cranes her neck, looking up at me. I stare blankly at her, trying not to focus on the little details of her features, how even in the simplest form, she is breathtaking. I let out a long breath through my nose, restraining my thoughts. "What are you doing with that? Please tell me it's yours?" I ask flatly. She sucks her bottom lip in for a moment, running her fingertips along the cat's head.

Shaking her head, she responds, "No, a lady brought her in today to the vet. She was crying, upset. She's having to move from her current home and can't take her cat. No one there could help. So, I panicked and said I would."

I tilt my head. "So it's yours now?"

She looks down at the cat before bringing her eyes back to mine. "I can't keep her here, I'm only allowed to have fish, or something that lives in a cage, like a hamster. I snuck her in here," she admits.

I furrow my brows, trying to piece together her plan. "So you want me to take it to an animal shelter? The closest one is probably over an hour away, but I can—"

Raina takes a step back, cutting me off. "No! And it has a name…her name is Mango."

You've got to be fucking kidding me. *Mango.* I pinch the bridge of my nose, trying to process whatever the hell is going on here. "Just spit it out, Raina. Why am I here, and why did I need to bring my truck?"

She huffs lightly. "I need you to keep her until I can find her a new home," she breathes.

She has to be joking. "Absolutely not!" I chime.

Her expression tenses as she pulls the cat closer to her. "Please, Ezra! I don't know what else to do…I could ask—"

I step toward her, closing the gap between us. "Don't say his fucking name," I growl. Her breath hitches at my sudden demand. She stays quiet, her brows pulling together while her green eyes dart back and forth between my cold stare and my lips. I break eye contact just for a moment, noticing the cat staring up at me. Its eyes are glowing green, very much similar to Raina's. I shake my head and bring my attention back to her. She's not the normal bubbly, feisty Raina I've slowly gotten to know. I can tell she's stressed, and maybe even a little anxious. The last thing I want is for her to feel that way, because I know that feeling all too well.

I relax my shoulders and my expression. "Raina…I—"

Banging sounds come from the door, and we both turn toward the noise. A voice I never care to hear again sounds from the other side. "Raina! I know you are in there! Why haven't you answered any of my texts or calls? It's been weeks!" He pauses, I guess expecting her to open the door. *She's actually not talked to him.* I assumed she hasn't seen him, but I figured they were still communicating. He bangs on the door again. "Is it because of that piece of shit bartender? What do you see in him anyway, huh? He's all scarred up…probably fucked up in the head…he's no good for you!" I feel Raina's eyes on me now. I continue staring at the door, imagining his annoying presence on the other side. How easily I could open that door and crush his face in seconds with my bare hands.

"I can't believe this," Raina says, her frustration evident beside me. "He's going to cause a scene and get me in trouble. Just let me deal with him quickly. I'm really sorry." I lock eyes with her for a brief moment as she turns to head down the hallway, planning to put the cat back in the room. I turn back toward the door, catching Scottie muttering shit under his breath from the other side. In an instant, a decision takes shape: I'm going to confront him myself, and after tonight, he won't be a problem for either of us again. I take off my leather jacket and hang it over one of the bar chairs, wanting my scars to be visible for him to see. As I walk toward the door, I can feel a heat rising inside me. Just knowing he's here stirs something deep. What if I hadn't come tonight? He would have shown up anyway, and Raina would have let him in, and he'd be here with her instead of me. It feels like he's trying to claim something that isn't his, something I'm not sure I have a right to. But that doesn't matter now. I'm determined to make my point and get what I want. I might end up regretting it later, but I'm set on taking control of this situation.

I throw the door open, resting my arm against the frame overhead. Confusion flickers across Scottie's face, and he looks instantly irritated. *This is already too entertaining.* I stifle a laugh.

"Great to see you, Steven."

His brow furrows. "It's *Scottie*," he murmurs.

"Right," I reply.

He tries to peer past me, searching for Raina, but I block his view with my body. He scowls, clearly annoyed. "What are you doing here?" he demands.

Someone's bold tonight. That's fine, I'll let him have his moment of bravado. "We were just in the middle of something…but do come in," I say, my tone icy. I step aside to let him enter. He hesitates for a beat but ultimately walks in, and I gently close the door behind us.

Scottie strides down the narrow hall, stopping where the kitchen meets the living room. He immediately turns his head to the right. "Raina…" he mutters under his breath. The sound of her name on his lips makes my blood boil, and I feel my patience hanging by a thread, ready to snap. I take a deep breath, keeping my eyes locked on him.

Raina appears beside him, arms crossed, looking up at him. "Why did you come here and cause a scene, Scottie?" she huffs.

He reaches out for her arm, but she pulls back. I step forward, tempted to smash the back of his head, but I refrain. "I've been trying to reach you for weeks…you haven't replied to a single text or call. What's going on?"

Raina's gaze shifts to me as I approach. She opens her mouth to respond to Scottie, but I jump in first. "She's been busy."

He snickers under his breath. "Busy with *you*?" he says sarcastically.

I shrug nonchalantly. "Yeah, something like that," I reply.

I stroll into the living room, quickly taking in the sight of the couch and loveseat facing each other. "We were in the middle of something…before you decided to drop in unannounced. Please, have a seat," I say, waving my hand toward the loveseat.

Scottie narrows his eyes at me, likely weighing his options about whether to leave, but I know his pride won't let him back down. He's determined to show Raina he's got what it takes. With that thought in mind, he ambles toward the loveseat. A satisfying smirk tugs at my lips as I watch him settle in. I shift my gaze to Raina and can see the confusion—and maybe a touch of concern on her face as she waits for my next move. Deep down, I know she may end up resenting me for this, but maybe it's for the best.

I give a slight nod towards the couch, urging her to take a seat. She glances at Scottie but quickly turns her focus back to me, sliding into one end of the couch. I move closer. "No, sit in the middle, Raina." Her brow furrows for a moment before she shifts to the center of the couch, now directly across from Scottie. *Perfect.* I crack my neck and position myself right in front of her, leaning down to meet her gaze. Her light green eyes search mine, her bottom lip caught between her teeth. I clench my fists at my sides and lower myself, placing both hands on either side of her. Just as she's about to speak, I gently press my index finger to my lips, slowly shaking my head to signal her not to say anything. She follows my cue. I take a moment to appreciate the view of her as she tilts her neck back to look up at me. My tongue glides over my lip; this moment with her is one I know I'll never forget.

I lean in, bringing my mouth close to her ear without actually touching her, ensuring that my breath softly caresses her skin. "Can I touch you, Raina?" I whisper. A gasp escapes her lips, and I notice her slowly nodding her head in agreement. A wicked grin spreads across my face as I reach my right hand to gently cradle her jaw. My thumb slips under her chin, guiding her head to rest on the back of the couch. I bring my mouth back to her ear, murmuring, "Good…now keep your eyes on me." Leaning back slightly, our faces are just inches apart. I take in the sight of her glistening lips before locking my gaze with hers. She obeys, focusing solely on me. As I kneel down and run my hands along the fabric covering her thighs, she watches me with her full attention. I hear Scottie shifting behind me, his voice dripping with disdain.

"What the hell is this?" he barks.

Without breaking my gaze from Raina, I tilt my head slightly in his direction. "I'll only say this once. If you so much as make a sound or try to get up and leave before I finish, I'll make sure you leave here crawling from both of your eyes being swollen shut," I growl, my voice low and dangerous. Raina bites down on her bottom lip, but remains silent. Rolling my shoulders, I brace myself for the sins I'm about to add to my list.

I run my hands back up her legs, gripping her thighs firmly before locking my fingers around the waistband of her beige scrubs. I notice her glance down at my hands resting against her lower stomach, but she quickly catches herself. Slowly, I begin to tug at her pants, her hands pressing firmly on either side of her. My heart races in my chest as I draw back the fabric, revealing pink lace panties beneath. I pause for a moment, licking my lips in anticipation. I want to take my time and savor every detail, knowing I may never have the chance to touch her like this again. It's a difficult truth I must face, because I already sense that she will be a desire no one else can ever fulfill. I gently slide her pants off her legs and feet, laying them on the floor beside us. Gliding my fingertips up her smooth skin, I feel goosebumps rise with each touch. I hook my finger under one side of her panties, pulling it back before letting it snap against her skin. She gasps, yet remains still. I caress her golden skin, tracing my fingers along the delicate line where it meets the lace. Her breathing quickens, and when I look into her eyes, I can see she understands how wrong this is, but there's also a flicker of desire in her gaze. She craves this as much as I do.

I finally glide her panties down, my eyes light up, revealing her. A breath falls from her mouth. It's just as I imagined it to be. Almost instantly, my mouth feels wet with saliva. A slight groan vibrates in my throat as I take her in. I can feel my dick growing in my pants, throbbing for attention. I ignore it, focusing on what I'm about to do. I grip the inside of her legs, spreading them further. She doesn't fight me, yet lets them fall apart. Her pussy is already gleaming with want and desire. I adjust myself, keeping her bare waist hidden behind my large frame. I want Scottie to see her face, though; I want him to watch her come undone, calling out for me.

I position myself, placing my hands around her legs, my thumbs hooking onto her inner thigh. My mouth is now not even an inch from her center. I lick my lips before flicking my tongue along her clit. She jerks a little at the sensation. I do it again, this time looking up at her through hooded eyes. Her mouth has fallen completely open. I watch her long lashes flutter with each teasing flick of my tongue. I pause for a moment, relishing in the sweet taste of her. I grip her thighs tighter, digging my fingertips into her skin. Her eyes are begging me to fuck her with my mouth. I knew she had a naughty side to her, which makes me crave her more. I add a little pressure with my tongue, pushing against her throbbing clit, while my lips gently suction around her center. A moan escapes her, causing my dick to grow harder. I remove my hands from her legs, placing them around her waist. I continue ravishing her with my tongue and mouth as I slide her down closer to the edge of the couch.

I remove my right hand from her waist, bringing it down between her legs, rubbing my thumb against her soaked entrance. I take my left hand and slide it under her shirt, planting it firmly against her stomach. I can feel her breathing hard, her stomach tensing. "Just relax, Raina. I'm going to take good care of you," I murmur. In one motion, I slide my middle finger inside her. She whimpers as I slide it back and forth, forming a slow, sensational rhythm. Holy fuck, the feel of her around my finger makes me crazy. The sensitivity from my scars is barely noticeable with the agonizing pleasure I'm feeling from this. I bite down on my tongue, fighting the thoughts that circle through my mind. *Keep it together, Ezra. We have company.*

It takes everything in me not to let go. There are so many things I want to do to her right now. Things I know would only complicate our situation further. I push the urges aside and bury my face between her legs. My tongue laps around her aching clit as my finger pumps in and out of her. I look up at her as she's biting down on her lips, trying to suppress the sounds begging to escape her mouth. I want to hear her moan my name, and selfishly, I want *him* to hear it. He will know by the end of this that he could never make her feel the way I can.

I suction my mouth onto her, swirling my tongue viciously. I look her up, catching Raina's head falling back onto the couch, but her eyes never leave me. "Ezra!" she squeals. *There it is. Scream my fucking name.* I pick up my speed, applying more pressure with my tongue as I slam my finger fully inside her. Raina's sweet moans fill the surrounding air. She's so close. I pull my finger out, continuing to devour her with my mouth. I bring my hand up, running my soaked finger along her bottom lip. She parts her mouth, letting her tongue run across the tip of my finger. I can't help but groan at the sight of it. I ease it into her mouth, sliding it back and forth across her tongue. She has to know how good she tastes.

Raina wraps her plump lips around my finger and begins sucking on it as I slide it back and forth. *This.* Fucking *this.* I can't compose myself much longer. I suck harder on her clit as she continues to suck and swirl her tongue around my finger. She is struggling to keep her eyes open as her orgasm takes over her whole body. Her moans are music to my ears, so needy, so fucking sexy. Her body begins to jerk under my left palm. She bites hard down on my finger, causing me to wince, but I keep feasting on her. Bringing my hand back from her mouth, I place it on her neck, gripping gently. "EZRA! Oh. My. God." Her moans turn into panting, her head falls back as she rides out her orgasm. As I slowly pull my mouth away, her back arches from the sensitivity. She gazes at me as she catches her breath. Her updo is a mess, and I can tell she is exhausted. Seeing her this way, though, she's perfect.

I rub my thumb over my mouth, wiping her sweet evidence away. I glance at my thumb before running it across my tongue. I close my eyes, savoring the taste of Raina Adele Hope. She still hasn't taken her eyes from me. Her expression is now unreadable. I'm sure she hates me now for doing this in the way I did. I pick up her panties, carefully placing each foot in, and doing the same with her pants, ensuring Scottie doesn't see her bare. I then quickly adjust my dick in my jeans and stand. I turn to face Scottie. Sweat is dripping down his temples, and he looks like shit. His expression reads something between *what the fuck just happened* and *I want to kill this guy*. It's valid.

I glance towards the door, signaling for him to get up and leave. He snarls at me, but quickly stands and strides to the door. He hesitates for a moment, casting a glance back at Raina, but she simply stares ahead, pulling her legs up to her chest. He shakes his head and keeps moving. I fall in step behind him. Once he's outside, I call out, "So tell me, Scottie, did she ever cry out for you the way she did for me?" I click my tongue as he shoots me a glare. "Just imagine if I had used my dick instead."

He scoffs loudly. "You're a sick fuck," he sneers.

I shrug off his insult. "I've called myself worse. Bye, dipshit."

With that, I slam the door in his face and head back to the living room.

Raina sits quietly in the same spot, and I can't help but wonder what's going through her mind. But I know that diving into that conversation now would be a mistake. I pull out my phone to check the time, realizing it's already after 10:00. Taking a deep breath, I approach her. As I run my fingers through my hair, I say, "I should probably be going."

She bites her lip and finally glances up at me. For a brief moment, I feel like I've hurt her with my words, but she quickly hides it. Clearing her throat, she asks, "Aren't we going to talk about what just happened?"

I was expecting that question. I may not know Raina completely, but I do know she's direct about her feelings and wants answers. It pains me to disappoint her, but I simply can't give her what she's looking for. I put up my defenses, keeping my expression neutral. "It's best if we don't, Raina." We lock eyes for a moment before she looks away, crossing her arms in disappointment. I turn away to grab my jacket and put it on. Just then, I hear meows coming from the hallway. Fuck, the cat. I close my eyes and take a few deep breaths, then open them, staring at the door. I should walk out, but I can't bear to be so cold. I've done enough damage already. I head towards the hallway. When I reach the door, I slowly open it, and Mango steps out, rubbing against my legs and purring softly. I pinch the bridge of my nose, feeling frustrated. Leaning down, I scoop her up. She stays calm, nuzzling against my chest repeatedly.

I make my way back down the hallway and find Raina standing up. "What are you doing?" she asks.

"I'm taking the cat…isn't that what you wanted?"

Her eyes brighten for a moment. "Oh…yeah…thank you," she replies. I walk over toward the narrow hallway, and Raina follows closely behind. In the kitchen, she reaches for a bag hanging from a drawer. "Um, everything she needs is in here…food, a litter box, bowls," she says.

I nod, taking the bag from her. We walk to the door in silence, and she opens it for me as I step outside. I pause and look back at her. "Raina."

She leans against the door, her gaze fixed on the floor. "Scottie was right. I'm no good for you. Neither of us is."

She looks up and offers a tight smile before looking down again. "I'll let you know when I figure something out for Mango." With that, she quickly shuts the door. For a moment, I lean my head against it, listening to her faint footsteps fade away. *What am I doing? How am I supposed to get her out of my mind now?* I was managing okay until tonight. Now that I've had a taste of her, I don't know if I'll ever be able to satisfy my hunger. I glance down at the small cat cradled in my arms. Now I'm cat-sitting. Scottie spoke multiple truths tonight: I am fucked up in the head.

19

I stare off into the distant mountains, admiring the way the snow blankets the mountain tops. Uncle Jesse sits in the driver's seat of his 1980 Ford F-Series pickup truck, strumming his thumb along the steering wheel to some old rock music playing on the radio. He's always lived the simple life, never needing more than he already had. I enjoy spending the day with him at his cabin. I don't get to do it much since he is busy with work a lot. My dad left last night, and that always means he'll be gone for a couple of days—or more. And I don't like leaving Mom alone when he's there. He's always yelling at her or me. I wish she had come with us to the cabin, but she always says I need to spend quality time with Uncle Jesse, since I don't get to spend much time with him. When we are together, Uncle Jesse never says much about my dad. I often want to ask him what he was like when he was younger, but I end up stopping myself. Other times, I've wondered if he truly knows him.

As I daydream, my mind drifts along the winding road, wrapping around the large rocks and navigating the countless bends that climb the mountain. As many times as Uncle Jesse has driven these tricky roads, I can almost picture him driving them with his eyes closed. His voice abruptly interrupts my thoughts. "Does it bother you that your mom never wanted you?"

I jerk my head to look at him, gaping in disbelief. "What?" I mumble, my voice barely escaping.

He chuckles softly, gripping the steering wheel tightly. "None of us wanted you... You were a mistake." My brows furrow as a wave of heaviness settles in my chest. Could he really mean that? Is it true? *I look away, turning to stare out the window as I feel tears welling up in the corners of my eyes. I can't cry. Dad has told me that men don't cry.*

He scoffs beside me, clicking his tongue. "Is that why you burned us alive...because you knew?" A sharp, needle-like pain shoots through my stomach at his words. For a moment, the smell of burned flesh clouds the air in the truck. I cover my mouth and nose with my hand, slowly turning back to Uncle Jesse. My eyes feel wide with shock as I nervously stare at him. Half of his face is melted away, exposing his teeth and jaw. I hold my breath, watching as it travels up his cheek; his eye now protrudes from its socket. I grab my hair, leaning forward and pressing my palms into my eyes. This can't be real, this can't be real, *I repeat over and over in my head. "Look at me, Ezra!" Uncle Jesse yells. The truck slowly fills with smoke, causing me to cough and gag. I cover my mouth and look back at him. He's no longer looking ahead at the road. He stares at me with a haunted expression. His right eye dangles along the bone where his cheek once was. I can't control the tears that stream from my eyes. "You've always been a worthless piece of shit." I can't comprehend what's going on. He's never spoken to me this way. His venomous words sound just like him—my father.*

"It's your turn to die, boy." His voice drips with malice as he slams the gas pedal, sending us hurtling around the curves at breakneck speed. I clutch the dashboard, gasping for breath as the

acrid smoke envelops us, thick and suffocating. Uncle Jesse jerks the wheel sharply to the left, veering us across the road. Straining to see what lies ahead, I find the smoke growing denser and darker by the second. Suddenly, BANG! The truck comes to an abrupt halt, jerking me against the passenger door, my head slamming into the window. Dazed and trying to catch my breath, confusion washes over me. My hand fumbles along the door, seeking the door handle. But before I can find it, I hear a low, sinister chuckle beside me. My heart races as that familiar laugh echoes in my ears. I turn my head slightly, squinting through the haze to catch a glimpse of the figure next to me. Just for a heartbeat, the smoke lifts enough to reveal his wicked smirk glowing in the dim light.

Nausea creeps into my stomach, traveling up my esophagus. Nothing makes sense right now. Why is this happening? Why is he here, and how? *As if he hears my rapid thoughts, he growls beside me. "I'm here to finish what I started." I panic, grabbing the door, feeling for the handle. Once I locate it, I try to open it, but it won't budge. I slam my shoulder into it as hard as I can, but nothing. He laughs beside me; the sound of a blade scraping against metal ring in my ears. My body freezes at the vile sound of it. I'm going to die. My breathing becomes unhinged as my chest tightens. Without warning, I feel something sharp poke at my neck, sending stings down my spine. I squeeze my eyes shut, unable to move. I'm frozen. I can feel everything, but when trying to lift my arm, my entire body is paralyzed. The blade slides across my skin. Hot, scorching breath beats against my ear. I can hear his heavy breathing. "Bleed out!" he snaps. Just as a whimper comes from my throat, a sharp, jagged pain shoots through my neck into my chest. My breathing instantly turns into gurgling as I try to reach for my throat. Thick, metallic blood pours from my mouth and neck as I sit helplessly, drowning in my fate.*

My eyes snap open in confusion, scanning the ceiling above

me. A heavy weight presses down on my chest, and I feel heat building. The frantic thumping of my heart reverberates through me. I clutch the bedsheet tightly, trying to steady my breathing. Glancing down, I notice something fuzzy lying on my chest. I blink harder, straining to make it out in the dim light of my room. Slowly, I lift my hand and brush my fingers against the furry creature. A soft meow breaks the silence. *Fucking Mango.* I scoff, quickly scooping her up and leaning over the edge of the bed, gently placing her on the floor. I've had her for a few days now. I tried to keep the little beast in the bathroom the first couple of nights, but she just scratched and meowed at the door until I let her out. I've lost countless hours of sleep to her annoying habits. But I keep reminding myself that she'll be gone soon—I'm just putting up with this for Raina, considering I owe her for my shitty decisions.

I reach over and switch on the small lamp before glancing at my phone to check the time—it's already past seven in the morning. Letting out a heavy sigh, I lean back against my pillow, pressing my hand to my racing chest. It's been days since I last woke up from a nightmare, and this one felt completely different. I shake my head, closing my eyes and starting to focus on my deep breathing. Wiping the sweat from my brow, I push my dark hair back from my forehead.

Mango jumps back up onto the bed, and I watch her closely as she rubs against my arm. I tense slightly, expecting the touch to irritate my scars…but it doesn't. Staying still, I continue to observe her. She eventually climbs onto my stomach, facing me directly. Her big green eyes blink slowly at me as she inches closer. I squint at her when she presses her little cold nose against my hand resting on my chest. Then, she steps over my hand and curls up, settling higher on my chest in a cozy ball. I draw my head back slightly, looking down at her. This is the first time she's ever done this, and I'm a bit unsure of how to respond. I've never really been around cats before. I reach to move her off me, but I hesitate, feeling the gentle vibrations of her purring against my chest.

As the soothing sound washes over me, I notice my heartbeat and breathing begin to slow down. *Why does this actually feel comforting? And why does she look so cute, curled up like that?* I suppose this is what Scottie experiences when he's home with Fluffy. I grunt and quickly shake off my slight admiration for the little orange beast.

A few minutes have gone by of me observing her sleeping. I gently slide my hands under Mango and place her on the other side of me. As I hop out of bed, I hear her let out a soft meow, prompting me to turn and look at her. Once she has my attention, she rolls onto her back, stretches her legs, and blinks up slowly at me. How ridiculous. She knows she's cute and is trying to win me over as some sort of crazy cat lover. Not happening, Mango. Not fucking happening at all.

20

I let out a frustrated sigh as I tuck my phone back into my pocket. Yanking my helmet off, I balance it on my bike's handlebars. I've texted her four times today, and not once has she replied. I know she's home—I checked when I drove by her apartment on the way here. However, I didn't see Scottie's truck around, which gives me a bit of relief. At least she's not with that jerk off. Still, I can't shake off this feeling of uncertainty. With her silence, it's like I'm completely out of control regarding what's happening between us. Is she angry with me? Or has she finally had enough? Can I really blame her? Honestly, I've been the one stirring up trouble since we first crossed paths, and I still can't figure out what the hell I'm doing.

I aggressively rub my face, staring at the house I lived in for many years. I am not looking forward to this afternoon's dinner.

I still haven't talked to Beck, and now here I am, having to meet the guy she's exploring a relationship with. I had almost talked myself out of coming multiple times, but I tried to remember what Blake mentioned. And well, this family has done so much for me throughout my life, so I knew this had to be done. With that being said, I did make a point of arriving right on time to avoid any awkward conversations before dinner. I had also hoped Blake would be here before me. He always knows how to fill in the quiet moments when things seem on edge. Mainly, because he doesn't know how to shut the hell up. But we love him for it.

I scan the vehicles in the small driveway and spot Beck's car parked. Behind it sits a dark blue BMW that I assume belongs to Jenson, while Eric's truck is tucked away in the garage. Naturally, Blake is nowhere to be found. Taking a deep breath, I hop off my bike. Suddenly, I hear the loud thump of music, and moments later, Blake rolls in with the windows down, blasting Bone Thugs & Harmony from the speakers. I can't help but roll my eyes and shake my head. He leans out of the window, bobbing his head to the beat. I cross my arms, letting him have his moment, refusing to give it the attention he craves.

He finally turns off his Jeep and steps out. "Well, if it isn't the cat whisperer himself," he teases. I just stare at him, keeping my expression neutral. He approaches for a hug, giving my shoulder a friendly pat. "Have you and sweet Mango gotten matching pajamas yet? You'd look adorable in some purple ones—*oof.*" Before he can finish, I throw a light punch into his stomach, just enough to take the wind out of him. Blake doubles over, clutching his stomach with one hand while the other rests on his knee. He chuckles, "Damn, Ez, I love you too." A small smile creeps onto my face. He knows I'm tense and anxious about this whole situation, and as always, he's trying to lighten the mood and steer my thoughts away from things I shouldn't be worrying about.

I give his shoulder a reassuring pat. "Come on, let's just get this over with."

He nods as we head toward the garage. "Oh, and by the way…I might have told Dad to order pizza instead," he adds sheepishly. "I figured it would make things a bit smoother than sitting down for a full dinner. It'll, you know, feel more laid-back." He chuckles lightly. I take a deep breath, grateful for his approach to the whole situation. This way, I can avoid an awkward meal with a pissed-off Beck and some guy I've never even met.

As we step inside, I find Eric in the kitchen, rummaging through the cabinets for plates while the TV plays softly from the living room. He glances over his shoulder, and an instant smile spreads across his face. He pauses his task and strides toward me, wrapping me in a warm hug. "It's great to see you, Ezra," he says, giving me a gentle pat on the back. He pulls back quickly, resting his hands on my arms and looking up at me. I notice he seems a bit shrunken since our last time seeing one another, and his hair has definitely gained more gray strands.

I nod my head in acknowledgment. "It's great to see you too, Eric."

He holds my gaze for a moment longer before giving my arm a firm pat and heading back to his task. I glance around, searching the living room for Beck, but she's nowhere in sight. Eric draws my attention again. "So, I heard you adopted a cat recently," he says cheerfully. I whip my head back, locking eyes with Blake. He throws his hands up with a smug expression, and for a split second, I feel the urge to punch him in the stomach again—harder this time. I turn my attention back to Eric just as a voice calls out from the living room.

"Did I hear you have a pet now?" It's strange not to have heard her voice these past weeks. I look over at her; she's dressed up a bit more tonight. Her dark auburn hair is curlier than usual, and she's wearing some makeup. With or without, she looks beautiful.

She walks toward me, reaching out for a hug. I can sense the tension between us, and our embrace turns out to be the briefest hug I've ever shared with her. As she steps back, she places her hands on her hips and glances up at me before quickly looking away. "So, you have a cat?" she asks.

"No, I'm just cat-sitting until she finds a home."

She bites her cheek, nodding slowly with a tight smile. It seems like she's about to say something, but her attention shifts to someone approaching from behind her. *This must be Jenson.* She steps aside to let him come up beside her. "Uh, so this is Jenson. Jenson, meet Ezra."

I observe him as he gazes at her intently, fully engaged until she finishes speaking. When she's done, he turns his attention back to me, extending his hand in greeting. I reach out, noticing his eyes momentarily dart to my tattoos and scars, though he quickly regains his composure. I can only assume Beck and Eric have filled him in on my unsettling past, preparing him to meet the damaged man who was left behind with no family. As I clasp his hand, I try to brush off the feel of his calloused palm against mine. "Beck and Eric have told me a lot about you. It's great to finally meet," he says. I nod firmly in response.

I step aside and lean against the kitchen counter, watching as he and Blake officially meet. I catch a glimpse of Beck's smile as she shifts her gaze between her brother and the guy she's into. My eyes wander to the living room, where everything looks mostly familiar except for the newer couch and a smaller coffee table. My gaze lands on the couch, sitting right where the old one used to be. Memories flood back of that intimate night and how quickly it spiraled into chaos for both of us. Since then, nothing has felt the same between us. Just when I thought we were making progress, I turned around and fucked everything up.

"Ezra, are you going to eat?" Eric calls out from beside me.

I quickly reply, "Yeah, sure. I'll grab a couple of pieces." After everyone has made their way around to get their plates, we all migrate to the living room. Beck and Jenson settle onto the couch while Eric slides into his small recliner off to the side. Blake plops down on the floor, propping his plate up on the coffee table. He motions for me to join him on the floor, but I wave him off, preferring to lean against the wall that leads into the kitchen.

Things fall silent for a moment, and I can feel my heartbeat start to quicken. But Blake breaks the tension, his mouth full of pizza. "So, how did you meet my sister?"

All eyes turn to Jenson, who steals a glance at her and smiles. "Well, after I transferred to the fire department here, your dad eventually showed me pictures of you all. When I saw Beck, I thought, *wow...she's stunning.* I just had to ask him if she was single or taken." Eric chuckles under his breath. "And he didn't hold back, either." Laughter fills the room, but I stay focused on Jenson, eager to hear more. "Anyway, he told me she was single, and I asked him to pass my number along so I could ask her out." Jenson laughs and glances at Beck adoringly. "He warned me she'd be tough to win over, and he was right...she brushed me off at first. But hey, she's coming around now." He nudges her playfully. I shift my gaze to her and see the light in her eyes. She clearly feels something for him. I take a moment to study his looks. From what I can tell, he doesn't have any tattoos unless they're hidden. He has blue eyes similar to the twins', but lighter. His hair is a short, sandy blond. Overall, a well put-together guy. I can't shake the obvious, though—he's everything I'm not.

"So, are you seeing anyone?" Eric blurts out, his question directed at me.

I blink, pulling my attention back to the room. Everyone's looking at me, waiting for an answer. I clear my throat, "N-no,

I'm not."

I notice Beck biting her lip, shifting her gaze between my eyes. "Well, there's a lucky girl out there waiting for you," he says with a grin. I brush it off and force a smile before heading back to the kitchen to toss my plate. Once there, I pull out my phone to check notifications—still no word from Raina. My worry is growing with each passing moment I don't hear from her. I feel I have no choice but to drop by her place and see what's going on. This is completely out of character for her. I need to make sure she's alright, and if she's fine, I have to find out why she's shutting me out. I'd rather just face the music now than keep wondering what I've done. Even though deep down, she and I both know I've done everything wrong and more.

"Everything alright, Ez?" Beck asks quietly from behind me.

I turn to face her, rubbing the back of my neck. "Yeah…I've got to head out, though."

She glances over her shoulder before looking back up at me. "Alright, I'll walk out with you." I make my way back into the living room, giving Eric a quick hug and thanking him for having me over. I then fist-bump Blake. Finally, Jenson stands up, shakes my hand once more, and nods his head firmly in acknowledgment.

Beck walks quietly behind me as we make our way to the driveway, heading toward my bike. My mind races with questions and things I want to express. I come to a stop in front of my bike, my fists clenched tightly at my sides. Turning to face her, I try to collect my thoughts so I don't mess this up any further. She stands there, arms crossed, rubbing them as if she's cold. I offer her my jacket, but she shakes her head. We share a moment of silence, our eyes locked. "I'm sorry, Beck," I finally manage to say.

A soft smile crosses her face as she tucks her hair behind one ear. "I'm sorry too," she replies softly.

Taking a step closer, I place my hands gently on her arms.

"I mean it, B…I'm truly sorry for how I've handled things all these years, leaving you in the dark, questioning what you truly deserve." She lets out a frustrated huff and pulls back out of my reach.

I pull my hands back, giving her the space she clearly needs. She looks away for a moment, crossing her arms tightly. "You always say that kind of stuff." I furrow my brows, unsure how to respond. When she meets my gaze again, her expression is intense. "You act like I don't know what I deserve, while also hinting that you don't deserve the same happiness." I glance down, feeling a knot of anxiety twist in my stomach. I hear her sniffle, and it draws my eyes back to hers. She bites her bottom lip, trying to hold back her emotions. "If anyone deserves more, i-it's you, Ezra. When are you going to see that?" A single tear slips down her cheek, and her lip trembles slightly. Instinctively, I pull her close, wrapping my arms around her tightly. I don't have the words right now to explain why I feel unworthy, so I stay quiet, choosing instead to focus on how much I've missed her presence.

She wraps her arms around my waist, resting her head against my chest. I let my head drop and bury my face in her hair, inhaling her familiar scent that brings back memories of all these years spent knowing and loving her. We remain quiet, savoring the moment together. "Beck," I murmur softly.

She snuggles deeper into my embrace. "Yeah?"

I place my hand gently against the back of her head. "Just be happy, okay? And don't worry about me…I'll be alright." I close my eyes for a moment, silently hoping she won't ask for a promise I can't keep. Because deep down, I know I may never truly be okay, and that's a burden I'll carry alone. One that's not hers to bear.

She steps back, wiping away any traces of tears from beneath her eyes. A strand of hair clings to her lashes, and I gently brush it away. She smiles up at me, then glances back at the house. "I should head inside. Jenson is probably wondering what's taking me so long…and we both know he's not safe stuck with Blake in there." We share a chuckle. She takes hold of my left arm, running her thumb along the leather of my jacket before turning to walk back to the house.

"Hey, Beck," I call out. She turns to glance back at me. "See you at work in a couple of days?" I ask.

She playfully rolls her eyes. "See you then," she replies, and a wave of relief washes over me. Things have felt so off not seeing her in our usual routine. Now, we can finally move forward. I get on my bike, taking one last look at the house that was once my home, with a family that has always accepted me since the first time we met on the street as kids. Despite all I've been through and continue to face, I am grateful to have the twins and Eric as my family.

21

I flick my cigarette butt away as I anxiously walk across the street, heading toward the entrance of Raina's apartment complex. I quickly look up at where her balcony is and see a faint light glowing from inside. She has to be here, unless someone picked her up. My thoughts begin spiraling. *What if she left with Scottie?* I will lose my fucking shit if she's with him. I don't care about the chaos it might cause. I will make sure he knows exactly how I feel about him and why he should have stayed away from her. I have already made myself very clear during our last encounter.

I feel my heart racing as I move, each step almost in sync with my pulse. I would run to her room if I knew it wouldn't draw unwanted attention. Yet, since discovering she lives here, my approach has shifted from trying to conceal my identity to casually walking in as if it's my own home. I press the elevator button impatiently, tapping it repeatedly while clutching my bike helmet tightly. My patience is wearing thin. *What's taking this elevator so damn long?* I tug at my hair, anticipation practically igniting my skin. I glance around, my gaze landing on the stairway door. *Fuck this.* I bolt over and yank it open, racing up the stairs and skipping three steps at a time. In seconds, I find myself on the third floor, standing in front of Raina's door. I press my ear against the cool wood, straining to catch any sounds of a TV or anything that might suggest she's inside, but all I hear is the rapid thump of my heartbeat.

I quickly pull out my phone, checking for any response from her, but as I suspected, there's nothing. I slip my phone back into my jeans and lightly knock on the door. Restlessly, I pace in front of it, pinching the bridge of my nose in frustration. Pressing against the door again, I strain to hear any signs of movement from the other side. Still nothing. I exhale sharply through my nose, feeling a mix of anger and concern bubbling up inside me. With a sudden surge of urgency, I bang my fist against the door, harder than I meant to. If this doesn't grab her attention, I might just have to kick the damn door down.

Just as the thought crosses my mind, the door creaks open, and I catch a glimpse of Raina peering through the crack. Once she recognizes me, she swings the door wide open. I open my mouth, ready to bombard her with questions, but I hold back and simply stare. *Something feels off.* Her hair is down but tangled, and I notice dark circles under her eyes, suggesting she hasn't been sleeping well. The vibrant green of her irises seems muted, lacking the usual spark. She's dressed in emerald-green pajamas, made of a silky fabric—the pants are long, and the top has delicate, thin straps forming a V at her chest. Something is clearly wrong. I just can't pinpoint what it is, and the frustration I initially felt toward her slowly begins to fade away.

She crosses her arms and looks up at me, asking, "What are you doing here?" Her voice screams exhaustion.

I take a moment to study her, trying to figure out what's going on. "It's nearly eight at night, and you haven't replied to any of my texts," I respond, keeping my tone calm yet firm.

She lets out a sigh. "Yeah, I haven't even looked at my phone all day." I wait, hoping she'll offer an explanation, but silence hangs in the air. I rub my jaw, working to maintain my composure. "You didn't think it would be a good idea to just let me know you were okay?" I step closer as the words leave my mouth. She holds my gaze, fatigue etched on her face.

"I wasn't aware that you cared," she retorts sharply, then turns and walks away, leaving the door wide open behind her. She's right in thinking that, even though it's false.

I step into her apartment, trailing behind her as she enters. It's dark, with only a dim lamp casting a glow in the living room. My gaze drifts down the hallway where I spot a flickering light at the end. She must be watching TV in her bedroom. As Raina moves into the kitchen, she grabs her phone off the counter. "Well...it's dead," she states flatly. I watch her pull a charger from a small drawer and plug it in. Looking up at me, she asks, "Happy?" Dropping the phone back on the counter, she walks past me, almost brushing against me. Even in her exhaustion, there's an undeniable feistiness about her. She heads down the hall, glancing back over her shoulder. "Would you like to follow me to my bedroom...to make sure I get there safely?"

A weak smile crosses her face. "Yes...I would," I reply. She scoffs at my answer, rolling her eyes as she steps into her bedroom.

I set my helmet down on the bar counter and walked toward her room. She probably thinks I'm some weird stalker or a total creep, but I need to find out what's really going on. It hurts to see her like this. I pause at the doorway, watching her closely. She slowly crawls onto her bed, settling against a large pillow. Then she reaches over, grabs a heating pad, and places it on her stomach. She tilts her head back and takes a deep breath. "What's going on, Raina?" I whisper.

She briefly closes her eyes, then turns her head toward me. "Um…well, it's that time of the month." I furrow my brows and lean against the doorframe. At first, it doesn't register, but then I get it. I always knew when my mom was dealing with it, and also when Beck was, while I was living with them.

She turns her gaze to the TV, flinching as she shifts uncomfortably. "Is it really that bad?" I ask, hoping to gain a better understanding as seeing her in this state fucks with my head.

She picks at her fingernails, clearly uneasy. "It is when you've got the condition I do."

My heart sinks. "What condition?" I ask, my concern deepening.

"It's called endometriosis…and it's a real pain in the ass." She chuckles lightly, though her expression remains serious.

I've heard the term before, but I know little about it. "What kind of issues does it cause?" I ask as she adjusts the heating pad on her abdomen.

"It varies from person to person, but for me, it's excruciating periods that leave me unable to go to work, stuck in bed all day, while taking meds that hardly make a dent in the pain." Her mouth opens like she has more to say, but she hesitates.

"Is that all?" I prompt gently.

She shakes her head, a hint of reluctance in her eyes. "Well, it…it also brings on a lot of pain after sex sometimes…a-and infertility." She quickly looks down at her hands, avoiding my gaze.

Fuck, that's a lot to take in, especially considering she's only twenty-one. It really pains me to think about her dealing with this every month, and knowing she's been here all day by herself, feeling miserable, just makes it worse. Clearing my throat, I finally say, "I, uh, I'm sorry."

She tries to run her fingers through her hair, but they get caught in a knot. With a frustrated huff, she replies, "It's okay…it'll be easier tomorrow. Honestly, the first day is usually the toughest." I nod slowly, doing my best to hide how her confession affects me.

I watch her as she opens the drawer of her nightstand and pulls out a small hairbrush. Sitting up, she starts to brush her hair, wincing at the knots she encounters. After a moment, she places the brush back on the nightstand and begins to part her hair in preparation for a braid. I clench my fist, feeling a strong urge to help her. Swallowing hard, I step into her room. "Can I help you?" I ask.

She pauses, glancing at me. "Help me with what?" I gesture towards her hair. For a second, she looks a bit puzzled, but then she nods, giving me the go-ahead. As I approach her bed, she shifts, pulling the heating pad off and laying it beside her. Then, she turns to face the headboard, crossing her legs. I gently take a seat, positioning myself so I'm facing her back while making sure to keep my shoes off her bed and blanket.

I take a deep breath through my nose, gently reach for her hair, and begin to detangle the small braid she started. My fingers glide through her silky strands, and I can't help but admire the natural blonde and gold highlights that remind me so much of my mom's hair. Memories flood back of her teaching me to braid; moments I cherished as they made me feel useful, as if I was repaying a small piece of love. I refocus on Raina, captivated by the sight of her exposed upper back. I spot a few faint freckles sprinkled across her shoulders, just like those on her cheeks and nose. I find myself imagining kissing each one, slowly counting them with my lips. Being this close to her feels dangerously intoxicating.

The silence between us is gently interrupted when Raina lets out a soft laugh. "What?" I ask, glancing at her.

"I never imagined you could braid hair."

I take a brief pause, feeling a bit self-conscious. "Is that odd?" I reply.

"Not at all…actually, it's really cute." Her compliment brings a smile to my face as she hands me a hair tie from behind her. "How did you learn to do it?"

I sense genuine curiosity in her voice. Taking a deep breath, I respond, "My mom taught me. I used to braid her hair for her."

Raina turns slightly, a warm smile on her face. "That sounds really special."

I relax my shoulders and finish weaving her braid. "It was, yeah." We fall into a comfortable silence as I tie off the end. "There…all done." She reaches back to touch the braid, running her fingers along it.

"Wow…you're really good at it." Turning to face me, she hugs her knees close to her chest, a playful smile spreading across her lips. "Thank you."

I nod, mirroring her lazy smile. Even when she's completely worn out, there's a beauty about her that's impossible to ignore. Being close to her, reliving a moment that means so much to me, it's hard to resist the urge to pull her in for a tight embrace. I imagine what it would feel like to draw her against me, wrapping my arms around her tiny frame. My gaze drifts to her chest, envisioning the way her perky breasts would fit perfectly in my hands. I can almost see the outline of her nipples through the fabric, enticing me to run my thumb over them and witness how they respond eagerly to my touch. I note how her chest rises and falls steadily with each slow breath. Our eyes lock, and I can feel the unspoken words hanging in the air between us. It's like my self-control is slowly unraveling at the seams, and the longer I stay this close to her, the more I worry that I might do something that I'll never be able to resist again.

With that truth, my teeth grind together as I quickly rise from her bed and head for the door. "I should get going. I need to check on the cat," I say.

I hear her sigh behind me. "Stay?" she asks, her voice sounding more like a quiet plea.

I glance back over my shoulder. "What?"

She averts her gaze for a moment. "Could you sit with me a little longer? It's…helped take my mind off how lousy I feel." She shifts back on the bed, picking up the heating pad and settling it back on her stomach.

How do I say no? My mind is urging me to leave, but my racing heart is pulling me to linger just a bit longer—for her. I steal a glance at the empty space on the other side of the bed, feeling an almost magnetic draw toward it. Shifting my gaze back to the door, I close my eyes for a moment. *Just a little longer*, I tell myself as I quietly make my way around her bed. I grab the pillow and prop it up against the headboard before sinking back onto it, making sure to keep some distance between us. I position myself so that only my feet hang off the edge, crossing one over the other. When I glance at Raina, she meets my eyes with a grateful smile before grabbing the TV remote and flipping through Netflix. Every once in a while, I find myself watching her, observing the way her expressions shift as she gets absorbed in some silly reality show that I don't pay attention to. She's caught me staring more than a few times, yet she remains silent. In this shared space, we simply enjoy the quiet company of each other, saying nothing at all.

22

I glance up at the sky, directing my gaze toward the mountains. The sun is setting soon, and I need to pick up my pace. I quickly spread out a large blanket and pull out things from the big bag I brought along. Once everything is neatly arranged, I rub my chin and make a few quick adjustments. *There, that looks good enough.* I relax my shoulders and pull out my phone.

> Me: I'm here. Wear something warm…meet me at the rooftop door. And don't be suspicious.

> Raina: The rooftop? I thought you were coming here? Are we still eating?

> Me: Raina…just come on.

> Raina: Fine. Give me like 10 minutes…and I'll be there…very unsuspicious like.

I smile at her response. She seems to be in better spirits today, which is good. I didn't want to leave her alone last night, but I knew I shouldn't stay. The ride home was me trying to piece together what her condition is, and once I was home, I went down a long rabbit hole on Google, researching it to the best of my ability. I wanted to understand it better, so much that I was up until after 3:00 a.m. I had to force myself to put my phone down to avoid texting her in the middle of the night. All the bullshit I read for hours had me staring at the ceiling, wanting to drive right back to her and comfort her. I can't explain what she's doing to me. And I know I'm going to make a fool of myself, or worse, hurt her heart. The longer this continues, the more questions she will have that she demands answers for. And the answers I have to give her will not be what either of us wants to hear.

I comb through my thick hair, frustrated at how unstable I am with this situation. I could leave right now and never contact Raina again. Yes, she would most likely fight me on it. Or show up at the bar demanding answers. I learned quickly that she is not one to back down easily. And that alone will draw me back in. I would need to tell her that this isn't what she thinks it is, and that I'm not interested in continuing whatever the fuck is between us. She would be livid, and storm out of the bar. And for a moment, I would feel relieved that I did what I had to, what needed to be done. But then I'd get off work, passing through town on the way home, and I wouldn't be able to resist checking in to make sure she was at her place. I would sit in the parking lot staring up at her balcony, hoping to see a glimpse of her. It wouldn't be enough to suffice my raging thoughts, so I'd find myself standing in front of her door, my fist twitching at my side, eager to knock. Desperate to be near her again.

I tense at the sound of a knock, jerking my head to the rooftop door. I quickly walk over, grabbing the handle. I pause, taking a few deep breaths. *What if she doesn't like it? Or reads too much into it?* I've never done anything like this for anyone before. This could go wrong for different reasons. "Ezra…can you open the door, or give me the code?" Raina chimes from the other side of the door. *Fuck.* Here we go. My jaw tightens as I twist the handle, opening the door for her. She steps out, immediately looking at me. Her eyes are searching for answers to what I'm up to. She looks more rested this evening, which makes me feel at ease. It lets me know she got some sleep last night and is hopefully feeling a little better than yesterday.

"Hey, you," she draws out, squinting her cute little eyes at me. "So what are we doing here—" Her words cut short when she looks to the right and sees what I have laid out for her. Her mouth falls open, and her eyes seem to light up. She quickly walks over, checking everything out. I suddenly feel anxious. *Maybe I shouldn't have done this.* I squeeze my fingertips into my palms, looking down at what I put together for her. I tried to go off things I remembered my mom and Beck liked to eat during that time of the month. It was like they had little cravings they had to satisfy. There are a variety of crackers and cheeses, sliced apples with caramel dip, and small sliced chicken salad sandwiches. I made them just like my mom used to for us.

I wait patiently for her to say something as she turns to gaze up at me. "Y-you did this for me?" Her voice almost squeaks in the cutest way.

I nod my head, pressing my lips together tightly. "I, uh, know you had a rough day yesterday…so I thought this would take your mind off of it a little." I rub the back of my neck, wanting to jump off the roof to escape the way my skin is crawling.

She smiles at me. "It's really nice, thank you." She steps forward, all but lunging into my arms for a hug. I tense, spreading my arms out, unsure what to do with my hands. She quickly steps back, embarrassment written all over her flushed face. "Oh my gosh. I-I'm sorry…I just never had anyone do anything like this, and—" Thinking no longer, I grab her, pulling her into my chest. My arms wrap around her back, keeping my hands on my arms. I feel the tension between us slowly dissolve into nothing. She molds perfectly into my arms, so small, so fragile. I close my eyes for just a second, trying to soak in what it feels like to be this close to her, to hold her in my arms. I could stay right here like this all night.

My eyes fly open as I quickly release her and step back. I rub my sweaty palms on the sides of my jeans. "You're welcome," I say flatly. She smiles up at me. I can sense the unsaid words on her lips, but she stays quiet, turning and sitting down on the blanket. I gaze down at her, still imagining her pressed against me. My palm presses into my chest; it almost aches where her head rested. I clear my throat and sit down beside her, leaving a small, painful gap between us. I can feel my body pulling toward her, just needing to touch her and be closer, but I ignore it, pushing it to the back of my mind.

She sits on her knees with her hands resting on her thighs. She has her hair down tonight; it looks freshly washed and combed. My fingers twitch, remembering the feel of her silky golden locks weaving between my fingers. "Did you put this together yourself?" she asks, gently tucking her hair behind one ear.

I nod. "Growing up with my mom and B—uh, Beck—I noticed quickly that they had certain cravings when it was that time of the month." I rub the back of my neck. *What if she doesn't like any of the food?* Hell, she could be allergic to something, for all I know.

"You really are always observing things…aren't you?" She gives me a cute side eye. I shrug my shoulders, flashing her a small, one-sided grin.

"I should have asked you what foods you liked, instead of

assuming you'd be okay with—"

She stops me, reaching over and placing her hand on my knee. "No, this is perfect…really, Ezra." Her voice comes out so angelic it could bring me to my knees. My eyes fall to where her hand rests on my knee. I squeeze my hands together, feeling my knuckles throb.

She draws her hand back, pointing toward the food. "Are those chicken salad?" I nod. She reaches for a slice, and I observe as she brings it to her mouth, taking a bite. She gets a couple of chews in before beginning to smile. "Mmm. Oh, my gosh…this is amazing!" Relief hits me all over. She blocks her mouth with her hand as she speaks. "Did you make these yourself?" she asks before slipping the last bite into her mouth.

"I did. One of my mom's favorites she used to make."

She glances at me, tilting her head to the side. "Well…she would be very impressed with these." I laugh, appreciating her compliment before I turn, looking out toward the mountains. The sky is a mix of pinks and oranges as the sun goes down behind the mountains. "It's so pretty," Raina breathes from beside me. "Can you take me there sometime soon?" I turn to look at her, pulling my brows together. "Take you where?" She looks toward the mountains. "To your place…I mean, only if you are okay with it? I'd really like to see Mango." She quickly grabs a cracker and places a piece of colby jack cheese on top.

I've never brought a girl to my house, ever. Beck's never even came alone. She's always been accompanied by Blake or Eric. I have had nothing serious with anyone to the point where I've wanted them in my private space. To me, the cabin is my place to escape everyone and everything. Where I can take my invisible mask off. So I don't know exactly how I feel about bringing her there. But I can't tell her no, I don't think I have it in me. She just wants to see Mango, and I'm okay with that. I clear my throat.

"Yeah…that shouldn't be a problem."

Raina stares at the last seconds of the sunset, as things get darker around us. "I know you are probably getting tired of her being there. I was going to wait to tell you until I knew for sure, but one girl from the office said an older lady came in with her cat for a checkup and was possibly looking to adopt one. Amber showed her a picture of Mango, and she loved her. She's supposed to get back with her next week if she wants to follow through with it. She has been coming to our office for years now. I haven't met her yet, considering I'm fairly new there, but Amber says she's a good person and brings her cat in regularly for checkups. So I feel pretty good about it." I watch her place her hand on her upper chest, finishing the last bite of her cheese and crackers. Realizing there's nothing to drink. I grab the large bag and pull out a water bottle for her. She smiles at me, instantly opening it to get a sip.

I focus back on what she said, feeling a little uneasy. How do I explain to her that I may have gotten used to Mango being at the cabin, and that her company has helped me in different ways? I don't want to sound like a little bitch. Also, I can't help but think about the comments I've made against Scottie for having a cat named *Fluffy*. I don't think the name Mango is any fucking better. I comb through my hair, trying to stay calm, looking everywhere but at her. "Isn't it a red flag with her being unsure about whether she wants her? I would, uh, hate to change Mango's routine again if this woman ends up not wanting to keep her permanently." My shoulders tense up as I wait for Raina's reaction to my thoughts.

I slowly bring my attention back to her. I can tell she's holding back a smile. She's attempting to chew on the inside of her cheek to hide it, but I can fucking see it. *She's eating this shit up.* I know exactly what my response sounded like—an excuse instead of admitting the truth. She picks up an apple slice, dipping it in the caramel. She takes one small bite and my eyes fall to her lips where caramel clings to her bottom lip. My eyes flicker, as I fight the urge to lean forward and lick it off. I clench my teeth to keep my tongue from running along my mouth. Just imagining her full lips against mine feels dangerous. I don't know if I'd be able to stop. Her tongue glides across her bottom lip, taking the caramel with it. I refocus, reeling myself back in. *Pull it together, Ezra.*

"I can tell Amber no…that we'll keep looking for someone who is sure of the decision. How does that sound?" She grabs another apple slice, not letting me see the smile that is trying to force its way out. I know what she's doing. I think she's fully aware of my concerns and is avoiding drawing attention to it. My shoulders relax as I nod my head in agreement. Thank God we can move on from that for now.

My thoughts immediately go back to what I discovered about her last night, and the information I read on it. I need to know more and understand how it affects her. It's all I've been thinking about. I'm hoping she is comfortable enough to talk about it with me so it can help ease my racing thoughts and the constant worry about whether she is okay or not. "So…can we talk more about your condition?"

She pauses for a moment, gazing up at me. "What do you want to know?" she asks.

I adjust, wrapping my hands around my spread knees. "Just the complications you specifically have…and if you are okay." I dig my fingernails into the palm of my hand, feeling it break skin, but my expression doesn't crack.

She stares at me, like she's trying to pull answers from my mind. "Are you worried about me…Mr. Stone?"

My eyes begin to burn with an invisible fire. I lean in, never breaking eye contact. My voice comes out deep and raspy. "I think you already know the answer to that, Raina." She gulps slowly, quickly looking away and taking a sip from her water bottle.

We go quiet for a moment, only hearing the sounds of cars passing by below. She runs her fingers through her bangs almost like she's procrastinating. I'll sit right here and give her as much time as she needs. She lets out a soft sigh. "It just started out of nowhere when I was nineteen…terrible cramping to where it would have me doubled over…crying in bed. My aunt talked me into going to the doctor, and eventually I was diagnosed with it. A procedure was done, and the doctor found multiple areas where tissue was growing. Anyway yeah…so here I am."

She takes another sip of her water. She doesn't look bothered at all, maybe she has just accepted it. "I had read that, uh, is there not a surgery that can fix it?"

A playful grin stretches across her mouth. "You read about it?"

I exhale sharply through my nose. "I did."

She chews on her bottom lip, squinting at me. "To answer your question. Yes…There is a surgery…it could help with the pain in different ways, but it most likely won't fix the infertility part and could actually cause more damage because of where the tissue is at…and, I just.. that's what was most important to me… so I haven't moved forward with it." She looks away, moving her hair from her shoulders. There it is. Her mask broke. Infertility means something to her.

"Do you want kids?"

She focuses back on me, only smiling with her eyes. "Yeah… yeah I did." She pauses for a moment, adjusting the way she sits. "I never got to experience…um…what it was like to be a whole family. Being raised by just my aunt…I don't know. I think I'd be a great mom…And since I was a little girl…I daydreamed about finding a good man one day…who loved our baby and me." She laughs, but it doesn't meet her eyes. "Anyway…life just doesn't always work out the way we want it to. And I'm okay with it now." My jaw tightens. She's not okay with it. Her expression and her body language say it all. It pains me to know that this is out of my control. And even if it wasn't, I could never give her what she wanted. "Do you want children?" She pulls me back from my thoughts.

I roll my shoulders. "No, I don't."

She tilts her head at me, clearly studying me. "Why?"

A deep breath escapes me. "Because I'm clearly not fit to be a father…nor would I want a poor child to be a piece of me." I quickly look away, ashamed of the truth.

We sit with my answer for a moment before I hear her shuffle beside me. "I disagree." I bring my attention back to her. She hasn't taken her eyes from me. "You care deeply, and seem to have a natural habit of wanting to protect those you care about… you couldn't ask for a better father." Her words make my chest ache with something I've never felt before. It travels into my throat, making it hard for me to swallow. I quickly stand, walking toward the railing. I pull out my Zippo and a cigarette, lighting it quickly. She sighs behind me.

"It's your turn."

I look over my shoulder at her. "My turn for what?" I ask.

She presses her lips together, then replies, "To tell me something personal about you…it's only fair. I've answered all your questions." She shrugs her shoulders, reaching for another apple slice. I turn back, looking out across the town. My head turns to the right, looking at where the railing is leaning. Okay. Fuck it. I'll tell her something that will change her mind about me being a good father and person, for that matter. I take a long drag, holding it in longer than I should. I then walk over to the railing, where I almost ended everything. I take my hand, wiggling it back and forth.

"I know what happened to this." She stays quiet, but I can feel her anticipation beaming from behind me. "I…um…I broke it." My heart immediately starts pounding hard.

"How?" she murmurs.

"When this place was first built years ago. I came here to this exact spot. I then climbed over the railing. I, uh, was planning to jump…I was so close to letting go and being done with everything…but then the railing bent forward and I slipped off the ledge…I could barely pull myself back up…I thought I was brave enough…but when I lost control for that split second…i-it terrified the fuck out of me. I kind of hoped they never fixed it, and I don't think it will be with how long ago that was." I take another hit from my smoke. "So…it's a constant reminder of the piece of shit I am. Too weak to face the consequences I caused. So no, Raina…I'm not fit to be a father, or a husband, for that matter." I aggressively flick the cherry off, replaying that night in my head.

A small hand touches my back, causing me to jerk. I spin around, finding Raina standing there, looking up at me, her eyes glassy. And there it is, fucking pity. The very reason I keep to myself. I flare my nostrils. She rubs the hand that once rested on my back. "Not wanting to die…doesn't make you weak, Ezra."

I step toward her. "No, Raina. You are wrong. I *wanted* to die. Right then and there, and many times before. But I later realized that if I died that day…I would have gotten the easy way out… That I murdered my mom and uncle…and didn't get the suffering I deserved. So I choose to live and be haunted by my past every fucking day. It's the only way to honor them."

Her brows furrow as she pulls her bottom lip into her mouth. "You didn't cause the fire…did you? They wouldn't want to suffer—"

Rage blurs my vision as I step closer to her, tugging at my hair.

"I could have saved them! But I didn't…I was a selfish piece of shit! What don't you fucking understand!" I breathe heavily from my mouth while heat forms around my entire body. My heart is ripping at my chest cavity as I glare down at her. My eyes move to her trembling chin, causing me to step back. Every bit of anger I feel dissolves at the sight of her. *Damn it.* Here I am showing her exactly who I am.

My hands clench into tight fists on either side of me. I open my mouth to apologize for my impulsive actions, but before I can form the words, she speaks first. "I think it's time for me to go back." She turns and heads toward the door. I look at the mess that needs cleaning up and decide I'll come back after walking her to her room. She slings the door, and I catch up just in time before it shuts in my face. She turns around, crossing her arms. "I don't need you to escort me. I'm an adult." She quickly turns and heads down the stairs. I choose to say nothing, following behind her silently, but giving her enough distance between us.

Once she reaches the door to the 8th floor, she looks over her shoulder at me, scoffing that I am still following her. Yep, she fucking hates me now. But she and I both know I would walk her to her room either way. I brush it off, following her to the elevator. She presses the elevator button harder than necessary, refusing to acknowledge my presence. When the doors slide open, she goes to the back of the elevator, arms crossed, avoiding eye contact. I choose to stay in front of her and hit the level 3 button. Once the elevator doors shut, my thoughts go haywire. Voices scream at me, reminding me of everything I am and am not. I rub at my temples, trying to ease the tension.

The voices are loud, but her silence is louder, and it's killing me. I have to fix this; I have to silence the voices. For once, fuck doing the right thing. What's one more mistake going to hurt? I've made plenty, and I need to distract my mind. I need *her* right fucking now. In seconds, I'm standing in front of her. I give her no time to react. I hook both index fingers into the loops of her jeans, picking her up and buckling her up against the small railing. I then take my hands, spreading her legs, and quickly pressing my body up against her to keep her flushed against the elevator wall.

She goes to push me against my chest, but I quickly grab both of her hands, pinning each one to the wall behind her. My hungry gaze falls to her open mouth, our breath just inches apart. She pulls her bottom lip in, biting it tenderly. *Fuck that.* I clash my mouth against hers; she doesn't fight it, instead she opens wide, letting our tongues meet for the first time. They swirl and lap each other in a perfect rhythm, eager to taste one another. I can taste the caramel on her tongue. This…this is what I've missed all this time. Raina wraps her legs around me, squeezing them tight. I drop her hands, letting mine cup her face, my thumbs pressing against her delicate jaw. Her fingers find their way into my hair, tugging and pulling. I growl into her mouth like a rabid animal. The voices are gone, and my head feels clear for once. But with that, I can feel my dick growing in my pants at a painful rate.

I suck her bottom lip into my mouth, nipping it lightly. She moans into my mouth, letting me know she's enjoying this just as much as I am. Someone clears their throat behind us. I pause, looking over my shoulder. A man and woman stand outside the elevator, the woman holding onto a stroller with a baby in it. I look behind them, realizing we are on the first floor. I look back at Raina, and she looks a mix of embarrassed and still living in the moment we just had. I keep my eyes on her as I try my best to reach into my pants to adjust my rock-hard dick so that I don't traumatize the family any more than I already have. Raina's eyes trail down to my waist, watching closely. I quickly grab her by her waist and help her down. She fixes her tussled hair, and we both scoot all the way over up against the wall, wearing a strained smile. The couple gives us a look of disgust as they enter the elevator, making sure to stay as far away from us as they can in here. I watch the woman look up at the man, her expression almost annoyed. Maybe she's wondering why he hasn't pinned her in this exact elevator.

The doors slide open on level 3. Raina quickly walks out, stopping between the doors. She looks back at me to say something, but glances at the couple before walking off. After the doors shut, I hit the level 8 button and lean my head back onto the wall. So badly I wanted to get off with her and finish what we started, but I know it would cause more chaos. Plus, it's getting late, and I have to get all my shit off the damn rooftop. I look over at the couple; they look confused now, probably wondering why I'm still in here with them. My phone vibrates in my pocket.

> Raina: Just so you know. I'm still angry with you, and I don't know if that was your way of apologizing, but I'm a little less mad at you now, if that says anything.

A small grin forms on my face as I reread her text. This girl is doing things to me. How do I explain to her that I have kissed no one like that since Beck? How do I explain to her what a kiss means to me? Or that kissing her was like nothing I've experienced before. It means so much more to me than I expected. I can't quite grasp what she's doing to my charred heart. And I really fucked up tonight. I showed her the dark parts of me that I've spent so much time concealing. She didn't deserve that. Sometimes when I bring up my past, I black out into a rage. It wasn't her fault, but my own. Yet, somehow, just her being near me can bring me back from that dark state that clouds my mind. Like I'm an all-consuming forest fire, devouring everything in my path, constantly yearning for more. And she is the rainstorm— the very force that could extinguish me for good.

23

One Week Later

"Tell me about Raina's friend. Do you think she'd be into a tall, incredibly handsome guy like me?" Blake croons from behind the bar.

I let out a long, exasperated sigh. The moment Raina mentioned her friend coming over, I knew Blake would jump at the chance to meet her. I flipped on the *open* sign and unlock the front door. "All I know is her name and age," I say, walking back toward the bar and stealing a glance at him. He's leaning against the counter, a goofy grin plastered on his face, eagerly waiting for any info I can share. I give him a glare. "Her name is Callie, and she's twenty-four…happy now?"

He straightens up as customers begin to filter into the bar. "I suppose we'll find out soon enough, brother."

Beck walks through the double doors, finally emerging from the back where she's spent over an hour organizing. It's such a relief to see things starting to feel normal again and to have her here, actively engaging rather than avoiding me. From what Blake has shared, she and Jenson are getting along well. Although nothing official is on the table, they've been spending a lot of time together. I've noticed a new light in her. She seems genuinely happy, and that's all I could wish for. "Why is Blake acting so strange?" Beck asks, standing next to me as we both watch him preen in the large wall mirror while mixing drinks.

I rub my jaw, trying to pull my attention back to her. "Uh… Raina is bringing a friend."

Beck chuckles softly. "I might just have to stick around a bit longer to witness this."

I grab my phone to shoot Raina a quick text.

> Me: Just warning you, Blake is eager to meet your friend. Please give her a heads up. He's determined and won't give up easily.

> Raina: She has been warned…we are about to pull in.

I decide not to give Blake a heads-up that they're almost here. I'm curious to see his reaction when they walk in. Turning back to Beck as she mixes herself a drink, I ask, "So, do you have plans later?"

She nods quickly. "Jenson is coming here later…we're going to hang out here with Blake for a bit." She takes a sip of her drink before adding, "What about you?"

I reply, "Raina is riding here with her friend who's been visiting for the last few days. We figured we'd chill here for a little while, then she's riding back with me to see Mango." Beck laughs. "What's so funny?" I ask.

"Nothing…it's just hearing you say the name Mango is kind of amusing."

I cross my arms and lean against the counter. "Why's that funny?"

She rolls her eyes. "You're this big guy covered in tattoos, and I guess I just never pictured you as someone who would have an orange cat named *Mango*." She takes another generous sip of her drink, eyeing me playfully.

"I don't own her; I'm just fostering her until—"

She cuts me off. "Psh, come on, Ez…we all know that cat isn't going anywhere." It seems I'm losing this argument, so I figure there's no point in fighting it. I'll let it slide this time, mainly because I am just pleased to have the old Beck back. I've missed her.

"Oh, crap…I see Raina," Blake mutters from beside me. I turn around just in time to catch Raina as she walks through the bar door, followed closely by a girl who towers over her. This must be Callie. She has long, straight, dark brown hair and is wearing a sleek, black leather dress paired with high boots. I glance at Blake, and he immediately bites his fist, his eyes wide with excitement. *Oh shit, here comes the Blake show.* Beck sighs next to me.

"Well, she's in for a wild ride. She's definitely his type," she mutters, but I barely register her comment as my gaze snaps back to Raina. She's wearing a flowy, blue dress that ends mid-thigh, paired with calf-length boots. With her hair pulled up into a high ponytail, she looks absolutely stunning, it almost hurts to look at her. My gaze drops to her lips, the same ones I devoured just a week ago. It's been seven long days since I felt the softness of her mouth against mine. I've replayed the memory of her body pressed against me on the rooftop and in the elevator countless times—and I've touched myself far too many times since, indulging in the thoughts of tasting her, holding her, and that intoxicating kiss. Everything about her is addictive, and I can't quite put my finger on what that kiss did to me. What was once hard to resist has transformed into an insatiable hunger. Now, it feels like I'll always be starving for her.

Raina and Callie make their way straight to the bar, settling right in front of me. Raina turns her head, giving me a smile, then playfully bumps her friend's shoulder. "Callie, this is Ezra. Ezra, meet Callie."

I reach out to introduce myself, but Blake suddenly appears beside me, quickly grabbing Callie's hand before I can. "Hey, I'm Blake, the bartender…What's your name again?" He leans against the counter, flipping his hat backwards. I glance at him, a bit taken aback but not entirely surprised.

Shaking my head, I redirect my attention back to Raina, whose chin rests on her hand as she gazes intently at me. Next to me, Beck clears her throat. "I just wanted to reintroduce myself. Um, hey, I'm Beck."

Raina's lips curl into a smile as she adjusts in her seat. "Nice to finally meet you, Beck!" I look back and forth between them, feeling a sense of relief wash over me. *After all this time.* This is one less thing to worry about.

Beck's phone rings beside me, and a smile breaks across her face. "I'll be right back." She answers the call and heads to the back.

"Can we grab a drink?" Raina's voice chirps in front of me.

"Do you want the usual?" She lightly taps her chin with her fingernail, pretending to think.

"Hmm, no. Let's do a shot. Callie loves tequila—" She gestures toward Callie and pauses for a moment. We share a quiet moment, watching Callie and Blake leaning over the bar. Blake is whispering something in her ear, and she giggles, covering her mouth. *Well, that didn't take long at all.* Not that I'm surprised. Blake has that charm that draws women in. He knows how to work his magic with words and easily approaches girls he likes. I'm more reserved and tend to keep to myself, and I'm pretty sure others sense a dark cloud hanging over me when they come near.

I turn my attention back to Raina, observing the way she smiles at her friend and Blake. I remember the first time I saw her walk into this bar, how I felt immediately drawn to her, as if we were linked in some inexplicable way. Despite my efforts to push it away, whatever she stirs inside of me, I somehow find myself wanting to be near her all the time. I glance at Blake, noticing how Callie's face brightens just by talking to him. Then I think of Raina and how she looks at me. Her green eyes seem to search mine, and when she smiles at me, there's never a hint of judgment. She's bursting with life, even as she grapples with her own challenges. And then there's me—a mere shadow of a man, weighed down by anger and loss. I can't help but wonder how we've come this far. What draws her to me? Why does she even acknowledge my existence?

"What are you thinking about?" Raina asks, pulling me from my thoughts. I quickly grab a bottle of 1800 tequila and two shot glasses from the shelf.

Turning back to her, I say, "Nothing." She sighs through her nose, clearly skeptical but choosing to let it go for now. I know she'll have questions later. I slide the shot glasses in front of them, catching Callie's attention. She and Raina clink their glasses together before downing their shots. As Raina swallows, her little nose scrunches up.

"Can we have another?" Callie utters. Glancing back at Raina, I see her nodding, raising a finger to signal for one more round. I refill their glasses with more tequila.

"That was awful," Raina groans. Callie chuckles, grabs her second shot, and downs it with a straight face. She turns to Raina, teasingly motioning for her to do the same. Raina takes a deep breath, slowly picking up her shot glass. Pinching her nose this time, she brings it to her lips. I can't help but grin. She's adorable, even in the smallest of moments.

"So, how did two hot-ass guys end up as best friends running a bar together?" Callie bursts out, glancing back and forth between Blake and me. Raina nudges Callie's shoulder, rolling her eyes. "What? I'm just curious!" Blake, being the storyteller he is, jumps in to explain how we first met, adding his own colorful touch to make the story more entertaining. Just then, I hear the double doors swing open as Beck steps back out, positioning herself between Blake and me. Callie, unable to contain herself, interrupts Blake, her eyes darting between the twins. "No way… you two are twins?" In perfect sync, they glance at one another, mimicking each other's movements without even realizing it. Raina giggles beside Callie, resting her head in her hands and shaking it slowly. While the twins have Callie's attention, I find it impossible to look away from Raina. There's an undeniable pull towards her, and the more I'm around her, the harder it becomes to maintain my distance. She's just mere feet away now, and I feel a strong urge to reach across the counter, pull her close, and breathe her in.

"Why are you looking at me like that?" Her soothing voice cuts through the bar's loud noises. I blink hard to clear my vision. She leans in, resting her chin on her palm, and blinks slowly at me. My eyes wander down to her chest, where the low-cut dress she's wearing tonight offers a glimpse of what typically remains hidden. She's usually quite modest, so these little teases burn a whirlwind of thoughts in my mind. I can easily tell she's not wearing a bra. "Are you going to answer my question, or just continue eye-fucking me?" Her sudden remark jolts me. I meet her striking green gaze, her blinks deliberate and slow. I can't shake the feeling that she's slightly buzzed. The way those words slipped off her tongue is too smooth to be accidental.

I lean against the bar counter, bringing my mouth close to her ear. Her index finger lightly brushes against her bottom lip, and I'm caught up in the sweet scent of her perfume, a reminder of how intimately close our space is right now. I shut my eyes, taking a deep breath of her fragrance before breathing it out slowly. When I open them back, I notice small goosebumps skimming along the side of her neck. I bite down hard on my lip, fighting the urge to lean in even closer. "Isn't it obvious, Raina?" I whisper into her ear. She stays silent, absorbing my words. My gaze is drawn to the rapid pulse throbbing at her neck, and the urge to kiss and bite that spot intensifies. I raise my left hand, gently twirling my finger around the small curl resting by her ear. "You drive me absolutely insane."

I look up, catching her mouth parting slightly before she bites down on her bottom lip to hold back a response. Our eyes lock, breaths mingling as our mouths hover just inches apart. She licks her lips, her gaze drifting to my mouth. "Show me," she breathes, peering up at me through her thick lashes. *Dangerous words, Raina.*

"Get a room, for fuck's sake," Blake jokes beside me, and I can feel my shoulders tense as I instinctively step back. I shoot him a look that clearly says his joke is annoying me. Turning my attention back to Raina, I see her wearing a lazy smile while Callie leans in to whisper something in her ear. As I scan the room, I notice that Beck has left the bar; I soon find her sitting on the couch with Jenson, both of them laughing about something. I can't help but observe how Jenson gazes at her with such admiration. It's a look I know all too well—he's falling for her. For a brief moment, I feel a pang of jealousy. Not because of what they're becoming, but because of my own past with Beck and where it ultimately led us. I once thought we were destined to be together, but I've realized that we weren't. It was a lesson for both of us about what love is and can be. The love we have will always

be there between us, we were just never meant to be anything more than best friends. And I'm okay with that. I think she is, too, at this point. Beck glances up at me, and our eyes meet for a short moment. She smiles, and I can't help but smile back and nod in acknowledgement.

I take a deep breath, bringing my focus back to Raina. I'm watching her, Blake, and Callie engage in easy conversation. It's clear they're getting along well, which I find reassuring. Eventually, Raina meets my gaze, and I gesture toward the double doors, signaling that it's time for us to head out. We exchange our goodbyes, and Callie decides to stick around for another night so she and Blake can spend some time together after the bar closes. Blake's excitement is hard to miss as they make plans. Raina and I step outside, both shaking our heads in amusement.

24

We pull down my long gravel driveway leading to the cabin. It's a chilly night, and I feel terrible that Raina had to ride on the bike in a dress with no jacket to offer her. She didn't seem to mind it, though. She was in awe the entire ride up the mountain. The night sky is clear with bright stars, and there are many clear spots where you can see the sky over the mountains. I was once a kid mesmerized by the scenic drive when I'd come spend the day with Jesse here. Over time, you grow accustomed to it just like anything else, but I still admire the view. I park the bike in its usual spot. Raina climbs off from the back, pulling off my helmet that's too large for her small frame. I hang it on the bike handle, cross my arms, and look up at the sky.

Raina moves to stand beside me. "It's so beautiful out here," she says, rubbing her arms and looking up at the sky. I lean back on my bike and glance up at the moon; it's almost full tonight. Everything's so out in the open here, it looks like the whole sky is right above us. My gaze falls back on her as she smiles, looking up. The moon's luminous light gleams down on her. She almost looks like she's glowing. She's so beautiful underneath the stars. My eyes stay glued to her.

"Yeah…it really is," I mumble, agreeing to her comment… but really referring to her. She looks down at me, tilting her head. She chews on the inside of her lip, kicking her boot into the gravel. "What's wrong?" I ask. She smiles only for a moment before walking toward me. She quickly slings her leg over the bike in front of me, facing me. "Raina, what are you doing?" I press, feeling a little confused by her actions.

She leans in closer to me, sliding her hands around my shoulders. I tense a little at her sudden touch. She sucks in her lips, meeting my eyes. "Kiss me." Her words are soaked in lust. My heart rate picks up as heat travels through my veins. She's never said anything like this to me. And doing this here, right now, I can only sense it will escalate into something more. Her fingers trail around the back of my neck, and I watch her eyes move down to the right side of my neck. She gently takes her fingers and traces along the scars and tattoos, stopping at the collar of my shirt. My breathing becomes labored from her touch. I've never allowed anyone to touch me like this, or my scars. She continues to caress my battered skin, and I feel my control slipping away with each sensual touch she gives.

I bite down hard on my tongue. "Sometimes I lose control when I'm near you," I breathe out.

She bites her bottom lip, studying me closely. "Maybe I want you to," she replies smoothly. A groan vibrates through my throat. I reach up, lacing my fingers through her hair, gripping it tightly. I gently tug at her soft strands, tilting her head more to meet my eyes. Leaning down, I bring my lips to her ear, my breath warm against her skin.

"That's a very dangerous thing to want, Raina." I hear a gasp fall from her needy lips, my mouth inches from her neck. I grip her hair harder as I kiss and run my tongue along her silky skin. The taste of vanilla fills my mouth as I lavish her neck. She grips around my neck, her fingers tugging on the back of my hair. She moans my name into my ear, causing me to stop. I release her, quickly climbing off the bike.

"What are you doing?" she asks breathlessly. I step backward, running my hand through my hair. My mind is racing with so many thoughts. I can't think straight. I want her so badly. I want this. But it can only lead to disaster. With the way things have been going, I know what comes next, and I know I won't be able to stop myself. And then what? I know what sex means to women. And I know what it means to me when I *care* about someone.

"W-we can't do this, Raina. Let's go in and see Mango…so I can get you back home."

Her expression falters as she looks back and forth between my eyes. She straightens up, climbing off the bike to stand in front of me. "Why do this then, Ezra? Why make me believe this is something when it's clearly not? Do you want to hurt me…is that what you want?" A sharp gasp leaves her lips as she looks up, searching my eyes for answers I want to keep locked away. Her eyes well up, and she bites down on her bottom lip, fighting back determined tears. Fuck, I can't see her cry. I've put us both in this mess.

Frustration swells inside me as I run my fingers through my hair and turn away. For a moment, silence envelops us. Even the night air seems to hold its breath, mirroring my anxious heartbeat. I exhale deeply, knowing I'm about to say something I'll regret. "Because you make me do stupid things, Raina." I shut my eyes tightly before turning back to face her. "I've tried to keep you at a distance, because clearly this is something…isn't it?" I step closer, watching as a single tear glides down her cheek. I reach for her chin, catching it with my thumb before it falls. Our eyes remain locked.

"I never wanted to hurt you, can't you see that? But the closer you get to me, the greater the chance I'll break your heart." My voice comes out shaky. "And yes, I wanted to push you away so badly. But every time I thought I had it under control, there I was, losing my grip, wanting to pull you closer and protect you." Her jaw quivers under my touch. "Let me be clear, Raina. What I want and what's right are worlds apart. I crave to be selfish. I want to take every part of you and claim it as my own." I take a moment to breathe, noticing how her tear-filled gaze locks onto mine. It's not sadness in her eyes, but desire. She wants this just as much as I do. How can I deny her? She's fucking intoxicating. "Right now, seeing you like this...It's hard for me not to want to pick you up, bring you inside, and fuck you into submission."

I draw her closer, leaning down until our foreheads nearly touch. Our heavy breaths tangle in the cool night air. The words I avoid linger on my tongue, caught in the reality of our situation. I close my eyes, biting my lip before looking down at her again. "But what I want can never be. I don't deserve you."

She quickly raises her hands, placing them atop mine. Her throat tightens as she responds, "You don't get to decide that for me, Ezra." Her green eyes blaze with something fierce. "Maybe you're right. This is who we are, and it's inevitable." She pauses, wrapping her delicate fingers around my palms. "But I don't care." Our lips linger, aching to meet. She guides my hands from her face, tracing them down her neck and chest. I watch, hungry, as she glides them along the fabric clinging to her breast and places them at her waist. An explosion of heat ignites within me as her words brand into my scarred skin. "Because right now, all I want is for you to pick me up...take me inside...and fuck me into submission."

Just as the words leave her lips, something wet hits my face. We both look up; the stars are gone, and the sky is a dark gray. In just seconds, large, scattered raindrops begin to fall. Raina and I look back at one another, mouths parted. Before we can process, an ice-cold downpour hits out of nowhere. The heat building inside me mixes with cold rain, causing a dangerous storm inside my veins. Fuck morals. I need her right now in this fucking rainstorm. Without hesitation, I lean down so our mouths can clash together. We both moan in unison when our tongues reunite. Seven fucking days I've yearned to be this close to her again. Years I've waited and gone without, only satisfying my sexual urges at a bare minimum with meaningless connections. Not once have I experienced this with anyone but *her*. And I can't fight it any longer.

Our soaked bodies mold together as my hands slide down her curves. I go below her dress, grabbing her bare ass in my hands. I squeeze, pulling her into me. Lightning strikes behind us, just as thunder rattles the mountains. I grip her tighter, lifting her up. She wraps her legs securely around my waist, clamping her hands around my neck. Our mouths stay connected as I carry her to the front door. I reach into my soaked pocket, searching for my keys. After a few minor struggles, I'm able to get the door unlocked and step inside, kicking the door shut with the back of my boot.

I head straight for my bedroom, letting her down at the bottom of the bed. She stands in front of me, dropping her purse and craning her neck to look up at me. She immediately pulls her boots off, and I do the same as she reaches for the shoulders of her dress to pull it down. "No," I demand. She pauses, her hands grasping the fabric. "Let me do it." She listens, placing her hands back at her sides. I step forward, looking her up and down. First, I reach for her hair tie, slowly pulling it out. I watch as her wet, wavy strands fall around her shoulders and face. I brush my fingers against her long bangs as they cling to her brows. She breathes heavily, observing every touch I bestow upon her.

I glide my hands along her breast, my thumbs grazing the cool, wet fabric. Her nipples are visibly hard underneath. She bites her lip from the sensation, and I groan at the sight of it. I grab her face, taking my thumb and pulling her lip from under her teeth. She releases it as my thumb rubs along the inside of her pouty lip. I move my hands to the fabric of her dress where it meets her shoulders, hooking my fingers underneath. I slowly begin pulling it down, revealing her shoulders, then her collarbone. My jaw tightens as her breasts peek from the fabric. *Beautiful. Fucking beautiful.* My eyes catch on something right below them. I pull the dress down further, and my eyes widen as I let the dress fall from her hips. Right underneath her breast in the middle sits a tattoo.

A monarch butterfly.

I pause, staring at it. *How?* My mother flashes in my mind. "W-when did you get that?" I point toward the tattoo.

She takes her hand, running it along the butterfly wings. "On my 18th birthday…what's wrong?" Concern laces her question.

I shake my head, combing my wet hair from my face. "Nothing." I focus back in, stepping closer to her and guiding her backward to the end of the bed. Once the back of her legs hits the mattress, she slowly sits down on the edge. I lean down, pressing my hand between her breasts, pushing her to lie back on the bed. She lets me have control, guiding her where I want her to go. I quickly grab under her legs and scoot her back on the bed. She's in nothing but her black, lace panties now. Moments of me eating her out at her place flash through my mind as I slide them down her thighs and off her legs. Her body is fucking delicious. Never did I think I'd let it get to this point…seeing her so vulnerable and needy for me.

I step back, looking down at her. I glance over at the dresser with the small lamp that I keep on for Mango. The light is dim. I breathe through my nose as I grab my damp shirt, pulling it over my head. Raina's eyes scan my broad shoulders and move along my body. I know she's identifying every scar I hold. I push the thought away and unbutton my wet jeans, sliding them down along with my boxers. My rock-hard dick springs from my boxers, showing how turned on I am by her lying naked in front of me. I watch her mouth fall open as she takes in every inch of me.

"Does it intimidate you?" I rasp out.

She takes a moment to assess me, biting her lip as she does. Her green, needy eyes finally meet mine. "No," she replies softly. "But I'm prepared to be stuck in this bed." *Good answer, Raina. Because when I'm done, you will not want to move the rest of the night.* I wrap my hand around the base of my length, slowly stroking as I gaze down at her. She doesn't break her gaze from my movements, even as she runs her fingers down her collarbone, gripping her tits and squeezing them tenderly while lightly pinching her hard nipples. I grip my dick harder at the sight of it.

She continues squeezing her left tit while trailing her right hand between them, past her butterfly tattoo, and down her stomach. My eyes flicker as her fingers begin rubbing slowly, caressing her pussy. She takes her index and ring finger, slightly spreading her lips, followed by rubbing small circles around her clit as she continues watching me grope my dick. *Holy fucking shit.* A soft moan falls from her mouth as she continues touching herself, followed by labored breaths leaving her chest. I let go of my dick, stepping forward. I place one knee between her legs on the bed and lean down over her. I place my right hand over hers, keeping it pressed against her center.

I drop my head down to look at where our hands rest between her legs. "I want to be the one to make you cum, Raina." I take my middle finger and press it against hers, running it back and forth along her throbbing clit, adding pressure with each movement. I press her finger against her entrance as it slides inside of her. She closes her eyes as her back arches from the pressure. I grip her hand, guiding it back out, and running it through her center. I lock eyes with her as I bring her hand up to my mouth. She sucks her bottom lip in as she gazes up at me. I slide her middle finger between my lips, sucking and licking it clean. My eyes slam shut, savoring her taste. I draw out her name, hitting each syllable. "Rainaaa…I love the way your name rolls off my tongue with the taste of you," I groan, sliding her finger back in my mouth for one more taste.

My dick throbs between my legs, aching to know what it feels like to be inside of her. I clasp my hands around her waist, sliding her further onto the bed. I stand quickly, striding over to my dresser before opening the top drawer and grabbing a condom. Seconds later, I'm on my knees, hovering over her. I rip open the condom, pulling it out and gently sliding it onto my length. Raina's eyes follow my every move. I position myself, sliding between her legs. My heart pounds hard against my sweaty chest. I align myself with her entrance, bringing my hungry gaze to hers. The anticipation is driving me mad. I slowly slide my dick in, not even halfway. Raina winces as we both moan in sync. I stop, biting down hard on my tongue, tasting blood. *Fuck.* She's so tight and warm. I try to pull myself together. "A-are you okay… does it hurt?" I rasp out, searching her eyes.

Her eyelids flutter as she looks up at me. "Yes…b-but in a good way," she whispers breathlessly. She chews on her bottom lip as she wraps her legs around my back. "I don't want you to be easy with me, Ezra. I'm a big girl." Something flips in my mind with those words.

I grab both of her wrists with my hands, pinning them on either side of her head as I slam my length all the way in. Raina's back arches up, but I keep her pinned down by her wrist. Oh my God. This. *This* is what I've tried so hard to avoid. Why? This is feels too fucking good. I continue to slowly pull back and slam back into her. I release her wrists, leaning down to gently lick and tug at her nipple with my teeth. Her moans get louder as I continuously thrust inside her. I take my hand and run it between her breasts, observing the details of the butterfly tattoo. I roll my hips as I plunge inside her, watching her eyes roll back. We are both already close to our release. I lean down, taking her parted mouth in mine. I kiss her with full intent, claiming her with every part of me, even though she'll never be fully mine. In this moment, I own her, and no one will ever fuck her the way I do.

I suck her bottom lip into my mouth before releasing her. My large hands grab her waist, flipping her onto her stomach. I quickly prop her legs up and wrap my arms over her thighs, yanking her to the edge of the bedroom. I gaze for a moment, never picturing that I would get to see Raina in this position. So fucking delicious. She arches her back for me while I run my hands down her spine to her ass, gripping it tight. I move my hands, hooking my fingers onto her hips as I position myself. I slide in slowly, bucking her ass up against me, savoring the feel of how deep I am inside her. My head falls back before I reel myself in. She squeals as I slap her hard on her ass. "Brace yourself, Raina," I growl out. I push her body forward as I pull back, only leaving the tip of my dick inside her. I take a deep breath through my mouth and plunge forward as I pull her ass into me. Raina moans at the impact. I can't last much longer. I've never felt this good in my life. How can I ever stay away now after having a taste of this with her?

I create a push-and-pull motion, slamming into her with each thrust. Loud slapping noises fill the air, mixed in with our moans and breathless words. Raina thrusts her weight into me, causing me to go deeper inside her. *Holy shit.* I pick up my speed, rolling my hips with each hard plunge. I can feel my release pulsing through me, ready to lash out at any second. I glide my hand up Raina's spine, grabbing her hair and wrapping it around my fist. She tilts her head to the side, her neck arching along with her back. I watch as she bites hard on her bottom lip. I take my other hand, reaching over her thigh before I press my palm firmly into her pelvis as my fingers locate her wet center. I run circles around her clit as I continue to thrust into her. Her moans are unhinged. I can feel her inner walls expanding. I want to hear her moan my name. I need it like a drug. "Call out my name, Raina," I demand. I grip her hair tighter, pressing harder into her clit with my fingers.

"Oh my gosh!" she squeals. I tug her hair harder, causing her head to pull back.

"Say it," I growl. A breathy moan slips from her mouth.

"Ezra," she whimpers. I groan at the way my name falls from her lips. *Good girl.* I slam into her one more time and grip my hands on her hips, keeping her ass pressed against me as we both ride out our orgasms. My dick jerks deep inside her as my head falls back. Raina's arms give out underneath her as my sweaty palms slide from her hips. We both fall forward, and I catch myself on the mattress to avoid all my weight lying on top of her.

I take a moment to catch my breath, then pull the condom off and quickly walk to the bathroom to throw it away. When I come back, I find Raina in the same spot I left her, but she's curled up with her arms wrapped around her legs pulled up to her chest. I can hear her whimpering, and the sound makes me panic. "Raina, what the fuck?" I kneel on the end of the bed, scooping her into my arms. I walk around to my side of the bed, pulling the covers back, and climb in, holding her tight to my chest. I grab the covers with one hand, never letting go of her. I pull them up to her shoulders. She nestles her head on my neck against my chin. Her small body is trembling against my chest and stomach. "What's wrong...d-did I hurt you?" I ask calmly, trying to mask the concern in my tone and failing.

I feel her shake her head against me. She sniffles. "No...no it's not your fault." I turn, resting my cheek against her head while running my fingers through her silky hair.

"Tell me what to do...what can I do to make it better?" I plead, feeling like shit that she's hurting like this.

"Just hold me...it'll stop, eventually." I can feel her tears falling along my neck. I close my eyes and I hold her tight, continuing to rub and play with strands of her hair.

A small meow sounds from under the bed. Mango hops up beside us, sniffing Raina's hand. I feel Raina adjust, her fingers running along the cat's fur. "Mango." The name barely leaves her tired lips. She sounds exhausted. I stare at the ceiling, my thoughts drifting away. I can't even begin to explain what this meant to me, or how it felt to be connected to her in this way. Negative thoughts push their way in, making me feel guilty for allowing things to get this far, knowing what it would do to her— and me. I was supposed to take her back home tonight, now here we are, lying naked in bed with her cradled on my chest. I've taken it too far, and I can't allow it to happen again. Just saying those words in my head causes my chest to ache. This would never work. Not because of her, but because of me.

I take a deep breath, pausing from playing with her hair. I swallow hard, feeling my throat tighten as the words cling to my tongue. "This can never be what you want it to be," I breathe.

What I want it to be. I repeat the last part in my head over and over. Hating myself for being a piece of shit. If only my life were different, then maybe I could make this work with her. But then again, if nothing had happened the way it did, then I would have never met her at the bar. She stays quiet, which is not like her. "Raina…did you hear—" I pause, noticing her limp hand she was petting Mango with, and her breathing has slowed. She's asleep. She never heard me. I sigh, almost relieved that she didn't, but also regretting when I have to address it and shatter her into a million pieces.

25

Butterflies, thousands of them, swarm above me in a chaotic frenzy. They crash into one another while some tumble from the sky, hitting the ground below. I make my way toward the ones lying lifeless on the grass. Their wings are burned, some charred, while others are missing pieces. I glance back up, squinting to get a clearer view. My eyes widen in disbelief. Their wings are on fire. It begins with one, igniting another in a domino effect. Some hover awkwardly, one wing ablaze. I watch in awe as their vibrant orange wings glow against the flames that are steadily consuming them.

I jerk awake from a strange dream, one I've never had before. I try to piece together what it could mean, realizing it most likely has no meaning at all. I'll take it over the usual nightmares I have. I actually slept great last night; it's been a long time. I feel well rested for a change. I rub my eyes with my palms and comb through my messy hair. Mango is in her usual spot on my chest. I did purchase her a large cat tree to keep in my room. That has helped a lot with entertaining her, and keeping her from constantly following me—although I do enjoy her company most days. I give her a few rubs, glimpsing something to my right. My heart stops for a second. Blonde hair peeks from the top of the comforter. I slowly pull them back to find Raina lying peacefully asleep, facing me. All that occurred last night floods through my mind. When I woke up, I had forgotten she had stayed last night. I am so used to being here alone that it slipped my mind. How could I forget what she did to me last night? The way it made me feel. It almost feels like a dream now, but a vivid dream that's seared into my entire being.

I gently lift Mango from my chest and place her beside me on the bed. Turning onto my side, I can't help but admire Raina as she sleeps. How is it possible for someone to look so stunning while being completely unaware? Her soft lips are slightly parted, almost as if inviting a kiss, while her wavy, golden hair spills across the pillows like wild vines. My gaze drifts to her freckles, so faint yet striking enough to capture my attention. I inch a bit closer, carefully counting each freckle with my finger held just above her skin. Once I finish, I rest my hand beneath my chin, drinking in this moment, knowing that it might be my last chance to see her like this. I want to etch every detail into my memory, especially now. I could stay here forever, quietly taking note of her. How she breathes, the way her lips puff up in deep slumber, the delicate curl of her eyelashes resting against her closed eyes.

She jerks in her sleep, causing the blanket to fall down and uncover her a little. My eyes trail down, remembering we are both naked together in this bed. Her breasts are pressed together from her lying on her side, and I can only see the start of her cleavage. I take a deep breath through my nose, clenching my fist at my side. I hesitate for a moment before carefully clasping the top of the blanket between my fingers and slowly pulling it down further. My heart races as I bite my bottom lip, my eyes widening at the sight before me. Her perky breasts lay together, and just below them sits the detailed monarch butterfly tattoo that almost looks lifelike. My fingers inch closer, drawn to trace every intricate detail of the tattoo.

Out of nowhere, Mango leaps between us, startling Raina awake. I quickly jerk my hand back as she opens her eyes and spots Mango purring right in front of her. That cat is a bit of an attention whore. A smile spreads across Raina's face as she begins to stroke Mango. "Hey there, sweet girl," she coos, her voice still heavy with sleep. Her gaze shifts to mine, and I catch a glimmer of last night's memories in her expression. "Uh…good morning," she stammers, suddenly aware that she isn't fully covered. She sits up against the headboard, tugging the blanket around her.

"Good morning," I reply. "Did you sleep well?"

She glances at me and beams. "I actually slept really, really well." I can't help but smile back.

"Well, I'm glad to hear that…um, how are you feeling this morning?" I recall her curled up and crying last night, and I hated every moment of it.

She shifts slightly in bed, wincing a bit. "I feel good…just a little sore down there," she responds.

I furrow my brows, noticing her gaze drop to her lower half. "Oh," I say, my voice flat. "I'm sorry…if I was too—"

She interrupts me with a giggle. "Ezra, it's a good thing. I had a feeling you were well gifted in that department," she blurts out, quickly covering her mouth with her hand and trying to mask her embarrassment. I fall silent, not wanting to draw any more attention to the matter.

Raina's green eyes scan over me. Her expression quickly changes, no longer embarrassed, but something more, something deeper. She moves, letting the covers fall from her shoulders, revealing her tits and stomach. She sits on her knees, turning to face me. "What are you doing?" I mumble.

She places her finger over my lips. "I've wanted to do this since the time you came to my apartment and made Scottie watch you fuck me with your mouth." Heat crawls through my skin. She brings her lips near my ear; my skin tingles as I feel her lips brush my neck. "I've imagined this so many times, while touching myself." My dick jerks at her comment, I can feel it harden at her sinful words. She takes her tongue, running it along my neck where my scars and tattoos mingle. I grunt at the feel of it. I can't explain the sensation it gives. It's painful, but it hurts so fucking good.

She moves down my chest, then along my arm, kissing and licking every scar. My fingernails dig into my palms as I try to stay calm. She gently moves my arm slightly, making sure to get the ones taking over my right side. I've allowed no one to touch me like this or my scars, yet somehow I can't find the words to stop her. She looks up, placing her hands where the blanket meets my stomach. She brings her eyes down to where my dick stands straight up underneath, licking her lips. I'm frozen, hypnotized by her. She slowly pulls back the covers, exposing my hard length. She swallows hard, taking it in. She quickly pulls a hair tie off her wrist and puts her hair up.

She moves from beside me, going between my legs and sitting on her knees. Her eyes catch on my inner thighs where the skin grafting is visible. For a moment, I see sadness in her eyes, but she quickly masks it, leaning down and kissing each spot tenderly. My eyes slam shut and my fist grips the sheets, almost pulling them from the sides of the mattress. A heavy gasp shoots from my mouth. She stops, reeling in on my hard cock. She scoots closer, positioning herself where she needs to be. I breathe slowly, trying to show I do have some form of control in this situation, but fuck, it's hard with her.

She grips the base of my length with both hands, and my stomach tightens at the feel of her soft hands on me. She slowly blinks at me as she lowers her head. She slides her tongue over the tip, causing my mouth to fall open. She leans up just for a moment, spitting on my dick and running her hands up and down. *She is so fucking naughty.* This view of her naked, taking me in her mouth, this will be my undoing. She wraps her lips around me and begins sucking and tugging with her hands. I groan deeply. "Fuck, Raina," I say through clenched teeth. She continues sucking me, looking up at me through her thick lashes. She grips my dick harder, sliding her mouth down me as far as she can go. The head of my dick hits the back of her throat, making a wet thumping sound. I release the sheets, clasping my fingers into my hair as my head falls back onto the headboard. "Raina, I'm about to cum."

She pauses, licking her lips. "I want to have sex," she breathes.

Fuck, I know I shouldn't, but damn do I want to. I tug at my hair, looking toward the dresser. I clear my throat, trying to calm my breathing. "There are condoms in my—"

She cuts me off, "I don't want you to wear a condom."

I stare at her, unsure what to say. I've never had sex without one. "Raina, I've always used a condom."

She adjusts her ponytail, quickly responding. "They make the pain worse afterward…just…do you trust me?" I gaze at her for a moment, really considering her question. I do. I do trust her. I nod my head. She bites her lip, quickly crawling up. She grabs my shoulder with one hand and grips my length in her other. She glances at me, her eyes flickering as she positions herself.

"Tell me when you're about to—" She looks down at my dick, and before she gives me a chance to respond, she slides down onto me. My hands go from my hair to gripping her thighs. We both gasp at the same time. I can't even comprehend how good this feels to have her on top of me. All these years, this is what I've missed out on.

She leans back, taking both hands and planting them on my legs behind her. I gaze deeply at her, wondering how I ever deserved to experience something like this with this beautiful human. I never want to forget this view of her, fucking ever. She thrusts her hips back and forth, sliding up and down my hard length. Her head falls back between her shoulders as we both moan and gasp in ecstasy. I can already feel my release ready to erupt at any moment. I remove my right hand from her thigh, tracing my fingers up her stomach to the middle of her tits. My eyes glaze over, watching the way they naturally bounce each time she slams down on me. She grabs my hand, wrapping it around her left tit. I tighten my jaw, squeezing and rubbing as she picks up her speed. I can feel her legs and abdomen shaking from doing all the work. I quickly grab around her waist, my hands look so big gripping onto her. I follow her motions, taking over so her legs can rest. I pick her up and slam her down on my dick while thrusting up at the same time.

We both gasp and moan at how good it feels. I need to hold it long enough to let her orgasm—I can tell she is almost there. I thrust and slam her harder until I feel her pussy tighten around my length as her head falls again. "Fuck, Raina…I'm about to—" I slam into her one more time before she pulls herself off of me and takes me in her mouth. She hollows her cheeks out, sucking the last remnants of my soul from my dick. I yell out her name as my body jerks from my release. My head falls back, my vision going white for a moment.

Holy shit.

Raina collapses beside me, wiping her mouth. We both lie speechless, trying to catch our breath. I rub my eyes, clearing my vision. I tilt my head in her direction. "Are you okay?" I breathe out.

She turns onto her side, looking up at me and nodding. "The cramping isn't that bad this time, thankfully." I wish she'd do the surgery, especially if it could help with the pain. It can't be enjoyable dealing with it monthly and or during sexual encounters.

We both lie silent, trying to comprehend everything that has happened in less than twenty-four hours. Raina eventually scoots closer to me, resting on her elbow. "Why do these scars look so different from the others?"

I watch her as she points at my left side. My chest tightens at her sudden question. I've never had anyone question them because I've kept them hidden all this time. I glance down at my side, noticing how different they look. *Because the fire did not cause those scars. I did. Sometimes I burn myself as a punishment. Because I'm a piece of shit that deserves pain and emptiness.* The thought sits in my thoughts unspoken. I quickly clear my throat. "I...uh...just didn't get burned as bad there." She pinches her brows together, but nods in understanding. I take a deep breath, relieved she's not pressing any further.

She rests her head in the palm of her hand, studying the tattoos on my arms as they intertwine with scars. A relaxed smile plays on her lips. "I think they're beautiful."

I tilt my head, puzzled. "Beautiful?" I repeat flatly.

She nods, her gaze steady. "Yeah...I mean, they're a part of you, right? They tell a story that you survived."

I scoff, running my hand through my hair. "Sure, they tell a story of a teenage boy who made a selfish choice and ended up burning his family alive."

She looks at me, but I can't meet her eyes. "You really shouldn't be so hard on yourself...give yourself some grace. You've been through a lot, and you could have lost your life—"

I laugh quietly, bitterness lacing my words. "That's exactly what I wanted back then…to burn with them. But here I am, living in the reminder of being a broken, unlovable being."

She sighs beside me, her hand gently resting on my arm as she continues, "The broken parts of you are what deserve the most love…you just haven't allowed anyone access to those pieces of you." My eyes finally meet hers, and a deep ache rises in my throat. I swallow hard, forcing it back down and locking it away. Her expression says it all. No. There's that familiar look. The same one Beck used to give me. This is exactly why I shouldn't have allowed this to happen. I'm such a fool.

I pull my gaze away from hers and rub my jaw, scanning the room for my phone. I jump out of bed, my heart racing as I search for it. Finally, I spot it lying next to my clothes at the foot of the bed. Several text notifications flash across the screen. "Shit, it's 10:30. I was supposed to meet Blake at the bar thirty minutes ago." I grab my jeans, reach into the pockets, and pull out my Zippo and cigarettes. Great, they're ruined from last night's downpour. I flip the Zippo open, and to my relief, it sparks to life.

Rushing to my dresser, I quickly grab some clothes and throw them on. Out of the corner of my eye, I see Raina slipping her dress back on and reaching for her purse on the floor. "Are you hungry? I could grab you something from the kitchen before we head out," I offer.

She gives me a gentle smile. "No, I'm okay. I just need to use the restroom."

I tie my boots and note, "It's just across the hall." I realize we left things in a bit of a strange place, but I really don't have time to deal with it now. Honestly, I'm not even sure how to approach it.

We pull into the parking lot across from her apartment. The ride here was mostly quiet, aside from Raina occasionally pointing out pretty scenery that caught her eye. I simply nodded and smiled at her in response. My thoughts were distracted by other things. I'm still thinking about last night—the way it felt to fuck her and hold her close. The way she caressed my battered skin, never judging me. The way she made me feel calm and in control, even as I lost myself in her. It feels like I'm being tugged in two directions, like a rope in a tug-of-war, and neither side promises a good outcome. Because at the end, I'll be torn apart and left to die alone.

I nervously tap my fingers on the steering wheel of the truck, my gaze fixed straight ahead. Raina shifts in her seat beside me. "Well…I-I really enjoyed everything," she admits.

I glance at her and reply, "Yeah, I did too." And it's true—I enjoyed it so damn much. She presses her lips together for a moment before leaning in to kiss me. I hesitate, quickly turning my focus back to in front of me, my teeth grinding together in the process. Out of the corner of my eye, I see her settle back into her seat.

"So, what is this with us?" she pushes.

I exhale slowly through my nose. "It's nothing."

She lets out a laugh. "Nothing? So last night and this morning meant *nothing* to you?" Her voice rises, filled with disbelief.

"No, Raina, that's not what I mean—"

She interrupts me. "So, since this is *nothing* to you, you're fine with me dating other guys and fucking them?"

My nostrils flare as my hands grip the steering wheel. "*Fuck no*," I growl back.

She laughs mockingly. "Oh! So you think you can claim me without ever actually being together?"

I let out a frustrated sigh. "Raina, no…I can't be what you want me to be," I confess.

"That's bullshit!" she retorts, taking her hair down and glaring at me, fiery in her eyes. "You've been everything I've needed. Haven't I made that clear by sticking around, even with your random outbursts and flaws? I'm still here," she says, gazing out the window. Silence fills the air in the space we sit in. She then whispers, "You're so selfish."

I scoff at her words. "Selfish? I'm doing this for you! I'm saving you from the burden of me."

"Don't pretend you don't know what I want. If you were doing this for me—for us—then you would be mine." Her voice quivers. I open my mouth, but words escape me. She stares straight ahead, biting the inside of her lip. A sniffle breaks our silence as she quickly wipes her nose. "I can't do this anymore," she mutters.

I swallow hard. "What?"

She turns to face me, her expression hard as stone. "I'm done with whatever this is. I just can't handle it anymore." With those words, she grabs her bag, swings the door open, and steps into the parking lot. I watch her as she circles around the truck. In a rush, I fling my own door open, eager to follow her and resolve whatever this is. *Our first fight?* Fuck, I don't know what I'm doing. I stride towards her, but she suddenly halts, spinning around to confront me. Her finger shoots up in warning. "No!" I freeze, caught off guard. Anger and pain flash across her face, but the hurt in her eyes hits me hardest. It's what I do best. *Hurt* people.

I shake my head and start walking toward her again. "Ezra, please stop!" Her lip trembles as she gazes at me. "I do not give you consent to follow me." The words barely escape her throat, but she means it, and her eyes plead with me to respect her wishes. I desperately want to dismiss her request and follow her inside. I need to make things right somehow. But I can't. She's clearly over my shit, and I've led her on for far too long. I want to express how I truly feel. I want to give her what she's asking for…yet the words are stuck in my chest like a letter left unopened, slowly going up in flames. Those unspoken feelings smolder deep in my charred heart, where they'll remain hidden, because she'll never know they existed.

I pull my brows together, taking her in one last time. She tucks a loose strand of hair behind her ear and shakes her head slowly. "You told me last night that you never wanted to hurt me…but you did a damn good job of it." With that, she quickly turns and walks toward her apartment. I stand there, frozen, until I see a light flicker on inside her place. I watch as she peeks through the balcony doors, glancing down at me before swiftly shutting the curtains without looking back. A sharp ache stabs at my chest, a heaviness that nearly robs me of breath. I clutch my chest through my shirt, closing my eyes and drawing in deep, shaky breaths. *Not now, Ezra. Not fucking now.*

I stumble back to the truck, fling the door shut and gripping the steering wheel tightly as I rest my forehead against the cool material. My mouth hangs open as I gulp in large amounts of air, but my chest constricts painfully, making it hard to breathe. I wheeze repeatedly, desperately trying to regain control. Raina's face flashes in my mind, along with every moment we shared. My eyes snap open, and all I see is red. I slam my fist into the windshield, cracking it as I yell at the top of my lungs. Everything we experienced last night and this morning. The way our bodies melted together. The way her body reacted to mine. The fucking way I felt because of her. Just like that, it's *done.* It's over.

26

One Month Later

Today is here again, and somehow another year has passed. Another reminder of how long she's been gone. Mango's dramatic purrs vibrate through my chest while I lie restless, staring out the window of my bedroom. I run my fingers over Mango's striped fur. She hasn't left my side since yesterday. The nightmares have come back with a vengeance. Sleep has hardly existed lately, and if I am asleep, it consists of me jerking awake throughout the night from some fucked up dream. So lately, I just lie in bed with my eyes closed, thinking about *her*—Raina.

Twenty-nine long days have come and gone since I last saw her green eyes standing in the parking lot. Twenty-nine long days since I've heard her voice or smelled the sweet notes of vanilla when she was near. Twenty-nine days since I felt her against me, caressing my skin. Twenty-nine fucking days since I counted her freckles along her cheeks and nose. I never even told her how many there were. Nor did I ever ask her if she had ever counted them herself. Now I'll never know.

I sigh, roll over, and grab my phone to check the time. It's 11:00 a.m. The last morning Raina and I had together flashes through my mind. I rub the back of my neck, checking my notifications. The same three people have texted. Beck, Blake, and Eric. Every year.

> Beck: Happy Birthday, Esther. We love you, Ezra. I'm here if you need me.

> Blake: Don't do anything stupid today. Be easy on yourself. Call me if you need me.

> Eric: Thinking about you today. Please call us if you need us for anything.

I scroll down my notifications, making sure I didn't miss any texts. Nothing from her, but I'm not surprised. Why would I hear from her? She doesn't even know today is my mom's birthday, and even if she did, she has no reason to reach out to me after everything. And I don't expect her to. There is just a small kernel of my mind that wishes she'd text or show up at the bar. Just to give me a reason to talk to her or see her again. Every time I'm at the bar and hear the front door open, I'm hoping that when I look up, it's her walking through it. But no, she's just a ghost that haunts my mind.

I've followed her wishes, I've left her alone. Have I had temptations? Yes. I've come so close to showing up at her door, so close that I've gotten off the elevator on her floor, only to force myself to leave. Or almost dialing her number, calling her just to hear her voice, but never following through. It's the least I could do after everything I put her through. Drawing her in then pushing her away. I didn't even have the fucking decency to at least tell her how I felt about her. I left her with nothing but a broken heart and unanswered questions. Which is really fucking foul of me, considering I've suffered silently since the fire, stuck with questions I can never get the answers to. That's the one piece of this I can find peace in, knowing she's better off without me in her life. I can't say the same for myself. It took me some time away to understand the different ways she had made me a better person. Those parts don't matter, though. It was never about me. She's still so young, and she deserves a good life without my chaos. And just as I wanted it, she won't have to suffer; only I will. Because I'll never be able to get her off my mind. She's branded there.

Blake and Callie have stayed in touch and even driven to each other multiple times since first meeting at the bar. I've found comfort in that, because he gives me little updates on Raina. Callie isn't fond of me currently, but can I blame her? Fuck no. But I'm glad she keeps Blake informed on Raina's well-being. She hasn't told Blake not to tell me anything, which I'm sure she knows he does. The only thing I don't know is if she is seeing anyone. Callie has left that part out. Does it bother me, not knowing? Yes. Would I selfishly be livid if she were seeing someone? Again, hell yes. Is my head extremely fucked up, and I don't know how to fix it? Another, fuck yes.

Everything else has mostly remained unchanged. Beck and Jenson officially announced their relationship a couple of weeks ago, which we all saw coming. Honestly, I couldn't be happier for them. It's wonderful that she found someone who shares the same profession as Eric. She has always looked up to her dad's career, and I know Eric takes pride in that. I do, too. It seems like everyone is thriving, and that's truly all I've ever wanted for those I care about. They each deserve happiness.

I finally drag myself out of bed and make my way to the

bathroom. As I lean against the counter, I can't help but grimace at my reflection. Dark circles have made a permanent home under my eyes, and my irises look dull and lifeless. It's clear that these past twenty-nine days have been a grueling ordeal on top of the usual struggles I face. And now there's today. I let out a heavy sigh, turning on the cold water to splash my face. The chilly water jolts me awake, injecting a small spark of life back into me. I pat my face dry just as Mango jumps onto the counter to say hello. I give her a few gentle strokes on the head. I just need to get through today; I've done it every year, so I keep telling myself this time will be no different.

I set a pot of water on the stove for tea, just as Mom always preferred. Gazing out the kitchen window, I take in the scene. Winter is creeping in, and the days have grown colder and more dreary. The trees stand nearly bare, stripped of color. I often imagined my mom celebrating her birthday in spring or summer, surrounded by warm sunshine and blooming flowers. She always loved this time of year. My attention drifts to the mailbox, and I squint, stepping closer to the window. The flag is up. I quickly go to my room, pull on some warmer clothes, and grab my Zippo lighter along with a cigarette.

I walk down my long gravel driveway until I reach the mailbox. As I open it, I find a single envelope inside. Flipping it over, my heart skips a beat—my name is written on the front in my mom's handwriting. There's no stamp or any other indication on who sent it, just my name. I glance both ways down the road and into the woods before heading back to the house. I pull my phone from the pocket of my sweats and tuck the envelope in there.

I pull up the surveillance footage, scrolling through last night's and this morning's recordings. Frustration builds as I find nothing unusual until I stop at 3:43 a.m. Bringing my phone closer to my face, I zoom in on a mysterious car that pulls up to the mailbox. I'm increasingly annoyed because I can't tell who dropped the envelope off or identify the vehicle. The camera is too far to capture any details. I keep watching and notice a hand raising the flag on the mailbox. The hand lingers for a moment before the car slowly pulls away, stopping right at the end of the driveway. A cold chill runs down my spine as I realize that whoever it was must be staring at the cabin, searching for me. As the car drives off, I desperately try to zoom in on the license plate, but I have no luck.

I take a long drag from my cigarette, pulling out the envelope and staring at it. My heart rate skyrockets as I run my trembling fingers over my name. She always had the prettiest handwriting. I take a deep breath, flipping it over and tearing it open. I pull out a piece of paper, slowly unfolding it. My heart stops. *What the fuck.* My cigarette falls from my fingers, and my eyes bulge as I read the words *DNA Test Report.*

My eyes immediately read.

Name of child: Ezra Gray Stone

Name of alleged father: Jesse Reed Stone

The alleged father is not excluded as the biological father of the tested child. Based on the testing results obtained from the analysis of the listed DNA, the probability of paternity is 99.9998%.

I grip my hair tightly with one hand, staggering back in disbelief as I almost lose my balance on the stairs leading to the front door. How could this happen? A whirlwind of questions floods my mind, leaving me confused and disoriented. Where did this paternity letter come from? I steal a glance at the driveway, desperate to piece together a puzzle that offers no clues. All this fucking time, everything I've believed has been a lie. I bite my tongue, casting another look at the letter before crumpling it in my fist and shoving it into my pocket. Jesse is my father. I killed *both* of my parents.

I shout at the top of my lungs, my voice echoing through the trees and mountains. Bursting through the door, I head straight to the kitchen, where the water has boiled over on the stove. I rush over, grab the pot, and toss it into the sink, sending scalding water splattering everywhere. I'm at a loss for what to do or think next. I try to replay the moments leading up to this, searching for answers. The two people who could have explained everything are gone, leaving only him—the man I've always called my father. My mind drifts back to the envelope and the mysterious figure who delivered it. All these years, there have been no signs of him, no trace of his existence. But who else could it possibly be?

I pace around the living room, wrestling with what to do next. What can I even do? Fucking nothing. It feels like I'm trapped with this massive piece of my life that's been buried for God knows how long. My mind is teetering on the brink of explosion. My gaze wanders around the room until it lands on the hallway leading to Jesse's room. *My dad.* Even calling him that feels surreal. I bolt toward his room, slamming the door against the wall as I enter. I pause for a moment, taking in the familiar sight. It looks just as it did when he left it behind before he passed. I've avoided stepping foot in here until now, but I'm desperate for answers—I need something, anything.

I start digging through drawers and rummaging through his closet, searching for something that might ease my nerves. I desperately need answers. An explanation of why and how this happened. It feels as essential as the air I breathe. I move to his nightstand, pulling open the top drawer but find nothing useful. Frustration simmers beneath my skin as I continue my frantic search. In a moment of anger, I yank the bottom drawer open, and that's when I notice a small wooden box. Curiosity piques as I pull it out and run my fingers over the smooth wood. I slowly lift the lid, my brow furrowing as I take in the contents. At the top rests a picture of my mom holding me, taken on the day I was born. I recall Mom's photo albums, but this picture wasn't in any of them. Jesse must have taken it and kept it for himself. My eyes well up as I gaze at my beautiful mom. She looks so happy and at peace, cradling me in her arms. The way she gazes at me is just as she always looked at me when I was growing up.

I squint my eyes, pulling the picture closer to my face. In the distance, I see the window, and sitting on the glass is a butterfly. A deep ache hits me in the gut. It's a monarch butterfly—the very one Mom told me about on my sixth birthday. I can't believe he captured this moment. Did he even realize its significance, and did Mom know he had this picture? A rush of emotions sweeps over me, leaving me unable to fully articulate what I'm feeling. I don't have a single photo of my mom. I lost everything in the fire. I pull the picture to my chest, pressing it tightly against me in an effort to hold back the tears. For just a moment, I feel grateful that I now have something more than just memories of her, and I couldn't have asked for a better picture.

I wipe my eyes and notice a folded paper lying beneath the photo. Setting the picture aside, I grab the paper and unfold it. I pinch the bridge of my nose, fighting to keep it together. As I drop the paper, the weight in my chest intensifies with every passing second. It's a copy of the paternity test. All this time, living here, I had easy access to it. Yet I remained completely oblivious to its presence just feet away. Frustrated, I slap the wooden box, sending it crashing against the wall. I grab the photo of my mom and me and storm out of the room, slamming the door behind me. Tucking the photo into my sweats, I lean my head against the door, taking deep breaths. I know I need a distraction right now.

I make my way to the bathroom, shutting the door firmly behind me as I pull out my Zippo lighter. My hands tremble as I lift my shirt, biting down on the hem to keep it out of the way.

Just as I flick the lid open on the lighter, Mango begins meowing and scratching at the door. I pause for a moment, squeezing my eyes shut, trying to shut her out. "Mango, go away!" I call out, but she keeps at it. Frustrated, I whip the door open, and she darts away as fast as she can, retreating to my room under the bed. Fuck this. I don't want to be in this house right now. With a quick grab, I snatch my keys from the kitchen counter and head straight for my bike.

I pull into my usual spot at the back of the bar, fumbling for my keys. After a moment, I slip through the back entrance, making my way through the double doors and straight to the bar area. I stand in front of the shelves lined with bottles, the memory of my last drink on my sixteenth birthday at the twins' house flashes through my mind. That night spiraled into pure chaos. A snarl escapes my lips at the thought, and without a second thought, I start grabbing bottles, chugging them down. The warm burn of liquor and tequila fills me as I take a swig from one before smashing it to the floor, relishing the shattering sound of glass breaking into countless pieces. Then, I grab an unopened bottle of bourbon, and instantly, *he* comes to mind.

My jaw clenches at the thought of him. All this time, I believed I was a monster because I was a piece of him, not realizing it was just me all along. "AHHH!" I scream in frustration, slamming the bottle against the bar counter and shattering the stem. I turn it around, my eyes narrowing at the sharp edges of the glass. Shrugging off the warning in my mind, I lift the bottle to my lips, drinking deeply, feeling the burn as it slides down my throat. The taste of bourbon mingled with iron fills my mouth. Slowly, I wipe my lips, noticing the fresh blood that stains my hand. My head begins to spin, the alcohol surging through my veins.

Raina occupies my thoughts, her green eyes and contagious smile etched in my mind. I ache for her presence, but a wave of nausea washes over me, followed by a heavy sense of dread. I turn to face my reflection in the mirror on the wall. Who am I? A twenty-seven-year-old who feels utterly useless. My life has been nothing but a series of blunders marked by trauma and grief. My mental state resembles a never-ending merry-go-round, spinning with emotions that I can't seem to grasp. The fire that took my parents away never extinguished, it lingers within me—coursing through my veins, always ready to erupt from my fingertips. I bite down on my lip, wincing at the sting of a fresh cut.

I look down at the bottle of bourbon in my hand. For the first time since I was thirteen, I focus on the voices screaming in my mind. My expression goes blank as I stumble away from the bar. I slam the bottle down and dig into my pockets, emptying everything onto the bar in a chaotic mess. Grabbing the bourbon again, I take another swig. Where it once tasted bitter and difficult to swallow, now it flows down my throat like cool water. I pull my shirt off, leaving it hanging on one shoulder and exposing my left side. My eyes dart to my Zippo lying on the counter. I slide it across the granite, gripping it tightly in my hand. I glance down at the scars on my skin, marked and etched with self-inflicted burns. My mind whispers, *do it...do it*, over and over.

I take a deep breath, my face like stone. I slowly pour bourbon onto my side, watching it seep down my sweats. I drop the bottle to the floor, breathing heavily through my nose and flipping the lid back on my Zippo. I grimace as I hold it at my side and flick it on with my thumb. Instantly, my entire side lights up with flame, traveling down my sweats. I groan, watching it as it burns my flesh and begins melting away pieces of fabric. I can feel blood dripping from my lip from biting down hard on it. The pain is unreal. This is what my parents felt in those moments. A sharp pain stabs at my chest, causing me to collapse onto the floor. I scream out in pain, swatting at my pants and side. I pant, gripping my chest, wishing I could reach through my chest cavity and rip my heart out. My vision blurs as my head becomes light-headed and dizzy. I blink slowly, looking down. Parts of my leg are exposed with large burns where my pants melted away. I roll my eyes to my side. I can't comprehend the damage I just caused. It is an agonizing pain, but I also feel so numb. I curl up into the fetal position, grunting at the painful movements. I can feel myself drifting away into a thick fog. I try to open my eyes, but they feel so heavy. I don't want to do this anymore. I don't want to live, I want to die.

27

oud voices swirl around me, cutting through the fog in my mind. I recognize the heated exchange of a man and a woman. They sound familiar, voices I've encountered countless times before. I force my eyelids open, blinking hard to clear the haze. As my vision sharpens, I see two figures looming above me. With a few more blinks, their faces come into focus. Beck and Blake are there, their expressions a mix of horror and concern. Beck has her hand over her mouth, eyes glistening with unshed tears, while Blake wears an expression tinged with both anger and hurt. I attempt to shift, but a sharp pain slices through my body, causing me to grunt in response. Looking down, memories flood back in an overwhelming rush of what I'd done to myself. I roll onto my back and let my head drop against the floor, rubbing my temples in an effort to ease the throbbing sensation.

"What the hell did you do, Ezra?" Blake's voice trembles, but it carries an edge of authority.

I let out a heavy sigh. "I had a moment."

Beck scoffs at my words. "A *moment*? Seriously?" I can't bring myself to meet her gaze. I can only imagine what's running through her mind, seeing me like this. I've done well over the years to keep her at a distance from my struggles. But now, I've hit my breaking point. I cough, fighting through the pain.

"How did you guys find me?" I ask flatly.

"Do you forget I can access the camera footage? I would have been here sooner if I hadn't been away from my phone when it went off," Blake hisses, clearly seething. I attempt a laugh, but a sharp pain shoots through my side, forcing me to double over and expose my left side.

I hear a sharp intake of breath from Beck. "Ezra, what did you do?" Finally, my eyes lock with hers. She's terrified and concerned, her expression says it all. I quickly break our gaze. Blake crouches down, examining my injuries. His hand covers his mouth in disbelief.

"Damn it, Ezra, you've taken this way too far," he mutters.

Beck steps forward, her expression a mix of confusion and concern. "Wait, what do you mean by that, Blake?" She turns her gaze back to me, her eyes scanning my side and leg. Suddenly, they widen, as if a lightbulb has gone off in her head. It's as if she's finally pieced together the secret I've been hiding from her all this time. "You knew about this? Is this why you always keep your shirt on? You've been hurting yourself, and I had no idea?" A sob escapes her lips, filled with disbelief. Blake looks at me, shaking his head, his brows furrowing as he struggles to contain his emotions. It's clear he's not doing this for me, but for Beck. He quickly stands up and pulls her in for a tight hug. She starts hitting his chest in frustration. "How could you keep this from me? What if I could have helped him?"

I shout, "Stop fucking talking like I'm not right here!" My teeth clench as I prop myself up, but my head spins, a result of sitting up too fast and surely the large alcohol intake. "There was nothing you could have done to stop me, B. It was better that you didn't know. This was never your problem to fix." My words come out harsh, but it's too late to take them back. Beck shakes her head at me, and my gaze drifts past her, catching sight of someone standing behind her. My eyes widen as Raina steps up beside the twins, her arms crossed tight, and I can see she's on the brink of breaking down. She's barely holding it together.

"What is she doing here?" I demand.

Blake rakes his hand through his hair. "When I saw you on the camera, lying on the floor with broken glass all around, I knew something was off and that she might be the only one who could break through your thick fucking skull."

I scoff at his words. "How did you even get in touch with her?"

Blake shoots me a glare. "How do you think? Callie. I had Beck swing by and pick Raina up."

I struggle, but I manage to plant both hands on the floor and pull myself up. Standing in front of the three of them, my gaze fixes on Raina. Her eyes speak to me, conveying disappointment, worry, and that familiar sense of pity—all the things I truly loathe. I run a hand through my hair, swaying unsteadily. "Well, I guess it's nice for you all to finally see me like this…it's been a long time coming." I stumble over to the alcohol, grab the nearest bottle, pop it open, and take a long chug.

"Ezra, stop!" Raina's voice halts me in my tracks. I've longed to hear it again. Turning around, I see her standing there, looking up at me. She slowly reaches for the bottle, gently placing it back on the counter. I look down at her, pressing my lips together, caught in the moment.

"Ezra, what's going on? Is this about your mom?" Raina asks, concern etched on her face. I tilt my head in confusion as she glances back at the twins. "Beck told me what today is. I'm really sorry, I didn't know, or I would've—"

I interrupt her, stepping closer. "You would have what, Raina?"

She furrows her brows at me before replying, "I would have reached out to you."

I let out a laugh, running my fingers through my hair before moving past her toward the bar counter where my things are thrown around. "Since you all need to know," I say, grabbing the crumpled piece of paper and tossing it at the twins. Blake barely manages to catch it. I lean on the counter as he unfolds it. Beck stands nearby, watching as they read. I can see their expressions shift in shock. In unison, they both look up at me.

"What's going on?" Raina asks from behind.

"Dude, what the hell...I don't even know what to say," Blake says, grabbing his head and pacing anxiously. Beck remains silent, her gaze fixed on me.

Raina emerges from behind the bar, grabbing the paternity results from Blake. As she scans the paper, I can see the confusion flicker across her face. She looks up at me and asks, "Wait, is this your uncle...from the fire?" I stay silent, letting the stillness speak for itself. She sets the paper down on the counter with urgency and walks back toward me, attempting to give me a hug.

"Don't fucking touch me!" I shout.

She halts, taking a step back. "Ezra, why are you acting like this? We're just trying to help."

I snarl loudly, "I don't want anyone's help! Haven't I made that crystal fucking clear?" I start laughing maniacally, my fists clenched at my sides. As I move closer to her, she recoils. "Please, tell me, what kind of help could you possibly offer? Are you going to bring my parents back from the dead? Are you going to erase the fire that happened? Go on, enlighten me." She keeps quiet, letting me vent my frustrations.

I continue towering over her, stepping forward, eventually

pushing her into the wall. Her eyes glaze over, but she stands strong, never breaking eye contact with me. "This is what you wanted, Raina…y-you wanted to see the real me, the broken me? Well, here I fucking am!" I pound my fist against my chest repeatedly. "Now hate me…fucking hate me…like I *hate* me!" I slam my fist into the wall inches away from her face, sheet rock crumbles, falling to the floor beside us. Her hands fly over her mouth as tears fall from her green eyes. I try to catch my breath, searching her face. For the first time since knowing her, I see fear in her eyes. *She's scared of me.* What have I done? I'm the monster I've tried to protect her from.

I stumble back to give us space before reaching out to touch her, but pull my hand back quickly when she flinches. *What the fuck am I doing?* I grab my hair, ripping strands from my scalp. I glance at Blake as Beck is in his arms, crying. All three of them are staring at me like they don't know me. I've been a monster all along, and I couldn't contain it anymore. I bring my blurry gaze back to her. "Raina…I-I didn't mean to. Fuck…I-I'm sorry….I…" Exhaustion envelopes me, like heavy weights pulling me down. I collapse onto the hard floor, defeated. My head droops between my shoulders. I squeeze my eyes shut, trying to find any control left in my worn body.

I feel soft hands gently resting along my jaw. When I lift my eyes to her, I realize she's kneeling in front of me, her gaze shimmering with tears. "Ezra," she says, her voice breaking painfully. She grips the back of my head and pulls me against her chest, cradling me like I'm fragile. A deep ache wells up in my throat, and I can't help but wrap my arms tightly around hers. Suddenly, a long, anguished cry escapes me, and my entire body starts to shake uncontrollably. She doesn't say a word. She just holds me like the broken man I am. In that moment, it feels like my mom is holding me again, comforting me as she always did. I can't hold back any longer, all the pain I've kept buried, the guilt, and the constant mental torment rush out of me. My body can't bear it alone anymore, and I finally let it all spill out.

I feel an arm slip around mine as Blake's voice comes from behind me. "Come on, get up, Ez." I take a moment to close my eyes before sitting up, wiping my face on my arm. I'm not sure how long I lay in Raina's arms, but it's almost dark now. Blake helps me to my feet, positioning himself in front of me. He rests his hand on my shoulder, gripping it tightly. I can see he's on the verge of tears, pressing his lips together and tightening his jaw. Suddenly, he pulls me in for a hug, being careful not to bump my open wounds. I hear him sniffle. "I love you, brother."

I take a moment to accept the embrace, closing my eyes again. "Yeah, I love you, too," I reply softly. Beck walks up next to her brother, gazing at me with puffy eyes from crying. I feel a wave of guilt wash over me for putting her in this position. I've fought so hard to shield her from my issues, only to end up hurting her again.

I reach out, opening my arms to offer a hug. She hesitates for a moment, but then leaps into my arms, making me grunt from the pain. I can feel her soft cries against my chest. Damn it. My sweet Beck. I nestle my head against her neck, gently rubbing the back of her head. "I'm so sorry, Beck...Please forgive me," I whisper.

She shakes her head, barely managing to respond, "Shh. It's okay." I pull her back, looking into her deep, blue eyes. As I hold her face, I use my thumbs to wipe away her tears. Her hands grip my forearms as I lean in and place a gentle kiss on her forehead. I quickly let go, wincing at the pain coursing through me.

"He needs to rest, but I need to dress his wounds first." I glance back at Raina as she gestures toward the couch. I don't protest. I've had enough for one day, and I lack the energy to fight back. I can feel my body shutting down from exhaustion, likely a combination of the alcohol and the trauma I've inflicted on myself.

I turn, heading toward the couch, almost stumbling over my own feet. Blake grabs my arm and walks with me the rest of the way. I sit down on the edge of it, resting my face in my hands. Beck walks up with a glass of water in her hand, gesturing for me to drink. I grab it and guzzle the entire cup. "Do y'all have a first aid kit here?" Raina asks the twins.

Beck nods, heading toward the double doors. Blake follows behind her, looking over his shoulder. "I have some extra clothes in the back," he says, disappearing through the double doors with Beck. There's an unsettling silence as Raina and I wait for them to return. She stays facing with her back to me. I want to speak, but don't have the right words just yet.

The twins return together, with Beck carrying the first aid kit we keep in the back and Blake holding some clothing. "I think it's best if you hang tight and rest until you're sober," Blake suggests.

My head is pounding, and there's no way I'm driving anywhere, especially not up the mountain on my bike. "I'll text you when I wake up and feel safe to drive." I pat the pockets of my sweats, looking for my phone, but coming up empty. I glance at the bar, but it's nowhere in sight. "Shit, I must have left my phone back at the cabin," I admit, trying to recall what happened earlier today, but it's mostly a blur.

"You guys can go, I'll stay here with him. I can text you, Blake, and keep you updated," Raina says, rummaging through the first aid kit. Blake nods, glancing over at Beck.

"Alright, y'all don't be doing no nasty shit, I can see y'all on the cameras." Raina and I shake our heads as he and Beck head out the door. I study her as she pulls a hair tie off her wrist and throws her hair up into a messy bun. She puts her hands on her hips, staring down at me. She chews on the inside of her cheek.

"We need to get your pants off...well, what's left of them," she says dryly. I scan over my sweats, feeling slightly embarrassed now that I have somewhat come to my senses. I give a quick nod, hooking my thumbs into the band of my pants. I hiss as the charred fabric rubs against my open wounds on my leg. She kneels down in front of me. "Here, let me do it," Raina instructs. I move my hands, planting them on the couch. She grabs the seam and slowly begins pulling them down as I lift myself up. She moves carefully, doing her best not to rub against my injuries.

"There." She throws them to the floor beside her. "At least your boxers are still intact." A smile creeps on her face, but it doesn't quite meet her eyes. I stay quiet, observing her as she inspects all my injuries on my leg and my side. She lets out a long sigh. "I need a couple of rags," she requests, meeting my eyes.

"There should be some behind the bar near the sink area." She gets up and goes behind the bar, locating two rags and getting one damp from the sink. Walking back, she pauses at the bar counter. She picks up the photo of my mom and me. She stares at it for a moment, then looks over to me.

"Who is this?"

I adjust on the couch. "That's my mom...and me when I was born."

She smiles down at the picture. "We kind of look alike, well... like our hair—" she admits. I nod my head. "She's beautiful, Ezra," she says.

"Yeah...she was." I wait for her to spot the butterfly on the window, but she doesn't. Instead, she sets the photo back down.

She walks back and kneels in front of me, gently patting my

leg with a damp rag. I press my lips together, gripping the couch tightly. Then she pulls out ointment, gauze, and a wrap. I watch her intently as she applies the ointment and skillfully wraps my leg. Next, she helps me pull off my shirt, which was still clinging to one shoulder, and starts tending to my side. I notice her flinch several times as she works on me. My side is in the worst shape with skin that's bubbled and oozing in various spots. I've grown numb to it over the years, but I can only imagine how difficult it is for her to see such flayed flesh. Trying to lighten the mood, despite feeling terrible all over, I smirk and say, "When did you become a doctor?"

Her eyes meet mine for a moment before she rolls them and replies, "Remember, I work at a vet. I've had to bandage plenty of cats and dogs."

I chuckle softly to myself. "Well, I guess next time I get hurt, I can just call you," I say, my tone light. Her expression shifts, tightening. She clearly didn't appreciate that remark, as if I were suggesting I might hurt myself again. Maybe that wasn't the best choice of words, especially with her focused on tending to my wounds. I decide to keep quiet for now.

"All done," she announces, tucking away the leftover supplies into the first aid kit and closing it. Her gaze meets mine, and I can't help but get lost in her eyes, reminded of just how beautiful she really is. My attention drifts to her lips, and an ache forms inside me—I've missed those lips. Slowly, my hand finds its way to her jawline, and she instinctively leans into my palm, eyes shuddering. My thumb gently runs along her bottom lip. These tender moments are everything I've longed for.

Raina's eyes snap open, and she quickly stands, brushing off her pants. "You should get some rest...you really need it," she says before turning to walk off. I reach out and grab her hand, drawing her attention. Her gaze shifts from my grasp to my face, and though her eyes are filled with questions, she keeps them to herself.

"Lay down with me?" I ask, longing for the comfort of her body next to mine. A bittersweet smile crosses her lips as she nods. I scoot back to make space, lying down and guiding her to settle beside me on the outside of the couch. She positions herself on her side, resting her head on my chest. With our hands still intertwined, I run my thumb gently along her palm.

I look down at her as we silently cling to each other's warmth. I can hear her take a few deep breaths while she focuses on our intertwined hands. Glancing back, I realize my knuckles are busted open and stained with dried blood from where I punched the wall earlier. Raina turns her head and buries it in my chest, a sob breaking free as her body quivers with emotion. *What have I done?* I pull her closer, wanting to shield her from the pain. "Raina...what's wrong?" I ask, my voice strained.

"W-why did you hurt yourself like this?" she cries, her words coming out in broken fragments. I look at the injuries I've inflicted in just hours. To see me like this. How must it feel for her or the twins? I can't fathom the hurt I've caused. "You're killing me, Ezra. I-I can't handle seeing you like this again," she admits, her voice trembling.

I bite my wounded lip, reopening the small injury that had been slowly healing, and the sharp taste of blood hits my mouth. I reach over and take her face in my hand, pulling her gaze toward me. She's hurt and scared for my sake, and that tears me apart. Why do I keep ending up hurting the people I love? I flinch at that thought, rolling it over in my mind. I try to hold on to it, keeping it buried, unready to confront that truth just yet. Her freckles glisten with fresh tears. "I'm so sorry I hurt you. I-I never wanted to cause you pain," I manage to say, leaning in to gently lick each tear from her cheek.

A quiet gasp escapes her quivering lips. Her eyes dart back and forth between mine. "Promise me you'll stop…for me?" she pleads.

I want to give her that promise, I want to do right by her, or at least give her this to ease her worried mind. I know I'm sick and broken, and I have so many things to heal from. I can't just shut it off and be the man she deserves; it's not humanly possible, at least not for me. My mind is getting fuzzy. I can sense my mind and body wanting to shut down in response to everything that's occurred. I focus back on her. I'll give her a promise, in the only way I can right now. I lean into her, clashing our lips together. She doesn't pull away, yet melts into me. Our tongues meet yet again, like they've searched for one another, destined to meet again. I groan into her mouth, savoring her touch and the way her tongue moves perfectly with mine.

She pulls my wounded lip into her mouth, and I wince, but it's a sweet pain. She swirls her tongue around it, tenderly sucking. When she finally pulls back, I notice the blood smudged on her lips. I can't help but run my thumb along the crimson stain. She playfully licks my thumb, taking my blood with her. The sight sends a rush through me. I lean in again, kissing her softly, savoring each gentle movement and how it revives my weary body. As I pull away, I rest my forehead against hers. "I've missed you so fucking much, Raina."

She wipes away a tear. "I've missed you, too." My eyelids start to grow heavy, and I fight to keep them open, wanting to stay locked in her gaze. Before I know it, I drift off, surrendering to sleep without even realizing it.

28

I jolt awake, breathless and wide-eyed. My gaze darts around the room, filled with confusion. Raina sits up beside me, gently placing her hand on my chest. "Shh, it's okay…I'm right here," she murmurs, her voice soothing. I lean back against the pillow, rubbing my forehead with my left hand as I try to calm myself down. *In through my nose, out through my mouth.* I focus on steadying my breath. Raina rests her chin on her hand, gazing up at me. She doesn't pry for details, and truthfully, I don't have any answers to offer. I don't recall what I was dreaming about at all.

I glance out the glass window behind the couch. It's still pitch dark outside. Turning to Raina, I ask, "What time is it?"

She shifts around, reaching for her phone on the floor. "It's 5:00 a.m.," she replies. I pinch the bridge of my nose in disbelief. Wow, I've actually slept that long. It's the best sleep I've had in weeks. I quickly sit up, relieved to find my mind clear, free from the haze of alcohol.

"I need to get home and check on Mango." A wave of anxiety

washes over me as I think about the cabin. I can't even remember if I locked the door or where I left my phone. What if I left the door wide open and Mango slipped out? I tug at my hair in frustration, feeling the weight of my worries.

Raina gets up off the couch, handing me the clothes that Blake laid out for me. I clench my jaw as I slide jeans on, but I'm thankful Raina bandaged me well. "I want to go with you," Raina blurts out. I stand up in front of her, ready to protest, but I stop myself. I'd rather her be with me, anyway. And with everything that happened, I'm still unsure what's going on. *He* crosses my mind again, but I shake it off, focusing on leaving to get back home. I grab my things from the counter, glancing at the mess I made. I'll come back later and clean everything up.

As Raina and I approach the back door, I come to a halt. "Damn it, I forgot my helmet," I say, frustration creeping into my voice.

Raina tucks her hair behind her ears and replies, "It's okay, I trust you." After a moment of thought, I realize that she'll have to ride on my bike regardless because there's no way I'm leaving her behind. With a nod of agreement, we step outside and hop on the bike. I remind Raina to keep her face tucked behind me. The air is chilly, and the light breeze is even nippier while riding. I'm grateful that she's dressed properly for the cold, I just wish I could offer her more layers. She wraps her arms around my waist, carefully avoiding my left side. Before we take off, I look back at her.

"Don't worry about me, Raina. Just hang on tight." I see her nod lightly, her grip around me tightening.

The cold air whips against my face, making my eyes sting as I navigate the winding roads up the mountain. I struggle to remember yesterday's events, especially the drive to the bar. The details are hazy, but one thing stands out to me: Jesse is my father.

That realization sends a chill down my spine, layering over the briskness of the air. I'm not proud of how things spiraled out of control yesterday, and my thoughts drift to the twins and the turmoil I caused them. This was never their fault. They never deserved any of this. All they've ever tried to do is support me and be there when I needed them.

My thoughts get interrupted when I spot headlights approaching from behind. I quickly glance over, squinting as the bright beams flood my vision. I brush it off and return my attention to the road ahead. Suddenly, I hear the engine revving. In my side mirror, I catch a glimpse of the vehicle, and I can see it steadily closing the gap between us. It's hard to make out the details with those blinding headlights in the dark. I decide to pick up my speed a bit, trying not to dwell or think too much into it. After all, I'm going slower than usual considering Raina's on the bike without a helmet.

The vehicle speeds up again, closing in on the back of the bike. I feel Raina shifting behind me. "Who is that?" she shouts.

I shake my head, glancing in the side mirror. "I don't know, just hold on tight." I try to stay calm, focusing on the sharp twists of the road while brainstorming a plan. Once we're up the mountain and off these curves, I should be able to lose whoever it is. These roads are very familiar to me. I've known them since I was a young kid. I cling to that thought, gripping the handlebars tightly as I hit the throttle. For a moment, relief washes over me as I glance back and see no sign of the car. But just as quickly, I spot headlights approaching again. The driver is picking up speed and heading straight for us. *Damn it!* I push the bike faster, smoothly navigating the sharp turns. Every so often, I catch a glimpse of the car, which seems to handle the curves just as well. They're staying right on our tail.

The vehicle speeds up, colliding with the bike tire and forcing us to swerve wildly to the other side of the road. Panic sets in as I realize we're trapped on this winding path until we reach the top of the mountain, with still about three miles to go. I keep my eyes glued to the road while watching the rearview mirror closely. Each time the car swerves our way, I dodge instinctively, veering to the opposite side. "Ezra, I'm scared," Raina murmurs from behind me.

"It's going to be fine—" I begin, but my words are cut short as the vehicle suddenly turns sharply, clipping the rim of the bike's back tire. The bike starts to wobble, and despite my frantic efforts to regain control, it tips over, sending us skidding across the road at a high speed. I gently tap the brake. The headlights of the bike catch the railing along the edge of the curve. "Hold on!" I shout to Raina as we crash into the railing, throwing us off the bike.

I hear a loud thump, followed by Raina gasping, as branches and leaves crackle beneath us. My eyes dart around, struggling to see in the dim light. I catch a glimpse of Raina in front of me, rolling unconscious and hitting small branches. Panic sets in as I scramble toward her, desperately flailing my arms and legs to move faster. Suddenly, I notice something alarming—a ledge right in front of her. *She's about to tumble off the edge of the mountain.* "No, no, *no!*" I scream at the top of my lungs. This can't be happening. I reach out for her, but she's falling faster than I can react. My heart races as I search for a way to save her. I just need a little momentum. I spot a sturdy tree rooted in the ground nearby. Gathering my strength, I slide past it and kick off, using it to propel myself forward. With my left arm stretched out, I widen my eyes in horror as the ledge looms closer to her.

"NO!" I shout, my voice filled with panic as I feel a sharp tear in my left shoulder. The same one I hurt on the roof of the apartments. I grip Raina's leather jacket tightly as she dangles from the ledge, my heart racing. Straining to lift my head, I glance down and see my boot wedged firmly in a small root, holding me in place. A wave of relief washes over me, and I let my head drop back to the ground, trying to catch my breath. My grip is slipping, and I struggle to keep hold of her weight. I concentrate, knowing that one wrong move could cost us both, and if she falls, I will go down with her. The thought torments me. I can't bear the idea of failing her again. Her life is literally in my hands.

I carefully place my right palm on the ground, twisting my body so my upper half is pressed against the earth while my lower half remains positioned forward. My boot barely clings to the root, and it's the only thing preventing us from plummeting to our deaths. Taking a quick, deep breath, I reach out with my right arm and grab Raina's jacket tightly, securing my grip with my left hand. My upper body begins to shake uncontrollably from the strain. I grit my teeth and shout as loudly as I can while I slowly pull her back over the ledge. I can feel every muscle in my body straining, battling through the pain. I gasp as I pull her close, resting my head against her chest in an attempt to regain my strength. A sharp burning sensation radiates from my left shoulder blade, making me wince.

I lift my head, trying to assess her in the darkness. Grabbing Raina's face gently, I call out her name, but there's no response. I swipe sweat from my mouth and taste blood—though it's not mine. Panic starts to set in as I search through Raina's pockets and finally find her phone. Turning on the flashlight, I shine it on her face. Her lip is split, and there's a deep gash above her eyebrow. She must have taken a hard hit. I cradle her face, careful not to touch the injuries. "Raina, wake up!" I shout, my voice echoing in the silence. Suddenly, I hear rustling above us, the sound of boots scraping against the pavement. I quickly point the light up, but can only see so far. I flinch when I spot a large figure standing near the railing by the road, just watching us silently. Resembling the dark figure from my night terrors. "What the fuck do you want?" I growl, tightening my grip on Raina. I notice a flicker of a cherry and a puff of smoke before the figure turns and walks away, melting into the shadows. Moments later, I hear an engine start up, the car fading into the distance.

I shift my focus back to Raina, pressing two fingers gently against her neck. My shoulders slump in relief as I savor the rhythm of her pulse thrumming beneath my fingertips. I dial 911 on her phone, feeling a flicker of relief when the line connects. A woman's voice answers, but just as quickly, the call drops. No, damn it! Come on! I repeat in my mind, striving to keep calm. I try to turn the screen back on, but it remains dark. "FUCK!" Her phone is dead. Running my hands through my hair in frustration, I realize there's only one other option. I quickly tuck her phone into my pocket, steadying myself as I pull my foot free from where it was stuck. I grunt in pain as I maneuver, then lift Raina's unconscious body onto my back. I squeeze my eyes shut, pushing aside the searing agony coursing through me. My body feels battered and worn, but I won't let her down. I have to get her the help she needs.

I start hiking up the steep hill, grabbing onto trees and rocks planted in the ground, battling my own exhaustion as I make my way to the top. I reach for the railing that nearly led us to disaster. Carefully, I step over it, gently laying Raina down on the road, supporting her head to prevent it from hitting the pavement. I quickly grab my bike, turning the key off and back on. It stalls repeatedly. What else could possibly go wrong? Frustrated, I kick the fender and let the bike drop back to the ground. I pull the keys from the ignition and tuck them into my pocket along with Raina's phone.

I glance down at Raina, feeling defeated. "Looks like we're walking." I crouch down, picking her up in my arms and cradling her to my chest. I tense, forcing myself up. I look ahead at the long journey ahead, hoping that along the way someone will drive by and help. I walk, focusing on the road, reminding myself over and over *she's going to be okay, she's going to be okay.* The thought crosses my mind. *What if that person comes back?* I keep telling myself I don't know who that person is, but deep down. I know. It's him. Who else could it be? My mind goes back to my thirteenth birthday. Before he left, he made sure to tell me that our paths would cross again, and that it would be when I least expected it.

I can feel my knees starting to tremble under the weight of my tired body and hers. I'm not sure how much longer I can hold on, but I have to keep pushing through. Glancing up at the sky, I see dawn breaking on the horizon. Time feels like it's slipping away. I can't even remember how long I've been walking. I need to find a way to distract myself. My thoughts drift to my mom. Just yesterday was her birthday, and I didn't get the chance to sing Happy Birthday for her. I know she can't hear me, but it's something I always do for her every year, just to feel a little closer to her on her special day.

I swallow hard and start singing the words over and over as I fight to keep going. Time blurs, and I lose count of how many times I've sung it. The last number I remember was forty-three. Now, the words barely escape my lips, reduced to a mumble as my mouth moves with difficulty. I can feel my consciousness starting to fade. I'm not even sure how I'm still on my feet, but I know I am. For a moment, I think I'm imagining it when I spot two lights approaching from a distance. Shaking my head to clear my thoughts, I focus again—the lights are getting closer. I try to run, but my legs feel like they're made of lead. I stumble, struggling to maintain my balance. Tightening my grip on Raina, I whisper gently into her hair, "It's okay. You're going to be alright."

I squint as bright lights draw closer, shining directly into my tired eyes. "Help!" I manage to cry out, but my legs finally give way beneath me. I collapse onto my knees, still cradling Raina in my arms. Struggling to lift my head, I watch as the car stops right in front of us, the headlights illuminating our desperate situation. I hear car doors slam open and shut, and I strain to see a man and a woman sprinting toward us.

"Oh my gosh! Are you two alright?" the woman calls out.

"Please, she needs help now," I plead, my head drooping as they gently lift Raina from my arms. I keep my eyes locked on them; the woman cradles Raina's head in her lap while the man frantically dials a number on his phone. My vision blurs, making their voices sound muffled, like their words are blending together. Suddenly, all I hear is a ringing in my ears. I slump forward, and before I know it, everything goes black.

I lean against the glass window that looks into Raina's room, my eyes fixed on the heart monitor and the IV attached to her hand. With a deep sigh, I turn as Blake approaches me. "Any updates?" I ask, feeling the weight of worry settle in.

He rubs his chin, tucking his phone back into his pocket, his gaze locked on Raina. "Callie and Raina's aunt are on their way here. Callie mentioned she has a pretty bad concussion and a small brain bleed, but thankfully, she's stable. They're keeping her heavily sedated for a couple of days to monitor the bleed." I massage my temples, frustration gnawing at me. Things might have turned out differently if she had been wearing my helmet. All I can think about is how close I came to losing her. I should have kept my ass at home yesterday, because if I had, we could have avoided this whole nightmare.

I can't stand seeing her like this. And what makes it worse is that I'm not allowed to even step a fucking foot into her room. Only immediate family and those whom Raina's aunt permits.

I wouldn't allow myself in there either after everything. I have no idea what Raina or Callie have told her aunt about me, or if she just found out I exist today. All she knows is that Raina was with a man, not wearing a helmet, then was run off the road and almost plummeted off the side of a mountain ledge. Blake pats my shoulder. "Dude, don't stress too much. She's alive because of you."

I laugh under my breath. "And she's in that hospital bed because of me too, Blake."

He shrugs his shoulders, sighing lightly. "Things happen. She chose to go with you. Let's just be thankful she is alive and going to be okay at the end of this." I turn to face him, ready to argue my point, but I catch myself. I'm trying to do better and be better. So I seal my lips and stare back at her.

"How did you manage it?" Blake suddenly asks.

"What do you mean?" I reply.

"Carrying her all that distance, especially with your own injuries?"

I crack my neck and shake my head. "Honestly, I don't know. It felt like I might break down at any moment, but I knew I had to push through for her…to save her," I confess.

Blake shoots me a sharp look, a sly grin creeping across his face. "You can deny it all you want, but that's love right there. You love her," he states, not as a question but as a certainty. I turn to him, a rush of excuses flooding my mind. I bite my tongue, too exhausted to engage in a back-and-forth with him.

"How far away are they?" I ask Blake.

"Uh, around an hour. Beck is on the way here too, so I'm going to stick around," he responds.

I nod my head. "Alright, well, I need to use your phone to get an Uber. I need to check on Mango, considering I haven't been there since my meltdown."

Blake turns in my direction. "Are you not going to wait for them to get here—"

I cut him off. "Fuck no. Do you think either of them wants to see me right now? Her aunt and I have never met, and we're not meeting here. I'll come back tonight when they're not here."

Blake crosses his arms, assessing me up and down. "Whatever, Ez, but you look like shit. Are you not going to let a doctor check you out first?" he presses. I rub my jaw in frustration.

"No, I made that clear in the ambulance. I'm fine. I got a little banged up from the fall, and my shoulder is most likely torn. They did redress my injuries from the bar. And let's just say they looked horrified, but didn't ask questions." Blake shakes his head, throwing his hands up. He then reaches into his pocket and hands me his phone to order an Uber.

My eyes burn as the Uber driver passes by where Raina and I wrecked. You can see a black skid mark along the railing where we collided with it, as well as small fragments from my bike. While I was waiting on an Uber, I called the only tow service around and had them pick up my bike and drop it off at the shop in town. I'll drop the keys off either later today or tomorrow. So much has happened in the last couple of days, I can't even comprehend it all. I haven't had a chance to sit down and think about the information I discovered yesterday. Now Raina is in the hospital. This is exactly why I needed to keep her away. I'm fucking toxic.

The Uber driver pulls halfway down my driveway and lets me out. Everything looks normal from the outside, but as I approach the front door, I realize it is cracked open. *Fuck.* So I did leave the door open. All I can think about is Mango and if she's okay. She must be terrified. I storm in through the door, and my eyes catch something on the kitchen counter. My heart skips a beat as I stare at the half-empty bottle of bourbon, purposely displayed for my arrival. I creep around the counter, quietly open a drawer, grab a small knife, and slide it into the back of my pants. I take deep breaths, preparing for what's next. I turn to head to the living room, unsure of where he's hiding. I look down at the tile. There lies my phone, face down against the trim.

I quickly look over my shoulder before crouching down and grabbing it. I tap the screen, pleased to see it's not dead. I quickly text Blake.

Me: 911. My house. He's here.

I slide my phone into the pocket of my jeans, feeling shivers run across my body. The thought lingers in the back of my mind: someone is going to die.

I slowly creep around the corner, looking into the living room. I freeze, as goosebumps travel up my arms and down my neck. I flare my nostrils in distaste. "Joseph," I growl. He sits on the couch in the dim light, holding a glass of bourbon while twirling something in his hand. I look closely, and my eyes widen. *My knife.* My stomach drops. I remember looking for it after the fire, wondering what had happened to it. This whole time, he's had it. Which stirs up more questions I can't comprehend.

He smirks at me. "It's so good to see you, Ezra. How long has it been?" I glare at him with rage in my eyes. He laughs obnoxiously. "If I do recall, the last time was when you drove this very knife into my side and kicked me out of my home." His expression goes blank as he twirls it around his fingers. "Did you know this knife was supposed to be mine? My father was supposed to give it to me, yet somehow it ended up in Jesse's hands, then yours." He takes a generous swig from the bourbon as he watches the blade. "Jesse hated our father for everything he was and wasn't. I was the only one who looked up to him and admired him." He brings his hand up to his face, tapping his temple. "Apparently, my mother didn't agree. She always told me I'd be just like him. A raging alcoholic…guess she was right."

I step forward. "What are you doing here? What do you want?" I demand.

He straightens his posture, widening his shoulders as he glares at me. "I made a promise, didn't I? That we'd see each other again?"

I scoff. "What's your point…why after all this time?"

He gives me an evil grin. "I needed you to self-destruct first." He guzzles the rest of the bourbon, throwing the glass onto the floor. I glimpse Mango high-tailing it to my bedroom. Thank God she's okay. "I see you didn't take the news too well." I glare back at him, fist clenched at my sides. I know exactly what he's referring to. "I have been so eager to tell you the little backstory on how my big brother fucked your whore of a mother." I growl, stepping forward. "Ah, ah, ah." He waves the bushcraft in front of him, motioning for me to step back. I can feel the knife I grabbed pressed against me. Now isn't the time, I need to stall. I do as he wishes, taking a few steps back. He grins at my obedience.

So many years I haven't seen him, yet he looks almost the same, aside from mild aging and gray streaking his hair. He still keeps his face shaved like he always did. I wonder how someone who drinks their life away is able to still hold youth as he does. Working in the bar, I've watched people age in under two years from drinking every single weekend.

"I had my suspicions about you when you were around six. Certain things you did reminded me of him. Your mannerisms, your eyes, your smile. I sat with it for a long time, thinking I was going crazy, until I began spiraling from my own mind. I could tell your mother had her suspicions, as well. Or maybe she already knew. You know, I've had an issue with alcohol for a long time. It started about six months before I met your mother and gradually, over the years, consumed me. I was angry all the time, disappearing for days, drinking my life away." He laughs. "Guess my mother was right…I was exactly like my father. Then there was the hero, Jesse, who worked hard, lived the simple life, and was always a fucking gentleman. He pissed gold in my mother and father's eyes. While I was called the troubled teenager who had no self-control," he seethes.

"Get to your fucking point!" I shout, my hatred boiling over.

He smirks slightly at my demand, then leans back, settling into a more casual position. "As you wish. It was on your thirteenth birthday that I finally discovered you weren't mine for sure. You've clearly inherited your terrible hiding skills from your mother. Want to take a wild guess where I stumbled upon it?" He pauses, letting the question hang in the air, but I just give him a withering glare. "Fine. It was tucked under her side of the mattress. I'll never forget the expression on her face when I barged into the bathroom. I had already slipped the envelope into my pocket, and she could see the realization in my eyes. And you know what I saw when I looked at her?" He leans in closer, his grin turning mischievous. "Fear."

I dig my nails into the palms of my hands, desperately trying to stay composed. He casually picks at his fingertips, unfazed. "Anyway, you know how the rest goes. I had it all planned out to strangle her in the bath she was drawing, but then Jesse Jr. swooped in and saved the day." I hiss at his remark. "Now, let's fast forward to your sixteenth birthday, shall we?" My heart races. My sixteenth birthday. *What is he about to reveal?* "I had everything mapped out, three years of planning. I fully intended to take you and your mother out. But, as luck would have it, things turned out differently. I spent the entire day watching the house. I saw you leave with those twins of yours and kept an eye on your mother while you were gone. I slipped in through your bedroom window around 9:30 that night, found my knife, and waited. I knew you wouldn't be able to resist coming back to your precious mommy for long." He clears his throat, and my heart feels like it's about to burst. But I need to know. I have to hear the words spill from his lips.

I can tell he's getting a kick out of this, and has waited a very long time for this moment with me. He continues. "At around 10:00, your mother got a phone call, and it was Jesse. I then found out that he was close to being there, and that you would be home by 11. Did you know that they were planning to sit you down and tell you the truth then? That was the whole reason Jesse was coming. They had it all planned out. I needed to act fast." He pauses, running his fingertip along the sharp blade. My heart sinks. That night they were going to tell me the truth about everything. My lip trembles, but I quickly mask it. "Long story short. I waited until I heard your mother go into the bedroom. I snuck and strangled her just like I had always wanted to do, but instead of in the water, it was on the bedroom floor. I promise it was quick. As you know, she was a fighter, but her tiny little neck just couldn't handle my large hands crushing her trachea."

I charge forward, gripping the knife I concealed. "You bastard!"

He quickly stands in a fighting position, holding the knife in front of him, pointed at me. "Shut the fuck up and let me finish."

I slowly lower the knife and scowl at him. He paces back and forth, never taking his eyes off me. "Now, where were we? Oh, that's right, I killed Esther, and then I used her as bait. I hid in the bedroom, waiting for Jesse to arrive, and even hoped you would. I knew the moment he walked in the door from the sounds of his boots on the floor. He called out for Esther multiple times.

Eventually, he made his way into the bedroom, finding her dead on the floor. He was hysterical. I even waited a moment longer, wanting to see how he reacted to her death. I knew instantly that he loved more than he ever led on, which angered me even more. I stabbed him multiple times with our family knife. Now, don't think Jesse didn't put up a good fight, because he did." He pauses, facing toward me. "But see, Ezra, nothing can out-fight someone who carries a rage deep inside them. And from the look in his eyes, I think he knew he was going to die that night. I give him props for giving it his all. He was always too gentle, anyway." He shrugs his shoulders at his own comment.

Steam swirls around my face, my heart pounding with rage as I glare at the man who shattered my life. He laughs, a cold, mocking sound. "Everything went how it needed to. I arranged their bodies to give it a cinematic flair, holding each other as they burned together. Oh, and the sweetest fucking thing. Your mother had an envelope on the dresser that I hadn't noticed before. I opened it and read it. It was the sweetest letter she had written…just for you." He raises a finger, a smirk spreading across his face as he starts digging through his pockets. For a swift moment, hope flickers within me that he has the letter. But then he suddenly snaps his fingers and grins. "Oh, that's right, I used it to start the house fire. I did at least leave behind my lighter for you to find. Glad to know you've put it to good use." In a flash, I rush at him, yanking the knife from the back of my pants and slicing it through the air. He raises a hand, swatting it out of my grip. The blade clatters against the floor and embeds itself in the wall, blood streaming down his hand and arm. "You got me good, boy." His expression goes cold as he comes at me, swinging the knife toward my stomach. I leap back, dodging it multiple times.

I swing with a right hook, catching him on the lower jaw. He stumbles back slightly, but quickly regains his balance. Before I can react, he brings the knife down, plunging it into my left shoulder. Pain shoots through me, and I stagger back, clutching my wound. He chuckles, watching the blood drip from the tip of the blade. "Now, isn't this family bonding at its finest? So much of our blood has been spilled by this very knife, and now I get to kill you with it too." He lunges at me, aiming for my throat with the blade. I quickly dart forward, ducking low to tackle him. We crash to the ground with a grunt. I scramble for the knife, trying to seize it from his grasp as we roll on the floor. I pound my fists into his side, desperate to make him loosen his hold. He presses his thumb into my stab wound, making me tense with agony. In a heartbeat, he overpowers me, flipping us around and pinning me to the ground with his weight.

He drives the knife down, digging and twisting it into my side. I groan loudly through clenched teeth as he slowly pulls it out, bringing the blade dangerously close to my neck. He lifts his shirt, revealing the scar I left on him so many years ago. "For fourteen years, this has been my constant reminder of you. Now, I get to watch you bleed out," he whispers, leaning in close. The knife hovers near my throat as he continues, "And the best part is that I barely had to lift a finger. You ruined yourself all on your own, making this exact moment so easy for me."

I look down at pools of crimson covering my shirt and the floor around us. I'm losing too much blood. I don't have much time left to finish what needs to be done. I won't leave him behind to torment the twins or Raina. I begin laughing hysterically, glaring at him as I choke out, "I've had scratches worse than that. Thank fucking God I can die knowing that my real father wasn't a little bitch like you." With that, I sling my head forward as hard as I can, head-butting him. He grunts, tumbling back. I grab his shirt, twisting it around my fist, throwing him to the ground, and straddling him, pinning his arms under my knees. I drill him in the throat, knocking the wind out of him. He wheezes, and finally the knife drops from his hand. I quickly grab it, sending it into his shoulder blade. He cries out, hissing in pain. I twist the blade in circles, hearing the muscle and tendons rip and snap. He tries his best to wiggle from my hold, but fails.

I press down hard on the blade, my weight bearing on it as his blood begins to pool around my grip. I lean in closer, forcing him to see my face. "How does it feel to realize you're about to die…all for nothing? The last thing you'll witness is a face that embodies the very people you despised most. It's downright tragic that you've lost a battle to someone as worn down as I am. But I suppose it's no surprise, is it? Because deep down, you, I, and my dead mother and father all know you'd never win a fair fight."

He grimaces at me as he strains to get from under me. I pull the blade from his shoulder and stab it into the side of his neck. He screams in agony as I bring my mouth to his ear. "Now, I get to watch you drown in your own blood." I rip the blade from his neck, and red liquid spews out everywhere. He tries pulling his arms from beneath me to grab his neck, but I calmly keep them pinned, keeping my eyes locked with his. He begins making a gurgling sound while choking on his own blood. His head jerks back and forth as life leaves his body. And I know the moment it does. *He's dead.*

I look down at the man who shattered my entire life and took away those I love. He has haunted my dreams and lingered in my thoughts for far too long. After twenty-seven long years, I can finally find solace in knowing he is truly gone. My head tilts back as I struggle to process everything that's happened. It's as if my body knows I've done what I needed to do, and the pain rushes back in. I gasp as I glance at my fresh wounds, blood oozing from them. My body has endured so much in just twenty-four hours, but I'm grateful it brought me to this moment.

A sharp pain jolts through me, and I collapse onto the floor. My teeth grind together as the agony courses through me, causing involuntary convulsions. I double over, desperately shutting my eyes. For a short moment, the pain subsides, leaving me almost numb, as if my mind is bracing me for a peaceful end. Rolling onto my back, I struggle to catch my breath, gasping for air that feels so distant. All I can think about are the twins. The good and bad memories we shared growing up together. I remember the day we first met as kids and how, from that moment on, we became family. Raina crosses my mind, stirring a different ache in my chest. My lip trembles as I reflect on the time we lost and wonder if things could have been different if I hadn't been such a dick. Now, I'll never get the chance to make amends or tell her how I truly feel.

My eyes snap open, and I quickly start searching my pockets, wincing at every little movement I make. I fish out my phone, struggling to hold it steady as my hands tremble. As I tap the screen, I see it's down to 2%. I dive into my contacts and dial her number. I need to leave a message. She has to hear this before I go. It goes straight to voicemail, just as I knew it would. I let out a whimper that escapes my lips when her voice sounds over her voicemail message. I shut my eyes, savoring her sweet tone one last time before the beep interrupts.

I take a deep breath into the phone as my mind starts to drift away. "Raina…I…I've needed to tell you this for a long time, and I'm really sorry it took us reaching this point for me to finally say it." A choked, gurgling sound escapes me. "I want you to know that I don't regret a single moment we shared. You made me want to be better…it just took me some time to understand that. Most of my happiest memories are tied to you." I let out a shaky laugh.

"That first time you walked into my bar, you had my attention. I tried to brush it off by acting like a complete jackass." The phone nearly slips from my grip as I clutch my side wound, trying to stifle the sounds fighting to escape. I know I need to hurry. I have to say it before it's too late. "I'm sorry…I'm so fucking sorry for everything I put you through." A sob catches in my throat. "I'm going to miss your voice, your little laugh, and those cute freckles." I close my eyes, recalling the morning I spent watching her sleep so peacefully. "At least I got to count them…there are twenty in total…eight on your left cheek, seven on your right, and five on your nose." I feel myself slipping away, the darkness creeping in. I choke on my words, pushing to get them out. "Raina…I… I…" The phone drops from my hand, as my body jerks uncontrollably, but then everything goes still.

The sounds of wheels scraping against tile mingle with frantic voices shouting back and forth. Flickers of light dance in my eyes, and everything fades to black before I catch glimpses of moving ceilings. A finger brushes alongside my floating body. "Don't you dare die on me, Ez," a familiar voice echoes in my mind. The persistent beeping fades in and out. I gasp and then vanish once more.

The sounds of birds singing float all around me, and the sweet aroma of honeysuckles fills the air. I hear some rustling to the left of me, catching my attention. My gaze falls on a vibrant flower garden, bursting with a variety of colors. As I stroll through, my palms brush against the silk petals, feeling their delicate textures. Suddenly, I catch a faint, familiar tune, a soft humming that draws me in. My brows knit together as I venture deeper into the floral maze. My heart skips when I spot golden hair sparkling in the sunlight. The sweet smell of lavender and rosemary surround my senses. A woman kneels with her back to me, carefully sorting through blooms in a wicker basket. Monarch butterflies fly gracefully all around her, some clinging to her hair and clothing. As I draw nearer, she pauses, and her humming is silenced. Standing up, she brushes her knees and tilts her head slightly, a warm smile spreading across her lips. My eyes go wide with recognition. "Ezra." Her sweet voice consumes me, breathing life back into me.

I jolt awake, breathless and disoriented. My eyes squint against an overwhelming brightness as I blink rapidly, struggling to clear my vision. A shadowy figure towers over me. I instinctively yank my arm, trying to rub my eyes, but something snags my arm, sending a slight sting shooting through me. A gentle hand presses down on my arm. "Ezra, it's okay, I'm here," a soothing voice reassures me. I clench my eyes shut again, then open them slowly, focusing on the small hand gripping me. With each blink, my surroundings become clearer. Gradually, my gaze travels upward, and a sigh of relief escapes my lips.

Raina.

She gazes down at me, her expression a mix of relief and sadness. My eyes are drawn to the stitches zigzagging along the top of her brow. I can't forget how her mouth was busted open; there's a small cut there, but it's healing now that it's been cleaned up. "Raina," I whisper, trying to take it all in. My focus shifts to myself, and I notice I'm hooked up to a monitor and an IV. Panic begins to set in as fragments of what happened flood my mind. I attempt to sit up in the hospital bed, but Raina gently presses her hand against my chest, easing me back down.

"Hold on, Ezra, everything's okay now."

I glance back at her, feeling a mix of confusion and concern. "How long have I been here?"

She sits on the edge of the bed, gazing out the window. "It's been three days. You were unconscious for three days," she replies softly. I can see she's putting on a brave face for my sake. I reach out and place my hand gently on her wrist, and she flinches slightly at my unexpected touch.

"What's wrong?" I ask, aware of the tension. She bites her lip, glancing back at me. Her eyes are misty with unshed tears.

"They nearly lost you twice on the way to the hospital." Her voice trembles as she speaks. "The twins told me the next morning, I had just fully woken up and was feeling somewhat like myself. I tried to get to you, but the nurses wouldn't let me leave my bed. I had to sit in this hospital knowing you were somewhere near me." She sniffles, wiping her nose. "They just released me last night, and I've been here since, waiting for you to wake up. The twins and Eric just left about thirty minutes ago."

I rub my fingertips along her wrist. "Raina, I'm here, I'll be okay." I furrow my brows, trying to recall the last thing I remember. Joseph's face flashes through my mind. *I killed him.* That's the last thing I remember.

I have so many questions spinning in my mind, and I'm not sure where to start. I'm just relieved that the first face I saw was Raina. She's okay. She's here with me. Raina shifts on the bed to get a better look at me. Taking my hand, she gently traces her finger around the IV that's under my skin. Her eyes glisten with tears as she meets my gaze. "The twins told me everything you did after the wreck," she says, her voice trembling. "You pulled me back from over a ledge and carried me up a mountain?" She pauses, wiping away her tears with her free hand and taking a deep breath. "You really carried me all that way?"

I run my fingers through my hair and nod. "I don't know how far I walked. It feels like a blur to me."

Raina gasps, her eyes widening in disbelief. "The police told Blake that it was almost three miles from the crash site to where the couple found us. You carried me all that way." She raises her hand to cover her mouth in shock.

I take hold of her wrist, drawing her closer. Rubbing small

circles along her soft skin. "And I'd do it all over again if it meant saving you." She gazes into my eyes, a silent thank you for saving her life. But I don't care about that, all I care about is that she is here in front of me, breathing the same air as me.

Raina clears her throat. "Um, I got your message." I tilt my head in confusion. She falls silent, allowing me to piece it together myself. *Oh no, the voicemail.* She searches my eyes, her expression hopeful. "Did you say those things only because you thought you were going to die? Or did you mean it?" Her voice pleads for answers. I bite my lip, feeling the tenderness where I cut my lip days ago. *This is it, Ezra, don't fuck it up.* I breathe through my nose and nod my head.

"I did," I admit.

She smiles. "When did you count my freckles?" she asks.

I chuckle, but it's cut short as I wince from discomfort all over my body. "The morning after you stayed over, you were asleep." She laughs softly, glancing down at our intertwined hands.

Her expression wavers, and I sense there's more on her mind. I decide to wait it out. "I didn't get the end of your message," she says. "You were saying something when it cut off. What were you going to say?" I look away, struggling to piece together the fragments of that moment and the message itself. I remember how crucial it was to me, how I never had the chance to say the words.

I draw my gaze back to hers, locking onto her eyes. "That I love you."

Her mouth drops open. "Do you really?" she whispers.

"I do," I manage to breathe out. As she covers her face, she pulls her hand away, tears spilling quietly into her palms. Concern etches itself across my face as I grip her thigh. A wave of negative thoughts washes over me. Deep down, I knew no one could truly love someone as broken as I am. I take a moment to collect myself before asking, "What's wrong? It's okay if you don't—"

She stands abruptly, cutting me off. "I need to tell you something, Ezra." Her voice trembles with nerves. I glance at the monitor, watching my heart rate spike unnaturally. Is she going to end things with us? Not that we were ever truly together, but is this it for good? I shift uncomfortably in the hospital bed.

"Raina, please tell me." She paces for a moment before stopping in front of me, her hands tightly clenched at her sides. She closes her eyes, takes a deep breath, and then looks at me.

"I'm pregnant."

31

7 months later

"Good! That's it! Keep pushing!" the doctor encourages from the bottom of the hospital bed. I grip her hand tightly, nerves running high. I glance down at her; she looks so uncomfortable and in pain.

"Is she okay? Can someone check on her again?" I ask, my voice tinged with urgency.

"She's fine. She's doing great," the nurse assures me, trying to calm my anxiety. I tug at my hair with my other hand, feeling helpless as she endures so much.

"Raina, is there anything I can do for you? Please, just tell me—"

She suddenly yells, clenching her teeth. "Just shut up and squeeze my damn hand, Ezra!" she commands. I shoot a quick look at the nurse, who struggles to suppress a grin. For once, I obey her. *My little feisty rainstorm.*

"Alright, here we go, just one big push—" A small cry interrupts the doctor mid-sentence. I quickly turn my gaze to him, and a wide smile spreads across his face as he lifts his arms. My eyes widen as I take in the sight of the tiny human cradled in his hands. He looks at us both and announces, "Congratulations, it's a girl!" Raina gasps in joy, her eyes sparkling with fresh tears as she meets my gaze. I squeeze her hand, gently rubbing my thumb along her palm. We had agreed to keep the gender a surprise, and I would have been over the moon either way. I just wanted Raina and our baby to be healthy.

I watch intently as the doctor carefully places our baby on Raina's stomach. A rush of pride floods over me when I catch a glimpse of her tiny face. "Oh, she has your dark hair, Ezra!" Raina cries, tears of happiness streaming down her cheeks as she gazes at our daughter. I can't believe it—*I'm a father.* A warmth spreads through me, an emotion I've never experienced before. The nurse holds out a tool toward me with a reassuring smile.

"Would you like to cut the umbilical cord?" I swallow hard, my nerves kicking in as I worry about messing it up, but I reach for the tool with my trembling hand. "Don't worry, I'll guide you," the nurse says, sensing my apprehension. I take a deep breath and nod at her. She points out the spot where I need to cut, and for a moment, I hesitate, glancing at Raina. She offers a reassuring smile, encouraging me to continue. Holding my breath, I press down on the tool, my heart racing as I watch it slice through the umbilical cord.

"There! All finished," the nurse says with a cheerful tone as she picks up the baby and starts to walk away.

"Wait! Where are you taking her?" I call out, feeling a wave of anxiety wash over me.

Raina gently grips my arm. "Ezra, they're just going to weigh her and check her out. It's okay, just breathe," she reassures me, offering a tired smile and giving my arm a soothing rub. I glance back at the nurse, unable to shake my worries. When another nurse enters, my nerves spike even higher. I never anticipated this situation would be so intense, and I've only been standing here supporting Raina.

"She's six pounds and one ounce, and nineteen inches long," one of the nurses announces.

"Is that good? Is she healthy?" I shoot back nervously.

The nurse nods quickly, her attention focused on the task at hand. "Yes, for being a bit early, that's a great weight and length." A sigh of relief escapes me. Despite the overwhelming stress of the moment, it's comforting to know that everything has gone smoothly and the baby is healthy.

Finally, the nurse who assisted during the delivery returns, cradling our little girl in a soft, light pink blanket. She gently hands the baby to Raina, placing her against her chest. "Alright, here's the big question…have we chosen a name yet?" the nurse asks. I glance at Raina, who is completely entranced by the baby. She smiles.

"We have. It's Esther Adele." My heart skips a beat, sending a rush of excitement through me, along with something else I can't quite grasp.

"Really?" I murmur, barely able to contain my surprise. Raina looks up at me, tears welling in her eyes. She presses her lips together and nods.

"That's a beautiful name!" the nurse utters as she walks back to the other side of the room. I turn my attention back to Raina, feeling a whirlwind of emotions I've never felt before.

"Did you just decide that?" I ask.

She shakes her head. "No, I've known for a long time that if we had a girl, I wanted her to have that name," she confides.

I lean down and kiss her gently on the head, feeling an overwhelming sense of gratitude. Words seem inadequate to express the depth of this moment and what it means to me. And for a moment, I can't help but wish mom were here to see it all. My heart swells with love as I admire my two girls forming their bond. Mine. They are *mine*. My eyes glaze over, witnessing the way Raina gazes at Esther. She was always meant to be a mom. She's a natural, just as I knew she would be. I can't believe we are here in this moment now together. My thoughts drift back to the day Raina broke the news to me.

Raina's confession lingers in my mind as I try to wrap my head around it all. We had sex twice, once with a condom and the other time I pulled out. I keep replaying the details from that night and the morning after, searching for anything I might have overlooked. Yet, every moment we shared is etched in my memory as if it happened just yesterday. I glance back at her while she paces nervously. "Are you sure?" I ask softly.

She pauses, running her fingers through her hair. "Yes. They had to check me when I got to the hospital. I found out shortly after waking up. My aunt and Cassie knew before I did." A wave of anxiety washes over me.

"How did they take it?"

Raina bites her bottom lip, flinching slightly from her injury. "Well, they were surprisingly okay with it. They handled the news better than I anticipated. I think they were mostly just shocked given my condition." She lets out a forced laugh.

I flex my fingers at my sides, still struggling to grasp the reality of the situation. "I'm just trying to understand how this could happen. I really thought we were safe, given everything."

She shakes her head, her expression heavy. "I thought so, too. I told the doctor that. But…he explained that there are several ways this could have happened. First off, it was during my most fertile time after my period. Then there's the chance the condom could have broken or had a defect. And even with the pull-out method, it only takes the tiniest amount." She pauses, taking a moment to collect herself. "*The doctor seemed stunned by my condition when he looked over my medical history. He mentioned that there could be various complications.*" *She stops, trying to hold back tears.*

"*What complications, Raina?*" *I ask, feeling the tension in the room. She furrows her brows, biting her lip.*

"*Just different complications during the pregnancy. I'm at a higher risk of miscarrying because of my condition—*" *Her lips shake as she fights to finish the thought.*

"*Come here,*" *I demand. She brings her watery gaze to me, slowly walking over and sitting on the edge of the mattress. I pull her into my arms, trying to ignore how sore I am. I rest her head under my chin, rubbing her back.* "*Whatever you go through, we'll go through it together, okay?*"

I hear her sniffling as she lifts her head. "*Do you mean that? I-I thought you never wanted kids? I don't want to be a burden for—*"

I grab her face, careful not to hit her stitches. I kiss her tenderly. God, I needed this for so long. Her mouth on mine. I release her, gently kissing where her lip wound is. I then hold her face, staring into her green eyes. "*I've said many foolish things, Raina. And honestly, I don't know what the fuck I'm doing. But I'll learn for you. I'll do better for you, f-for our baby.*" *She gasps at my words.*

I rub my thumbs along her jaw. "*I fucking love you, which means I will love this baby growing inside you.*"

She smiles at me. "*I love you, too,*" *she whispers. Something flips in me. Hearing those words come from her mouth for the first time. She fucking loves me? How did I become so lucky to be loved by someone like her? I pull her in again, sliding my tongue past her lips. I moan into her mouth, remembering the way she tastes and how crazy she makes me in all the best ways. I need her now, in this moment, more than I need air. I pull away, but our lips remain touching, as we breathe each other in.*

"*Lock the door,*" *I groan.*

"What?" she breathes out.

"Hurry and lock the door." I release her, and she does as I say, looking back at me multiple times.

She turns around, pressing her body against the locked door. "Now come here and take your pants off." I say stern-like.

"Ezra, what? No...you are hurt badly."

I pinch the bridge of my nose, slightly grinning. "Raina, I'll be okay. My dick isn't broken." She sucks her lips in, holding in a smile. With no hesitation, she walks back over to me, unbuttoning her jeans. I watch as she pulls them down along with her panties. I lick my lips, remembering how deliciously intoxicating she is. I lean over, wincing as I rip the monitor plug from the wall, then quickly pull the IV out of my hand. Raina gasps, opening her mouth to say something, but she stays silent. I lay back, propping up on the pillows. "Get on top of me." She looks back at the door, as if thinking someone will come in. When she looks back at me. She looks feral.

She leans in, pulling the covers back. My dick stands straight up beneath my hospital gown. I watch her eyelids flutter as she takes it in. She then pulls the gown up to my stomach, revealing my dick and where my stab wound is bandaged on my side. I hear a long breath come from her. She climbs onto the bed, carefully as she straddles me. She focuses on me as she slides down onto me. We gasp in unison. We both have wanted this again for over a month now. And it's felt like an eternity. I grip around her ass, squeezing and tugging.

She begins rocking back and forth slowly, taking her sweet time fucking me. My eyes roll back as I try to savor how tight and wet she is wrapped around me. I bring my eyes back to her, unable to believe that she is all mine. This. Her. How did I ever deserve it? I grab her waist, pushing and pulling with her, adding more pressure for both of us. She drops her head back between her shoulders, mouth parted.

"Raina, look at me," I moan out. She continues riding me, bringing her hooded gaze down. "You are mine, yeah?" She bites her bottom lip, nodding slowly. "And I am yours…I have been this whole time," I breathe. I grip her tighter, picking her up and slamming her down on my length over and over. "Tell me you love me, Raina." I grab her breast, pinching her hard nipple between my fingers.

She squeals, "I love you." I bite down on my bottom lip. I could hear her say that over and over. I can feel my release seconds away. I run my hand along her tattoo, pushing her back as she plants her hands behind her. I slide my middle finger down her center, rubbing circles around it. She gives a breathy moan. "Ezra, I'm about to—" Before she finishes her sentence, I add pressure to her clit, as she slams down on me, filling her fully with my dick. We both groan as we ride out our orgasm. "Fuuuck, Raina." My head falls back onto the pillow as I try to pull myself back together. I look up at her. She has her head resting on her shoulder, looking down at me, panting. I take her in, every piece of her. She is mine, and I am hers. Forever.

"Ezra, would you like to hold her? The doctor needs to check me and go over a few things," Raina says, pulling me back from our shared memory. I glance down at little Esther, who is making soft cooing sounds. I instantly feel a bit anxious. I've never held a baby before.

"I-I really want to, but I'm afraid I'll hurt her," I stammer.

Raina tilts her head with a reassuring look. "You're not going to hurt her. Just pick her up like this and settle into the recliner with her." She nods her head toward the chair sitting by the window. Taking a deep breath, I flex my hands at my sides. Raina gently lifts Esther, and I support her with my hands underneath. "Yes, just like that. Just make sure to cradle her head." I nod, nervously drawing her to my chest and gazing down at her. Raina glances back and forth between me and our baby, a genuine smile spreading across her lips.

I walk slowly over to the recliner and sit down. I hold her close to my chest; she is a cute little thing. I glance at her dark hair, feeling a bit of pride. I was convinced that regardless of whether it was a boy or a girl, they would inherit Raina's stunning golden-blonde hair. Mom would have been tickled. She always loved my hair. I wonder what color her eyes will be. Raina had told me before that most babies are born with blue eyes and that their eye color can change as they get a little older. I hope she has her mom's green eyes. I picture what it would look like with the dark hair.

I gently run my finger along her tiny hands, and she instinctively grips it while looking up at me. My heart melts over and over again. I've never experienced anything like this in my life. This little one, who's been in the world for less than thirty minutes, has already captured my heart and begun to mend its broken pieces. Her delicate hand feels so small in comparison to my finger, and I never want her to let go. Leaning down, I touch my forehead to hers and say, "Aunt Beck and Uncle Blake are going to fight over you. Oh, and Mango's going to love you." I can't help but smile as she makes sweet little noises I've never heard before. But then, a wave of sadness washes over me. My mom should be here, meeting her granddaughter for the first time; she would have been absolutely smitten. I think of my dad, Jesse, and how special he was to me. Despite the traumas of my younger years, I try to remember that he and my mom did their best to raise me and that they loved me. I find comfort in that truth. All I want now is to make them both proud.

I let out a soft sigh, gazing out the window as I gently trace my thumb over Esther's tiny hand. Suddenly, my body goes still. It can't be. I blink hard, unable to believe what I see. Perched on the window, fluttering its vibrant wings, is a monarch butterfly.

I want to call out to Raina, but the words escape me. Memories flood my mind of my mom telling me about the butterfly at the hospital when I was born; in that same moment, we watched a butterfly making an appearance in her flower garden on my 6th birthday, the very day Raina came into the world. Different emotions swirl through me as I reflect on our intertwined stories, and I can't help but wonder if Raina and I were destined to meet. I think about the tattoo on her chest, my mom's fondness for these butterflies, and the symbolism they carry. I watch the monarch linger a little longer before it flies off into the distance, and for that brief moment, I feel my mom's presence with me. A single tear rolls down my cheek.

I look over at my beautiful Raina, my rainstorm, who has calmed my fire, admiring her as my woman and as the mother of my child. I love her with every fiber in my body. All the years I spent beating myself down, feeling undeserving. All it took was for a feisty little blonde to walk into my bar with a dipshit named Scottie. I lightly shake my head, stifling a laugh at that whole situation and what transpired. My eyes fall back to the little miracle baby in my arms. I know she can't speak, but I can feel that she already loves me and depends on me. I want to be the father that my mom never had, that Raina never had. I want to fill the gaps and pieces I missed out on growing up. To be the family I yearned for all these years. My whole world lies right in front of me. I want to love and protect Esther and Raina with my entire being. If anyone tries to harm them, I will fucking kill them; I'll do whatever it takes to keep them safe. After all, they are mine, and I am theirs.

EPILOGUE

Ezra,

If you're reading this letter, it's because Jesse and I have confessed the truth to you. I wrote this for you to read after your sixteenth birthday, when you were ready to. I can only imagine how you are feeling with the information we've given, but I hope you can understand why we waited. There were many reasons. Mainly, because we wanted to make sure you were old enough to understand and process the news. Never once did I or Jesse want to hurt you. You have been through so much, more than most at such a young age. I feel like I've failed you as a mother, as your protector. And that's something that I will live with for the rest of my life.

And I'm so sorry that you had to go so many years thinking that you were a piece of someone who hurt our family and carried demons. I've tried to remind you often that you are nothing like him...that your heart is pure. You blame yourself for different things when none of them were ever your fault. I wanted to tell you the truth after Joseph left, but I was so scared to. I didn't know if he'd come back, or if you wouldn't understand and resent Jesse and me for it. It would have just been too much for you to take in after everything that happened that night. You have already faced so much pain, I couldn't bear adding more to it. You needed time. We both did.

Ezra, I need you to know this. I've made mistakes throughout my life and felt many regrets. But not once have I ever regretted being your mother. You are and always will be my reason for breathing, for never giving up. You have given me more love than I could ever ask for from a son. And I'll never forget the first time I heard your little heartbeat. It was just moments after I found out that I was pregnant with you. I felt it, like something told me you were a boy. And I knew then that no matter what happened with Joseph, I would never be alone again…because I had you. You saved me.

You remind me so much of Jesse, but also me. We are so proud of who you are. Never forget that.

You are good, Ezra. You deserve to be happy…never think otherwise. One day, a girl will unexpectedly come into your life. A girl who reminds you of me, who has been through similar things in life, where maybe she didn't have a father or a man to protect her in different moments. She will be something fierce, I just know it. And that will draw you to her. You will try your hardest to fight the connection you feel, but the more she comes around, the harder it will be for you, because, just as you always do for me, you will want to care for her deeply and protect her. It's just who you are, and I love that about you. Just please remember to "be loved" while loving her. Because you deserve the love you give.

In your heart, I know you feel you wouldn't be a good father, because of your past and Joseph. But you are so, so wrong. You will be the best father one day. And you won't understand that until you hold your baby for the first time. I have this strong feeling that if that day comes, it'll be a little baby girl. I hope she has your hair. It makes little sense to you right now, but you will protect her with your entire being. You'll love her just as you love her mother and me. And I hope I'm here to see it all, but if for some reason I'm not, know that I am nearby. And the day that sweet baby is born, if you have a little visitor stop in, know that it's me. I'll always be here, no matter what.

I love you, Ezra Gray.
My resilient boy. My monarch butterfly.
Love, Mom.

ACKNOWLEDGMENTS

Wow, what an incredible journey this has been for me! Looking back at the start of my writing journey in early 2024, when I created my debut healing romance, *The Rhythm of Their Souls*, I realize just how much has unfolded. Grief and healing became significant parts of my life after losing my two beloved sisters, Megan and Stacy, in 2023, followed by my best friend Jess in 2025. Writing has truly been my haven. A place where I can be myself and pour my pain into fictional characters. A place where I can escape my mind and express myself in a way that has stuck with me since I was a young child, who wrote sad poems and songs in my bedroom in the middle of the night to cope.

I can't fully articulate the impact that becoming an author has had on my mental health. I have met so many amazing people along the way who have become lifelong friends. Readers from all over the world who have supported me as a friend and as an author. Some I've gotten to meet in person, and continuing to meet. I adore this community, and I can't thank you all enough for finding me and sticking by me. I love each of you more than you know.

To my fellow indie author friends, I've met along the way. Some of you helped me from the beginning when I was clueless about what I was doing; you didn't have to, but you wanted to. One of the many things I love about indie authors is that we do not see each other as competition; we all genuinely want to see each other grow, and we always cheer each other on. We are a support system for one another, and that's how it should be.

Finally, I want to express my gratitude to my husband and children for being my greatest supporters. I truly couldn't pursue my passions without their unwavering love and encouragement. They have stood by me during the hardest times and losses, and for that, I'll always be thankful for our little family.

ABOUT THE AUTHOR

L.D. Pack is a devoted wife, a homeschooling mom of two, and an animal lover living in North Carolina. In her free time, she enjoys reading, caring for her small farm, and creating lasting memories with her little family. Since childhood, she's had a passion for expressing herself through writing, poetry, and music. Little did she know that one day, her dream would be to use her talents and experiences to craft stories that resonate deeply with others.

To stay updated with L.D. Pack and her book releases, please follow her socials.

Instagram: l.dpackauthor

Tiktok: lindsay_writes

www.ingramcontent.com/pod-product-compliance
Lightning Source LLC
Chambersburg PA
CBHW031148160726
47991CB00004B/1584